OTHER BOOKS WRITTEN BY
LESLIE A. RASMUSSEN

After Happily Ever After
The Stories We Cannot Tell

WHEN PEOPLE LEAVE

Happy reading,
Best wishes,
Leslie P

Happy reading,
Best wishes
Rishi R.

WHEN PEOPLE LEAVE

A story of love, lies, and finding the truth

LESLIE A. RASMUSSEN

Copyright © 2024 by Leslie A. Rasmussen

All rights reserved

No portion of this book may be reproduced, stored in a retrieval system, or transmitted in any form by any means—electronic, mechanical, photocopy, recording, or other—except for brief quotations in printed reviews, without prior permission of the author.

This is a work of fiction. Names, places, characters, and events are fictitious. Any similarities to actual events and persons, living or dead, are purely coincidental. Any trademarks, service marks, product names, or named features are assumed to be the property of their respective owners and are used only for reference. If any of these terms are used, no endorsement is implied.

Editor: Annie Tucker
Cover Design: Danna Steele, Dearly Creative

Paperback ISBN: 979-8-9889712-7-6
eBook ISBN: 979-8-9889712-5-2
Library of Congress Control Number: 2024924819

Connect with the author: https://www.lesliearasmussen.com

To my mother, Katherine Rieder, whose support has meant so much to me, not to mention her incredible way of convincing strangers to buy my novels. Thanks, mom, you're the best.

And to Bruce, Hunter and Jake, my three favorite men who will always be the lights of my life.

"When there's a breakdown in the family, it's the ones that love you the most that hurt you the deepest."

—*Iyanla Vanzant*

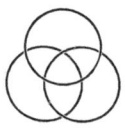

CHAPTER 1

Morgan

When Morgan found out that her sisters Charlie and Abby had left messages for their mom for two days and still hadn't heard back from her, she became concerned—so much so that she couldn't concentrate on anything else. If she hadn't lived nine hundred and fifty miles away, she would have gone over there herself.

Morgan called Sylvia, Carla's housekeeper. Sylvia had cleaned her mother's house every other week since the girls were little. However, Sylvia told Morgan she had been sick with the flu and had not been to Carla's in over a week.

Morgan tried to convince herself there was nothing to worry about, but her instincts were screaming for her to do something, so she called Carla's best friend, Ginny. Ginny hadn't talked to Carla in a few days either but said if Morgan couldn't get a hold of her in the next few hours, she'd drive to Carla's house.

Work had been hectic that day, so when Morgan got home, she was more tired than usual. She hung her jacket in the closet and put her slightly dripping umbrella in the stand.

It rained so often in Oregon that her umbrella rarely stayed completely dry.

She heard a knock on her door. Through the peephole, she saw two police officers standing on her doorstep, one male and one female. The look on their faces made her stomach lurch, and she suddenly felt the temperature in the room drop twenty degrees. Hundreds of thought balloons were above her head screaming, 'Don't open the door,' but she opened it anyway.

"Hi, I'm Officer Gardner," the policeman said, "and this is Officer O'Reilly," he gestured to the policewoman, who nodded. "Are you Morgan Weiss?" he asked.

"Yes…"

"The LAPD called us after doing a wellness check on your mother," Officer O'Reilly said. "Her friend called when she didn't answer the door."

"Is she okay?" Morgan asked.

Officer Gardner and Officer O'Reilly looked at Morgan somberly.

"No. I'm sorry to have to tell you this, but your mother has died," Office O'Reilly said.

"You have the wrong person," Morgan said.

"Carla Weiss was your mother, correct?" Officer Gardner asked.

"She *is* my mother. Are you sure it was my Carla Weiss?"

Morgan knew the answer; she just needed to hear it again, yet that was the last thing she wanted. She wished she could put her hands over her ears and drown out anything they were about to tell her.

Officer Gardner nodded. "Yes, they got a positive ID."

Morgan felt so light-headed that she had to grab the door jamb.

"Maybe we should go inside so you can sit down," Officer O'Reilly said.

In a haze, Morgan moved away from the door so they could enter. Officer O'Reilly led Morgan to a chair in the living room.

"What happened?" Morgan began to breathe heavily.

"The LAPD will tell you the details," Officer O'Reilly said gently.

"Please just tell me."

"They said it was an overdose," Officer Gardner said.

"That doesn't make any sense; she barely even drank." Morgan swallowed hard against the lump in her throat.

"They said there was an empty bottle of Xanax on the floor. The prescription had been refilled recently," Officer Gardner said. The word "suicide" hung in the silence between them.

The sob that Morgan had been trying to hold back overtook her, and she let out a wail that seemed to come out of her entire being. Officer Gardner stood there looking uncomfortable while Officer O'Reilly put her hand on Morgan's back.

"Why would she do that?" Morgan squeaked out. She could barely speak; her tongue had gone numb.

"We don't know, ma'am," Officer O'Reilly said. "Can we call someone for you?"

"No, I'll...I'll..." Morgan's voice cracked. "I'll call my sisters."

As Morgan walked the officers toward the door, she wished their exit meant this nightmare would end, but she knew it was only beginning.

"Your mom's neighbor Esther has her dog," Officer Gardner said. "The responding officer found him by your mom's side."

"Are you sure you're okay?" Officer O'Reilly asked.

Morgan nodded; she couldn't make any words come out of her mouth. She closed the door and slid down against it. *This doesn't make any sense. Mom was one of the happiest people I know.*

CHAPTER 2

Carla

Carla loved being alive until she wasn't.
Carla tossed and turned in bed, rolling from her stomach to her left side, then to her right side, then back to her stomach. Her legs became wrapped in satin sheets and her duvet lay crumpled on the carpet. She dreamed that she was lying on her bedroom floor while flying horses danced above her in a Cirque du Soleil ballet sequence. She could smell the hay on their breath as they whinnied and snorted. Carla bicycled her legs toward the ceiling as she tried to grab hold of one of them. It pained her not to be able to ride; she wasn't fast enough to catch the horses. They rotated around her head like part of a merry-go-round, one that squeaked so loudly it needed oil.

Carla emerged from the dream enough to feel her mattress swaying gently back and forth. Even semi-conscious she assumed they were having a small earthquake. *Probably only a 3.5, maybe less*, she thought. As a longtime Los Angeles resident, she wasn't a stranger to the ground moving beneath her, so she barely opened her eyes to see that the day hadn't even dawned. Carla pulled her sheet over her shoulders, turned from her stomach to her side, and tried to fall back to sleep. But just as she relaxed into it, the shaking started again.

Oh no, it's the big one! She jumped out of bed, pushing her feet into the ground to steady herself. She raised her hands as if she were about to fight off an attacker instead of Mother Nature. She waited in the dark anticipating what would come next, but the only sound in the room was the whoosh of heat fleeing through the vent.

Albert, part bulldog, part dachshund, part wrinkled loaf of bread, stared at her solemnly. After a moment, he put his paws up on the mattress and pushed on it, causing it to shake again.

"That was you? You scared me, young man." Carla said to Albert.

She wiped the sleep out of her eyes and glanced at the clock on the dresser. It was only 5:30 a.m.

"It's Sunday. You have to let me sleep for at least one more hour." She sighed, kissed him on his furry head, and laid back down. She stretched her legs out, feeling the cool, silken sheets surrounding her body.

As she felt herself drifting off, Albert let out a loud bark. Carla jerked upright, staring at him with raised eyebrows. Albert never barked.

He barked again, even louder and more insistent this time.

"What are you trying to tell me?" She wrinkled her forehead and whispered, "Is someone breaking in?" He put his tail between his legs and ran out of the room. Something inside Carla told her she needed to follow him as he ran ahead to the front door, whining.

She dropped to the floor in the living room and crawled over to the window, where she painstakingly and as surreptitiously as she could, pulled a slat away from the blinds. Her eyes opened wide and she had a hard time believing that what she saw was real. Martha, her eighty-year-old neighbor's garage was engulfed in flames.

Carla flung open her front door, the stench of burning wood hitting her nose. She waved her hands in front of her face to protect her eyes from the smoke and ash that blew toward her. At any minute the gentle breeze could turn into gusts, carrying the fire through the entire neighborhood.

Carla took off running despite wearing pajamas with holes in the armpits. Being a realtor, she knew the layout of every house in her Studio City neighborhood. She raced across the street, yelling toward the second-floor window where Martha's bedroom was. Carla prayed she'd see Martha running out the front door any second, but Martha was likely still asleep.

Several neighbors must have heard Carla's screams because they ran toward Martha's house.

"Call 911!" Carla hollered.

She opened Martha's gate and sprinted into the backyard. The fire hadn't reached the back of the house yet, so she tried the back door. Even with Carla's admonitions, Martha sometimes forgot to lock it. Of course, today she'd remembered.

Carla was not a tall woman, but she was strong. She picked up a garden gnome and smashed through the window in the back door, turning her head away to avoid flying glass. She reached inside, unlocked the door, and ran up to the second floor, finding Martha asleep, curled around her cat.

Strands of Martha's alabaster hair crept out of her sleep bonnet, almost covering her eyes. Next to the bed sat eyeglasses the color of red peppers with cat-eye lenses that looked as if they should be on a pop singer, not an elderly woman with a thimble collection.

Carla shook her gently. "Martha, wake up."

Martha slowly opened her eyes. At first, she stared at Carla as if she didn't know who she was, then sat up so quickly that she knocked her cat, Fluffy, off the bed. Fluffy ran past Carla and out of the room.

"Why are you in my bedroom?" Martha asked, her voice slightly scratchy.

"Your garage is on fire."

"My garage is *on fire*?"

"We need to get you out of here!" Carla said, handing Martha her glasses.

Carla knew Martha would be embarrassed to be seen in her granny nightgown even though she was a granny. Carla grabbed Martha's robe from the chair, and the two of them hurried down the stairs and out the back door.

When the smoke hit their lungs, they began coughing. They made it to the side gate when Martha stopped so suddenly that Carla almost fell over her.

"We need to get Fluffy!" Martha yelled over the approaching sirens that pierced the silence of daybreak.

"Go to the front yard," Carla said. "I'll find her."

Carla turned and ran back inside the house. The flames had spread from the garage to the living room, and the smoke was thicker now, so she had to cover her mouth.

"Fluffy! Fluffy!" Carla called out as loudly as she could through her fingers. She tried not to breathe deeply as she looked under the couch and the dining room table, but no cat. She finally found Fluffy in the kitchen, licking the sides of her food bowl.

Carla snatched the cat, who never let anyone other than Martha pick her up. As Fluffy squirmed in her arms, Carla tightened her grip.

"You idiot, the house is on fire," Carla said, quickly moving toward the back door.

By the time Carla reached the front yard, she was struggling to breathe, covered in soot and dripping in sweat. A crowd had formed on the street, and they cheered when she appeared with the cat. She carried Fluffy over to Martha, where two paramedics were examining her.

One of the paramedics stopped Carla as she turned to leave. "Ma'am, wait. I want to examine you; you must have inhaled a lot of smoke in there."

"I'm fine." She made a show of taking a big breath in and out. "See, not even a cough." Carla ignored him when he called after her.

A vibrant, golden sun had risen just enough to illuminate the sky behind the house as if to compete with the fiery yellow flames reaching toward the heavens. Carla guessed at least ten firefighters sprayed the facade as the inferno fought to stay alive.

As Carla made her way across the lawn, she saw that her neighbors, Marvin Monson and his ten-year-old son, Jason, were watching the firefighters battle the flames. It was still too dark to tell whether Marvin was sober, but at least she could be sure Jason was. Next to the Monsons were Harriet Gadler and her husband, Louis, who were both seventy years old but a study in contrasts. While Louis was perpetually hunched over as if he were looking at his shoes, his wife still went to the gym four days a week and had biceps bigger than women half her age.

"Carla!" Harriet yelled.

Carla pretended she didn't hear, but Harriet began gesturing wildly, so Carla had no choice but to go over to her.

"Oh, my goodness, you're so brave," Harriet said, then turned to her husband. "Lou, tell Carla what a hero she is."

"It's true. You *are* a hero," Louis said, raising his head just enough so Carla could glimpse a smile.

"Any of you would've done the same thing," Carla said to her neighbors.

"Not me, I have a bad back," Marvin Monson said, shaking his head, causing his blonde cowlick to sway like a feather sticking out of a cap. Someone who didn't know Marvin might think his messy appearance was because he'd just woken from a sound sleep, but he looked disheveled even when he went to a formal event.

"I'm going back to bed," Louis said, then hunched toward home.

"He wouldn't have done anything," Harriet Gadler said. "He barely takes out the trash."

"I would've helped if I'd gotten here before the firemen," Jason said with all the ego of a pre-teen boy.

"I know you would have," Carla said. Using that moment to escape the attention, she dragged herself home.

Once inside, Carla rewarded Albert with a handful of dog treats, pulled a blanket off the couch, curled up, and fell asleep. She didn't open her eyes until late afternoon when the sound of her stomach growling woke her.

On Monday morning, as soon as Carla finished her latte and pulled the latest comps of house sales for her new client, she headed to work. She liked to get in early before the sounds of printers pushing out papers and phones ringing took over.

At 9:00, the assistants chattering about their weekends echoed off the walls. At 9:15, the partners would come in. Carla had to be at a meeting in the conference room at 9:30. At 9:33, she grabbed her notes with all her new listings, opened the glass door, and headed for a seat at the large, oval table. She wanted to be a few minutes late to avoid the small talk.

As she sat down, the partners and their assistants looked up. All of them had goofy smiles on their faces. *Do I have something hanging from my nose?* she thought.

When they all stood up in unison, Carla was more confused. *It's not my birthday.*

The group broke into a rousing rendition of 'She's A Jolly Good Firewoman.'

Carla squinted at them. "What's going on?" she asked with a half-hearted laugh.

"You're a hero!" Rosa, one of the assistants said, running around the table to give Carla a bear hug. "I've watched this at least five times," Rosa said, holding her phone up to Carla and showing the footage of Carla pulling Martha to safety with the fire raging behind her. A second video showed Carla coming out carrying Fluffy in her arms as the neighbors cheered.

"How did the news get that?" Carla stammered.

"Someone must've sent it to them," one of the partners said.

Carla put her hands on the conference table to steady herself.

"Reporters have been calling here all morning, they want to interview you," Rosa said, rubbing her hands together. "Isn't that exciting?"

Carla picked up her things before a panic attack could rear its head. "I'm sorry, but I can't stay." She rushed out the door and straight to her car.

By the time Carla got home, her cell phone was littered with voicemails from area codes she didn't recognize. *How have all these strangers gotten my phone number?* she wondered.

Some people would have relished being celebrated, but Carla felt violated. After Carla's daughters, Morgan, Charlotte, and Abby, were born, she kept a very low profile. She ensured her phone numbers were unlisted and avoided social media.

Without listening to them, Carla deleted all the messages, then dropped her phone onto the couch as if she'd picked up a pot of boiling water with her bare hands. She began pacing around her living room. After walking the perimeter eight times, she realized it was only ten a.m., so she couldn't have a glass of wine. Instead, she settled for a cup of green tea.

She took her phone and her mug into her bedroom. All she wanted was to get under the covers and hide from the world. She pulled her sheets back and slid under them, fully dressed including her shoes. She eyed her phone on the nightstand as if it were a middle-school bully about to hurl insults at her. Then she turned away. *Do not look at your phone, do not look at your phone.* Unfortunately, her curiosity got the best of her after only a few minutes. Her pulse sped up when she saw alert after alert pop up. The videos were now on Next Door. The local news. And all over YouTube.

"Why can't people just leave me alone?" she asked as Albert looked up at her as if she were talking to him.

Carla put her head in her hands, her panic hitting a pitch higher than the soprano's aria in *La Bohème*. She willed herself to get up and get a Xanax out of her medicine cabinet, then popped it into her mouth like an M&M. She hoped it would help, but as her head buzzed and her heart pounded, she doubted if anything could calm her.

As she wondered if her daughters knew what had happened, the unique ringtone she had set for her oldest, Morgan, chimed from her cell, answering her question.

"Mom, why didn't you tell us that you saved Martha from a fire," Morgan said. "I saw it on Instagram."

"It's on Instagram, too?"

"It's everywhere. Have you told Charlie and Abby?"

"No. And I wouldn't have told you if you hadn't found out on your own."

"Why not? You should be proud."

"Because it's no big deal, and I don't want to talk about it anymore."

"I don't get you. I just wanted to let you know how impressed I am."

"Thanks," Carla said. "You know I love you."

"I know, Mom, I love you, too. I'll talk to you later, I need to get ready for work." Morgan hung up.

Carla hung up. As she dropped her phone on the bed, it rang again. She grabbed it reflexively.

"Okay, what did you forget, Morgan?" All Carla heard was silence on the other end. "Hello…?" she said. She looked at the phone; there was no caller ID.

"Is this the Carla that used to live in Brooklyn, New York?" The voice on the line was deep and gruff.

"W-w-who is this?" Carla stammered, her vocal cords feeling paralyzed.

"Answer my question, and I'll answer yours," the voice said.

Carla hung up quickly. She shook so vigorously that her phone fell out of her hand and onto the floor.

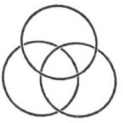

CHAPTER 3

Morgan

Morgan studied herself in the bathroom mirror. She was only thirty-four, but the gray hairs peeking out of her eyebrows betrayed the kind of life she'd led.

When she had moved into her tiny one-bedroom apartment in Portland, Oregon, she assured herself it would be temporary. She'd been there for three years now. The kitchen had a mid-size refrigerator and a stovetop with only one working burner. The place resembled a dorm suite that hadn't been updated since the eighteen-hundreds. In the living room, there was a worn brown leather love seat against one wall and a small particle board desk her next-door neighbor had put on the curb. To add some life to the place, colorful artwork prints covered every wall, but in truth, some of the "art" work covered up bubbles in the paint.

Even with the few possessions Morgan owned, the apartment was crowded—even claustrophobic--but the longer she lived there, the more deeply she burrowed into her cocoon.

The sheer fact that she could never lose her keys or phone in a place the size of a school locker made it worthwhile.

Morgan grabbed her phone from the kitchen counter to call her sister. Charlie would likely be at work, so Morgan wasn't sure she would be able to talk. Morgan tried to avoid her reflection staring at her from the toaster as she waited for Charlie to answer. When she had been in the bathroom, she'd missed the stray black hair sticking out of her chin. *Am I becoming the witch from Hansel and Gretel? I need to stop looking at reflective surfaces.* She was about to hang up and go pluck the hair when Charlie answered.

"Have you seen Facebook today?" Morgan asked, not bothering to say hello. Sisters didn't need formalities.

"No, was there another adorable husky howling at its owner?" Charlie asked.

"It's not a husky this time," Morgan said. "It's Mom. She's gone viral."

"What're you talking about?"

"Go online and check out Facebook."

Morgan could hear the clicking of Charlie's computer keyboard. While she waited for Charlie to sign on, she tried to use her fingers to pull the hair out of her chin, but she couldn't catch a hold of it. She turned the toaster away from her so she didn't have to look at it.

"Oh, my God, it's on more than just Facebook," Charlie said.

"It's crazy," Morgan said.

"I can't believe Mom saved Martha and her cat."

"I know. Mom hates cats."

"Funny. Have you talked to her?" Charlie asked.

"Yes, but she didn't want to talk about it. She's either being modest or weird."

"Does Abby know?" Charlie asked.

"I don't know, I called you first," Morgan said. During the following, she returned to the bathroom, grabbed the tweezers, and yanked the chin hair out as if she were pulling a nail out of a wall. She cringed and rubbed her chin; it hurt more than she expected.

"Do you mind if I tell Abby?" Charlie asked.

"No, then she can't ask me to babysit," Morgan said.

Charlie laughed. "What did her kids do this time?"

"I watched the kids so Abby and Alex could have a night out. After they left, I wanted to make myself a cup of coffee, so I put all four of the kids in front of cartoons. When I came back into the family room, one of them had switched the channel on the TV to Dateline, and the kids and the dog were all tied together with yarn. The little gremlins giggled and jumped around the whole time, making it almost impossible for me to get them untied. I was drenched in sweat when Abby and Alex got home."

"Abby deserves a medal…or a purple heart. And if you tell her I said that, I'll remind her about the time you wore her new sweater to picture day at school," Charlie said.

"How dumb was I not to realize Mom would put my senior picture on the mantel."

"I don't think I've ever seen Abby that mad."

"Yeah, if I hadn't smelled my shampoo, I never would've realized she'd put ranch dressing in it," Morgan said.

"Abby could be vindictive when she was a kid."

"I didn't always like her until she grew up. She may be the reason I don't want to have kids of my own."

"You don't mean that," Charlie said.

"I didn't inherit the maternal gene like you and Abby."

"Well, if Rick and I stay together, I don't think we're ever having children," Charlie said. "He couldn't handle competing for my attention."

"I'll pretend I haven't said this a million times. You *have* to leave that guy. Cut the cord. Eleven years is long enough to wait for him to propose."

"He'll propose at some point."

"And that's a good thing?" Morgan asked. "If you were one of your clients, what would you advise them to do?"

There was a long beat of silence, and then Charlie said, "I gotta go. I'll call Abby later. Bye." She hung up before Morgan could say another word.

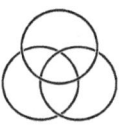

CHAPTER 4

Charlie

She was born Charlotte, but to her, the name sounded like either a Southern belle or an old woman with floppy jowls and a Mint Julep in each hand, two things she didn't want to be. She'd been going by Charlie since the first time she saw a *Peanuts* comic strip and identified with Charlie Brown. He kept hoping things would work out for him no matter how many times he failed, which described Charlie's relationship with men. Well, one man. She'd been with Rick for a long time, and deep down—or maybe not so deep down, she knew he was wrong for her, but she hadn't been able to bring herself to end it.

"I'll break up with Rick for you; I'm great at break-ups," Morgan had said to her more than once, but Charlie knew it had to come from her. *I wish my torso were born with a backbone,* she thought.

After she'd walked her last therapy client out of her office, Charlie collapsed into a chair. She loved her office, it fit her personality. Charlie thought of herself as a little bit shabby and a little bit chic.

Charlie stood and re-tucked her Gap turtleneck back into her long, flowing Armani skirt. She'd become skilled at pairing designer pieces with less expensive brands and knew precisely the styles that would look good on her. As she had a deep insecurity about her figure, she never wore anything tight or showed cleavage, which could also be because she didn't have any. She hated her A-cup breasts, which she assumed came from her dad's side of the family; her mom and sisters were more voluptuous.

Right before she fell headfirst down a manhole of self-loathing, she remembered that she had told Morgan she'd call Abby.

When Abby answered, Charlie heard the equivalent of a prison riot—when it was actually Abby's four rambunctious kids. Charlie could envision all of them crawling on Abby like ants on a cookie.

"Hold on," Abby said. The muffled sounds that followed meant Abby had covered the phone with her hand, but Charlie could still hear everything.

"Remember what we do when Mommy is on the phone?" Abby asked.

"We bug you even more!" the kids yelled out.

Charlie heard Emma trying to copy her older siblings, but at eighteen months, her words were mostly unintelligible.

"Levi, can you take everyone into the kitchen and ask Daddy for a snack?" Abby asked.

Charlie heard a lot of shuffling and then a door slam.

"Ow…" Abby said.

"What's wrong?" Charlie asked.

"I got hit with a broom."

"The kids hit you with a broom?"

"No, I'm in the closet," Abby said.

"You're where?"

"Forget it. What's going on?"

"Have you heard about Mom?" Charlie asked.

"Is she okay?"

"Martha's house caught on fire, and Mom saved her. Someone filmed the whole thing, and she's exploding on social media."

"You're kidding. Mom doesn't even like to have her picture taken."

"Morgan talked to her; she's not happy."

"I'll check in on her after the kids go down for their nap… or are in jail, whichever comes first." Abby laughed.

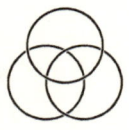

CHAPTER 5

Abby

Abby, the youngest of Carla's daughters, lived in Encinitas, California. As Abby was geographically closer to her mother than her sisters, she and Carla had a special bond. Carla could relate to Abby's struggles, having once had several young kids of her own close together. Abby often turned to her mother for advice. She was grateful that Carla never judged her or tried to take charge and only offered her opinion when Abby asked for it.

Abby sometimes joked with her mother that although she was technically the baby of the family, she considered herself the most mature of her sisters. She was the only one who took the responsibilities of adulthood seriously—at least when she wasn't overwhelmed and hiding in her broom closet. If she brought the baby monitor in with her, it wasn't exactly what she'd call peaceful, but it gave her a few minutes. This tactic had worked until one day, her oldest son, Hudson, tracked her down and told his siblings that their mom was playing hide and seek. Abby had very few moments of peace after that.

When Abby learned her mother saved the neighbor, she couldn't help but think how brave her mom was. *I wish I could do something to warrant that kind of attention. My life isn't all that exciting unless you count chasing naked toddlers around the house.*

Abby had never been a risk taker; she was the sister most likely *not* to try something different. The older she got, the more she avoided anything that would have challenged her other than motherhood. Being a parent was exhausting, but at least her kids were healthy and independent, sometimes too independent, as they didn't always listen to her.

She hadn't questioned the choices she made for her life until recently when she ran out of milk and needed to take all the children with her to the grocery store. She pushed Addison, two and a half, and Emma, eighteen months, in the stroller. Hudson, six, and Levi, five, were walking down the cereal aisle when she saw her high school drama teacher reaching for a box of Kashi cereal. Ms. Harper had been the most supportive and encouraging drama teacher Abby had ever had. She saw something in Abby, pushing her not to be afraid to be vulnerable on stage and to embody a role. She always told Abby she was destined to become a successful actress one day.

Abby didn't want Ms. Harper to be disappointed that she hadn't lived up to her expectations, so she turned and tried to herd the kids out of the aisle, but four kids under the age of six moved as quickly as a slug and a snail racing.

When Abby was about to turn the corner, Levi reached for a box of chocolate Cheerios and five boxes came tumbling down on top of him. He giggled so loudly that Ms. Harper turned toward them.

"Abby? Abby Weiss?" Ms. Harper said, walking over to Abby.

"Ms. Harper?" Abby said, feeling her face grow warm and knowing her cheeks had turned a tell-tale rosy tint.

"I can see you've been busy these last few years," Ms. Harper said, looking at the kids. "They're adorable."

"Thank you."

"Your mom had been my most promising student," Ms. Harper said to Hudson and Levi, who stared at her. "She's very talented."

And now she must think I'm only talented at having kids.

"That's sweet of you to say," Abby said. "But I have to get the young ones home to nap." Abby's legs itched to get out of there.

"Maybe when they all go to college, you can pick up where you left off," Ms. Harper said.

By then I'll be playing Grandma, Abby thought. She said goodbye and dragged the kids across the store to the produce section. As she picked through the apples to find ones that were still firm, she wondered if the life she'd chosen was as fulfilling as she'd once thought.

Over the last year, she had been feeling like the world no longer saw her as a person who added something vital to it. She was now seen as an overburdened mom with a pocketful of Goldfish crackers.

She was barely thirty but felt older. She had always been considered pretty, but it had been a long time since a man flirted or tried to pick her up. She assumed that was because she usually had four kids in tow and a wedding ring. But she still wanted to know that other men besides her husband found her attractive. On the rare occasions when she was alone and remembered to wear something cute and brush her hair, it was like she wore a sandwich board advertising that she was off the market.

And then there was the one day when she thought her luck had changed. She had left the kids with Alex and went to buy detergent when she noticed an adorable guy seeming to follow her through CVS. She didn't think it could be a coincidence that he kept ending up in the same aisle she was in. Her heart rushed with the unfamiliar feeling of flattery.

When she stopped in the laundry supply section, she heard footsteps coming up behind her. She casually looked over her shoulder as the cute guy sauntered toward her. Her stomach did handsprings. She licked her lips and brushed her hand through her hair.

The handsome man stopped directly next to her. "Excuse me. I hope I'm not bothering you."

"Not at all," Abby said, flashing him her best smile and hoping she remembered to brush her teeth that morning.

"You have a pacifier attached to your shoe," he said.

Abby saw Emma's binky stuck to the Velcro on her right sneaker. "Oh…uh, thank you." She reached down and grabbed it, tossing it in her purse.

"No problem. I'd hope someone would tell my wife if she was dragging something around."

Abby nodded, then turned and left the store without the detergent.

CHAPTER 6

Carla

Carla had raised her daughters alone—without a husband or family to help her. She did her best with what she knew and somehow exceeded her role models.

Carla's childhood was not a happy one. Her mother, Beverly, acted in B movies, or more accurately, C movies, although if you asked her, she'd say every role was crucial. She took any part offered, especially the ones that took her far away from Midwood, New York, and her family.

When Carla was eight, she overheard her mother telling a UPS driver that Carla was an 'oops' baby. "If I would've known more about birth control," Beverly said, "I wouldn't have had any children."

Carla's father, Mort, wasn't much better. He'd come home after a shift at the lumber factory, grab a beer, watch any sport on television, and not speak to his wife or kids the rest of the night.

Carla's brother, Roy, was six years older than she was. She idolized him, even when he wasn't nice to her. She'd trail him everywhere, begging him to play Hide and Seek. The last time he agreed, she realized he'd gone off to a friend's house, leaving her crouched in the Buckthorn bush in her neighbor's yard. Hours later, Roy sauntered up the driveway, shaking his scraggly curls like a Labradoodle and laughing at Carla as she berated him. When she told her parents about this, they repeated their admonitions that you can't trust anyone, even family.

"You come into the world alone, and you can only rely on yourself. People will only disappoint you," her parents had drilled into her since the age of three.

Even Emily, her closest friend growing up, wasn't privy to most of the thoughts in Carla's head. Carla didn't share much other than that she loved chocolate mint ice cream; her favorite color was silver, and her mom was Jewish and her father Episcopalian.

Carla and Roy were raised as Jews, but her father's last name was Christian. She loved how ironic it was when she would tell people her name was Carla Christian, but she was Jewish.

On the rare occasions when Beverly was home, she'd make popcorn and let Carla and Roy curl up on the couch with her to watch the thirty-two seconds of screen time she had on whatever show that was airing, even if it wasn't appropriate for children their age. Rarely did Beverly have more than one sentence before her character would run off-screen to fetch something and never come back. Carla would tell her mother how proud she was of her, hoping to bask in the rare occasions when her mother would honor her with a smile.

Carla was often left alone as a child, so her social life mainly consisted of the characters in her favorite books. She'd pretend they were her friends and wish the adults were her parents.

Roy had a different reaction to his loneliness. He would find friends, places, and activities that got him into trouble. When he wasn't home, which was most of the time, Carla would go into his room to take a whiff inside the box where Roy kept his marijuana. The pungent, woodsy smell made her feel adventurous and scared all at the same time. Once, Carla even pulled out his pipe and inhaled. Suddenly panicked that she'd done drugs, she felt her throat constrict as if there were a rock stuck in her windpipe, and when she ran to get water, she slipped and fell down the stairs. She never took Roy's pipe out again.

Carla didn't tattle to her parents about Roy and the pot; she didn't want him to get into more trouble than he already did. One morning, when Carla went into Roy's bedroom to wake him up for school, she saw tiny pink pills scattered beside his bed. She knew they were Xanax because sometimes she had seen her mother taking them. Carla picked the pills up as quietly as possible, put them in a plastic bag, and pushed them under his bed behind his *Mad* magazines.

When Carla was ten, Beverly was on set somewhere and Mort had gone to a friend's house to play poker. Roy was babysitting Carla, and when he tucked her in bed, he gave her a long warm hug.

"You be good," Roy said.

He'd never been that gentle with her before. A few minutes later, she heard a car start. She jumped out of bed and pulled her curtains back just in time to see Roy's car backing out of the driveway. Their block didn't have streetlights, so Carla tried to see his taillights for as long as she could through the vast blanket of black. Her whole body felt like it might seize up; he had left her completely alone. She prayed that Roy would feel guilty, and she'd soon see his headlights pulling back in the driveway.

Carla watched out the window for a while, then let the corner of the drapes drop. She didn't care if her mother complained that their electric bill was too high, she turned on every light in the house, including all the table lamps. As the hours passed, and Roy didn't return, Carla got her blanket and lay on the floor to wait for him.

"What are you doing in the living room?" her mother asked, waking Carla up when she came home at four a.m.

"Waiting for Roy." Carla yawned, which made her words slightly garbled. She stretched her arms over her head and twisted her torso from side to side. Her back hurt, and her shoulders ached. The ground was hard, not like her soft cushiony bed.

"He's not here?" Beverly ran upstairs with Carla at her heels.

"I'm going to kill him." Beverly stomped into her bedroom to wake up Mort. Carla followed, then thought better of it and went to her bed.

Later that morning, Beverly and Mort had coffee and waited for Roy's return. The screen door creaked as Carla poured Honey Nut Cheerios into a bowl. A heavy, dull knock reverberated through the house.

Beverly hurled herself toward the front door. "Lose your keys again, Roy?" she barked. She pulled the front door open wide. Carla saw a policeman standing on the front step, staring down at his black uniform shoes.

"What did he do now?" Beverly asked.

"Tell him we're not bailing him out this time," Mort yelled from the kitchen table.

Carla came up behind Beverly.

"Uh, I'm so sorry," the policeman said, looking up. "Your son, Roy… He, uh…"

"Out with it," her mother snapped. "What idiotic thing did he do this time?"

"He died. We found him in his car in the parking lot of Denny's with a shotgun."

Beverly jerked backward knocking Carla to the floor. It was almost as if retreating into the house would reverse the news. Beverly put her hand over her mouth and ran out of the room.

Carla heard herself screaming as though it were coming from someone else. Her father came rushing in and grabbed Carla to see if she'd hurt herself. Then the policeman told him what had happened to Roy. Carla would never forget the way her father's face aged in front of her eyes.

Beverly never got over the fact that her son committed suicide. She didn't get out of bed for months, her eyes slowly sinking into her face and her skin turning the color of old parchment paper.

Beverly and Mort blamed each other for Roy's death, which led to their eventual split. Since Beverly got very little money in the divorce, she told Carla she'd have to work harder, meaning she would be home even less. Beverly took jobs even if the cost of traveling exceeded what she got paid. To Carla, it felt like her mother wanted to be anywhere but home with her.

Mort moved to Chicago and lived with his sister, Marcy, for a year until he became enamored with one of the women who played in Marcy's Mah-Jong group.

"Your father is pursuing that little tramp like a rat searching for scraps in a Chinese restaurant," Beverly told Carla. Mort married her a year later and disappeared from Carla's life.

Carla's days became a relentless cycle of school, laundry, food shopping, cooking, and cleaning, and every night when she went to bed, she'd hug her pillow tightly and cry. She couldn't understand, even if things were bad, why someone would kill themselves.

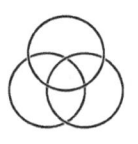

CHAPTER 7

Charlie

Carla's funeral was held in the smallest room at Mount Sinai cemetery. A raised platform held an urn with Carla's ashes, a flower arrangement, and a recent picture of her. The room was painted a pale shade of gray, and soft lighting and quiet instrumental music played in the background. The subtle scent of sandalwood floated through the air. Charlie knew these elements were designed to create a peaceful atmosphere to mourn a loss, but the sound of the wind outside contradicted any sense of calm she might have felt. The wind was so fierce that it caused the branches of trees to scrape against the windows like hungry werewolves trying to break in.

Charlie, Abby, and Morgan sat in white plastic chairs in the front row. Abby's husband, Alex, had to stay home with their children. Charlie scowled at all the empty chairs as if they were betraying her mother's memory.

"I put the obituary on Facebook *and* in the newspaper," Charlie said as if the low number of mourners were her fault.

There was a total of just over twenty people scattered around the room, and because of Carla's recent fame, five were curious strangers.

Carla's co-workers and a few of her neighbors, including Martha and Esther, sat in the third row next to Carla's best friend, Ginny. Charlie nodded at the women from her mother's book club. She knew them because when she was in town visiting her mother, Carla would convince her to go to a meeting, even though Charlie hadn't read the book. One of the women looked back at Charlie with such pity that she had to turn away.

The rabbi Morgan had found on the internet did a beautiful job incorporating what they had told him about their mom, even though he referred to her as Cara a few times.

During the service, the sisters fell apart in stages. When the rabbi described their mother as someone who loved her girls more than anything else, Morgan got choked up. When he went on to describe how Carla had raised the girls alone and put all her energy into making sure they had everything they needed to become successful adults, Charlie began to cry softly. When the rabbi ended the service by saying that Carla would live on through her daughters and grandchildren, Abby covered her mouth to stop a sob.

After the service, a short line of people waited to offer their condolences. Martha, first in line, bawled as if Carla had been *her* mother.

"Your mother had so much to live for," Martha wailed. "I should be the one in that urn; she saved my life!" Charlie tried to comfort her but gave up when she realized she couldn't.

After Martha moved away, the women from the book club stepped up together.

"Your mom was so nice; we're going to miss her," the first woman said.

"Carla joined our group eight years ago," another woman said. "She was on the quieter side, but she loved historical romances, kettle corn, and chocolate-covered graham crackers."

"Thank you all for coming today," Abby said.

Ginny approached each of the sisters, hugging them as if she could infuse them with all the emotional strength she could muster.

"Please know I'm here for all of you for whatever you need," Ginny said. "Call me any time."

"Thank you," Morgan said.

After everyone had left, Morgan went over to thank the rabbi. Abby picked up the urn, Charlie grabbed the three bouquets of flowers, and then the sisters walked outside to Abby's minivan.

Abby handed the urn to Morgan, who got into the front passenger seat. Charlie opened the back door and got in. Abby walked slowly around the car and slid into the driver's seat. The three of them sat there so long that the parking lot emptied, and the cleaning crew entered the building.

"It's sad that Mom didn't have more friends," Morgan said, breaking the silence.

"That might be because when she wasn't working, she spent most of her time thinking about us," Charlie said.

"I always liked that. Does that make me selfish?" Abby said, shrugging her shoulders and looking down at the floor like a dog that knew it was in trouble for something.

"No. Mom loved us, and she knew we loved her. We visited her a lot, and we talked to her on the phone at least once a week," Charlie said to the guilt inside her head.

"Did you guys ever notice that when you'd ask Mom about herself, she'd change the subject?" Morgan asked.

"Yes. She'd ask me a million questions about the kids and barely tell me anything about what was going on with her," Abby said.

"I'm a psychotherapist; how could I not have seen that she was always dodging my questions?" Charlie asked.

"It just seemed like who she was," Morgan said.

Charlie nodded. "What do people do after they say goodbye to the most important person in their life?"

"When Alex's grandfather died, we went to Alex's aunt's house and honored his memory by eating cold cuts," Abby said.

"I want to honor Mom, but I'm not hungry," Morgan said.

"Me either," Abby said.

"If we're going to eat anything, we should get corned beef sandwiches from Art's Deli," Charlie said. "Those were Mom's favorite."

"So, if she were here, that's what she'd want," Morgan said.

"I don't think any of us know what Mom would've wanted," Abby said. Morgan and Charlie nodded solemnly.

Abby blew her nose and started the car but left it in park. "Do you think her death could've been an accident?" Abby asked.

"Taking an entire bottle of pills is no accident," Charlie said.

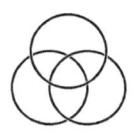

CHAPTER 8

Abby

Since Morgan was the first one to the front door of Carla's house, she unlocked it. When they walked inside, Abby couldn't take her eyes off how neat and organized everything was.

"Whoa," Abby said.

When Abby visited her mom, there would usually be a pile of clothes on a chair and a set of towels on the corner of the couch waiting to be folded. Dishes were always drying in the sink, and their mother had kept every *People* magazine from the last ten years. A few dishes were carefully stacked on the counter, and there wasn't a magazine in sight.

The house was dust-free and sparkling clean. The kitchen smelled strongly of Lysol. The books on the shelf in the living room were organized, and a jigsaw puzzle with only a handful of pieces was waiting to be put in. It looked like their mother had moved out, except for her cherry-red lipstick on a coffee cup on the side table in the living room.

"Mom didn't want to leave us a mess to clean up," Charlie said, her voice cracking. "When I talked to her at the beginning of last week, she was fine. Or at least she sounded fine."

"You guys should've seen this coming before I did. I have four kids and a husband to take care of," Abby said, then picked up the mug and put it in the dishwasher.

"Are you blaming us?" Morgan said. "How could we know she'd kill herself?"

"I'm sorry, you're right," Abby said, then her hands began to shake. "What if this is my fault?

Mom visited me three weeks ago, and the kids didn't give her a moment's peace." Abby put her face in her hands.

Morgan put her arm around Abby's shoulder. "Mom didn't kill herself because your kids are nuts," Morgan said.

Abby suddenly looked up. "Did you just say my kids are nuts?"

"She didn't mean nuts; she meant…wild," Charlie said.

"No, I meant nuts," Morgan said. Abby pulled Morgan's arm off from around her.

"Come on, you know how much mom loved your kids," Charlie said.

Abby knew in her heart that was true. The sisters plopped down on the couch and, almost in unison, put their feet up on the coffee table.

"If Mom were here right now, she'd say, 'No shoes on the table,'" Morgan said.

All three of them slid out of their shoes and let them drop to the floor.

"Do you think Mom was lonely?" Abby said, biting her lip. "People who are lonely might take their own life."

"If our father were alive, maybe he and Mom would've gotten back together, and then she would've had someone else to love," Charlie said.

"Mom said that a few years before he died, he walked out on us, saying he didn't want to be a father anymore. That's not the kind of man she would've wanted back," Morgan insisted.

"I wish I could remember him, but I was an infant when he left," Abby said, curling her feet up on the couch.

"I was three, so I have almost no memories of him," Charlie said.

"I remember some things," Morgan said. "Like that he used to tickle me until I couldn't stop laughing, and I'd almost pee my pants," Morgan said.

"It's hard to believe that's the same man who didn't want us," Abby said.

"Someone can have good moments and still not be a good person," Charlie said.

"At least we had Mom," Abby said. "She made sure we had a happy childhood."

"Do you remember when she took us to Solvang for the weekend?" Charlie said.

"That was fun," Morgan said, then laughed. "Remember that first night when we went to dinner, and she told us we couldn't have any of the rolls on the table because it would ruin our appetite."

"And then she shoved them and the butter packets in her purse so we wouldn't have to spend money on breakfast the next morning," Charlie said.

"And when the waiter noticed the empty basket and asked if we wanted more bread, Abby screamed from her booster seat that Mom had stolen all of it, and she didn't get even one piece," Morgan said. "Abby always ratted everyone out."

The girls erupted in giggles, quickly becoming guffaws and then silence.

After a few minutes, Abby went into the kitchen and scoured the cabinets for the one vice she knew her mother had. While the food they'd bought at the deli sat on the counter, Abby plopped a large bag of mini-Oreos on the coffee table, and each of them grabbed a handful and stuffed them into their mouths.

"What are we going to do without her?" Abby asked.

"I have no idea," Morgan said, standing up and pacing behind the couch. "We're missing something here," she said.

"I know. People don't kill themselves without a reason," Charlie said.

"She didn't seem depressed," Abby said, then pushed the Oreos away, her stomach beginning to ache. Then she stood up and paced alongside Morgan.

"I was going to tell you guys this later, but I'm going to take a leave of absence from work and move in here. I need to find out why Mom did this," Morgan said.

Abby stopped pacing and looked at Morgan.

"I'm going to join you," Charlie said.

"Thank you. I'd rather not do it alone," Morgan said, seemingly less anxious than she had been a few minutes before.

"Wait, what about me?" Abby whined like a four-year-old left with a babysitter when her parents went out on a Saturday night.

"Uh…you have four young kids?" Charlie said.

"So, because I procreated, you want to leave me out?" Abby's voice went up another octave.

"I think we both assumed it would be hard for you to get away for a week or two," Morgan said, sitting back down.

"She's my mom, too," Abby said. "I loved her, and besides, I haven't had a break in years!"

"Will Alex be able to handle things if you leave for that long?" Morgan asked.

"He'll be fine," Abby said, unsure if she believed it. She clicked on the notes app on her phone and began typing furiously. "I'll go to the grocery store, cook a week's worth of meals, and put them in the freezer. Then I'll pay all the bills, clean the house, and hire someone to watch the kids during the day."

"I'm exhausted just listening to you," Charlie said.

"Great, then we have a plan," Morgan said. "We all head home and get our lives under control," Morgan said.

"So, we meet back here in four or five days?" Charlie asked.

"Or, in Abby's case, a month," Morgan said. As Morgan and Charlie laughed, Abby gave her sisters the finger, making them laugh even harder.

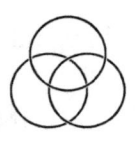

CHAPTER 9

Morgan

Late that afternoon, Albert, asleep on a towel in the backseat of Morgan's rental car, was softly whistling air through his nostrils. Morgan headed south on the 405 freeway toward the airport hoping the traffic would be light, although that was rare in Los Angeles. She tried to zone out, but the music on the radio kept distracting her, so she turned it off.

How could I go two weeks with only a five-minute call with my mother? she thought. Her remorse pulled her down like an anchor plunging to the sea floor. Lately, things at work had been busy, and the little free time she had she spent working her program--the one thing that kept her sane and sober.

Morgan loved her mother, but her relationship with her was complicated. Carla had done her best as a single parent, but for Morgan, seeing her mom struggle was a constant reminder that her father had left them. The feelings of abandonment made Morgan crave bourbon.

Morgan was five when her mother told her that her father would not be joining them at their new home.

"Your dad left us," Carla had said when Morgan got home from school.

"Where did he go?" Morgan asked.

"That's not important," Carla said.

"But I didn't get to say goodbye," Morgan said.

"We're better off without him," Carla said, ending the conversation.

Even at that young age, Morgan couldn't understand that the father who left was the same man who taught her how to play the harmonica when she was four. The "music" she played sounded like a crescendo into madness, yet he happily encouraged her. That same year, her father also taught her how to ride a bike. While all the other kids her age still used training wheels, he convinced her she didn't need them. He bought her a tiny spring-green Schwinn, and although she kept falling off, he continued to encourage her without getting frustrated.

Looking back, Morgan wondered if her happy memories were real or if her mind had fabricated a fantasy so she could torture herself on what she missed out on in life.

When Morgan turned seven, Carla told her and her sisters that their father had died. Knowing that she'd never see him again brought out all the emotions that Morgan had pushed down when he left. She became angry that her dad could no longer come to his senses and return home. Morgan refused to go to school, vacillating between sobbing and denial.

Not having any male role models affected her, Charlie, and Abby differently. None of the Weiss daughters had grown into adults without being scarred.

At twelve, Morgan started drinking with her first boyfriend, who was two years older than her. At fifteen, she smoked weed with her eighteen-year-old crush, and at seventeen, a college guy introduced her to opioids. Her desperate need for the wrong kind of male attention had not only been her downfall but was embarrassingly cliché.

Morgan dropped out of high school her senior year but had trouble keeping a job. She'd worked at a market, at a McDonald's, and even drove an ice cream truck. Being high and moving a heavy machine that played jingles as kids ran after her was a sure way to get arrested. She got her first DUI when a group of six-year-olds witnessed her jump the sidewalk and crash into a stoplight pole.

Four years ago, she joined Alcoholics Anonymous, got sober, and received her GED. Since then, she'd struggled through completing two years of community college.

During her first year in college, when she sat across the desk from one of the school counselors, Morgan heard words that made her smile from deep inside.

"I think it's time you got tested for learning difficulties," Harvey, the counselor, said.

"You think I have a learning disorder?" Morgan asked.

"I can't diagnose you, but my educated guess would be an audio processing issue and ADHD."

Morgan stared at him.

"What?" Harvey asked.

"It's just hearing you say that hit me like a bolt of thunder."

"You mean lightning?"

"See, I do have a learning disorder," she said. "All this time, I thought I had a hard time in school because I drank myself stupid."

Morgan floated out of that meeting with happy tears in her eyes. She wanted to sing joyfully and hug the first person she saw, but she changed her mind when she got on the elevator with a slovenly guy with hair coming out of his ears.

Morgan planned to get formally diagnosed, then find the money to go back to school, earn her bachelor's degree, and become a substance abuse counselor. She tried hard to save money, but her car died, her refrigerator broke, and her job didn't pay enough for her to work less and go back to school.

As tough as these obstacles were, there was one thing that stood in Morgan's way more than money: her fear of failing. From her disastrous years in school to all the times she was drunk at important family events, Morgan couldn't get the look of disappointment on her mother's face erased from her mind. If she had gone back to school to get her degree only to drop out again, she would have gotten her mom's hopes up for nothing.

School wasn't the only thing Morgan hadn't been able to follow through with. The first time she tried to get sober, she thought she could do it on her own. That didn't work. The next time, she took Charlie's advice and went into therapy. This would be the first time she spoke to anyone about her past mistakes. Morgan was relieved that things were progressing slowly and the therapist hadn't pushed her out of her comfort zone. Until two months later, when her therapist started the session a little differently.

"I've been seeing you for a while and noticed we haven't yet delved into why you first began drinking," the therapist said. "Is it possible that you were trying to numb the feelings of abandonment of a father you barely remembered?"

Morgan clasped her hands together for a minute, then began cracking her knuckles.

"I know this is difficult," the therapist said, "but it will help you if we explore how not having a male role model in your life has affected you."

"I don't need to talk about it," Morgan said.

"From what you've already told me, there are some things we should go deeper on that will help you work through old trauma."

"I don't want to talk about my father," Morgan said sharply.

Morgan finished the session with clenched teeth. When the hour was over, she headed to the nearest bar.

After a brief slip, Morgan returned to sobriety with a vengeance. She threw herself into AA, relied on her sponsor, and went to conferences as often as she could. AA became a new addiction—one she could thrive on.

Sobriety was Morgan's first goal, and her second was to get a job where the people she worked with appreciated her. She accomplished that when she was hired at Bloomington's Mortuary. When Morgan applied, the competition was far from fierce, so having been arrested for a DUI didn't seem to bother her soon-to-be employer.

"The job is yours as long as you can stay off Facebook long enough to reorder embalming fluid her boss Carl said during the interview. "With our last employee, we got so backed up we had to put up a sign for two weeks that said, *If deceased, drive to Samson's Mortuary.*"

Morgan liked the job, but even more, she liked the security that there would always be dead people, so being laid off for lack of work wasn't likely. Her responsibilities mainly consisted of paying vendors and overseeing the stock of coffins and urns. She made a deal with Carl that she could hide in the back when a funeral took place. She didn't want to deal with mourners; sad people depressed her.

Morgan's plane landed back in Oregon half an hour early, so it was only ten p.m. when she pulled up to her apartment with Albert in tow. Her building, the color of curdled milk, boasted an oversized sign that said Lake Oswego's Luxury Living. The only factual words in that sign were Lake Oswego.

Morgan could have afforded to live in an apartment with all the amenities in an area where she wouldn't have felt safe, but she chose a crappy building in a nicer neighborhood. A building where elderly men in their shortie pajamas, knee socks, and crocs sunbathed next to the pool. A pool that had water the color of wet cardboard and smelled like a gaggle of teenage boys' sneakers. Morgan worried that if she even dipped a single toe in that pool, it would fall off, which meant she'd have to trash her collection of flip-flops.

She headed down the ramp into the underground parking structure and backed into her spot, trying not to scrape her car on the yellow pole again. When she opened her car door, Albert sprinted like a kid getting out of school for the summer.

"Albert, wait!" Morgan yelled as she grabbed him and hoisted him into her arms. He was much heavier than he looked.

Albert had been Carla's constant companion for years, so the warmth of his fur against Morgan's chest made her think about her mother and how much she had already missed her. She balanced the little sausage in her arms while reaching for her apartment key in her purse. Albert's juicy tongue slid from her chin to her nose as if he knew she was now his meal ticket.

Albert ran inside Morgan's apartment like he had always lived there. She couldn't help smiling; it would be nice having the company. After all the partying she'd done in her youth, the quieter life she led now suited her, but at times it could be lonely. Her friends were mainly a few women from her program, most of whom were married. Morgan wasn't interested in dating because she had been prone to being with the wrong men; the right ones didn't want her.

Albert wandered into the living room. Immediately, his hackles raised as he stuck his nose under the couch. She now knew exactly where her cat, Brigitta, was.

"You'll get used to our guest, Brigitta," Morgan called out. "But for now, I'll protect you." She picked up Albert, brought him into her bedroom, and closed the door.

Then she picked up her phone and called her boss. "Hi, Carl, it's Morgan."

"Hi, I've been thinking about you. How're you doing?" Carl asked.

"Not great. I'm home for a few days, but I need to head back to California and take care of some things. I hope taking a short leave of absence from work is okay."

"Of course, the dead don't wait, but I can. Take care of yourself, and don't worry about us. If we get backed up, I still have the sign sending corpses to Samson's Mortuary."

Morgan thanked him and hung up. She thought about what she needed to pack for a more extended stay. The weather in Los Angeles was warmer than in Oregon, so she stuffed some of her lighter clothes from her closet and drawers into her biggest suitcase. Then, she googled AA meetings close to her mother's house and printed the list. She needed to stay on track, especially during this time. Following her program had become the one constant she couldn't do without.

Morgan did laundry, then packed again, grabbing a few more toiletries to add to her suitcase. She wasn't leaving for four more days, but she liked to pack early, so she had more time not to forget something. She left room in the suitcase for the three books she kept on her nightstand. *The Subtle Art of Not Giving a Fuck* by Mark Manson, John Purkiss's *The Power of Letting Go*, and Nick Trenton's *23 Techniques to Relieve Stress, Stop Negative Spirals, Declutter Your Mind and Focus on the Present*. Morgan wasn't one to see a bright light at the end of the tunnel; she only saw a tiny flicker. All of these books helped her stay positive and continue moving forward.

The next few days went by quickly. When it was time for Morgan to head back to her mom's, she went into the closet to get the cat carrier. Brigitta, who had been watching from the bathroom, scurried by Morgan, racing under the bed so fast that some of her fur flew into the air. Morgan stuck her tongue out and fished the hair out of her mouth.

"Brigitta..." she called out but knew it was useless.

Morgan got down on her stomach and looked under the bed. Next to a long plastic container holding mementos from her past and journals that she had written in over the years were two of the most beautiful copper eyes staring back at her.

"Come on, honey, we have to go." Morgan pushed the crate toward the bed, hoping Brigitta would get in it.

"There's a salmon treat in there," Morgan said in a sing-song voice.

Brigitta shook her head as if to say, 'No flipping way.' Brigitta didn't like to swear; she was a lady.

"We aren't going to the vet. We're going on an airplane, and then we'll be staying at a much nicer place than this." Brigitta yawned indifferently and still didn't move. Morgan tried a different tack: "If I leave without you, you will starve and shrivel up and die under there, and then my whole room will stink."

When Brigitta still didn't come out, Morgan reached her hand under the bed and grabbed Brigitta, hoping she wouldn't claw her.

"Ha, I got you now," Morgan said.

She stroked Brigitta's fur, which was the color of oatmeal, and Brigitta purred happily. Morgan put her in the carrier, then got Brigitta's food and catnip and took them to her car. Lastly, she retrieved Albert and her suitcase and headed to the airport.

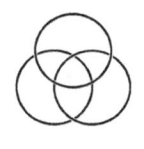

CHAPTER 10

Charlie

Charlie drove the twenty minutes home from Phoenix airport to her condo in Scottsdale. When she pulled up in front of the terracotta stucco building with the red tile roof, no matter how bad her day had been, she was grateful she could own a home in such a beautiful building.

As she exited the car, the sweltering sun radiating off the pavement made it appear that steam was rising from the surface. She let out a cough caused by the dust floating in the air. Charlie could barely walk without slouching as she dragged herself to her front door. The whole flight home she thought of nothing else but the tragic way her mother died. She told herself not to take her mother's suicide personally, but she couldn't make sense of why her mother wouldn't want to be part of her life anymore.

Charlie walked inside leaving her suitcase at the front door. She grabbed an afghan off the arm of the couch and curled up under it. She picked up the remote, hoping an episode of *Family Feud* would distract her.

Steve Harvey asked, "What's something someone keeps in their car for emergencies?" One by one, the contestants came up with an answer. When the grandfather in the family answered, Charlie erupted off the couch.

"Did you seriously just say condoms?" she hollered at the TV so loudly she almost didn't realize her phone was ringing. She fumbled in her purse to find it, tossing out receipts, her sunglasses, and her wallet. She cursed the purse for having so many pockets. It seemed to ring louder, as if the phone was aware she couldn't find it. Then she turned her purse upside down and shook it and finally the phone fell out of a pocket on the side of the purse. A pocket she never knew was there.

"Hi, Rick," she said a little curtly.

"Hey, are you home from LA yet?" he asked.

"I just got in."

"Oh, good. Could you go to the market for me? I have my poker game tonight at Darryl's place, and I won't have time to get to the grocery store for days."

"Sure… okay," Charlie nodded.

"I desperately need milk."

"Low fat or two percent?"

"Whichever. And I need a few more things."

Charlie opened the notes app on her phone and began furiously typing as Rick read off a list.

"I got it," Charlie said, typing some more.

"And can you make sure the cottage cheese is the one with the small curd?"

"Right, I know."

"You are the best, thank you. You know I appreciate it."

"I know you do. Talk to you later, bye, I love…" Charlie said before realizing Rick had already hung up. She dropped her phone back inside her purse, making sure it didn't go into the mystery pocket.

Charlie met Rick during her senior year in college, and the fun had gone by the wayside during her second year of grad school. It was more important that she had a man who wouldn't leave her, although lately, she wondered if that would be so bad.

Although Charlie thought she loved Rick, she was relieved she had avoided moving in with him when he'd asked her. He'd always bring it up in the least romantic way.

The first time was while they were eating Thai takeout on paper plates and watching the horror movie, 'Friday the Thirteenth.'

"Why don't we bite the bullet and move in together," he had said. "We could save a lot of money."

Charlie gave Rick all kinds of excuses for why she couldn't do it. The first time, she told him she needed quiet to study for her psychology boards. After she passed those, she told him her lease wasn't up, and she wasn't allowed to have anyone else move in. At the time, she'd been renting month to month, but he didn't need to know that. She didn't want to live with him until he proposed, which still hadn't happened.

Later that evening, Charlie unlocked the door to Rick's apartment. She found the house in complete darkness, which reminded her of her childhood when her mother would run around turning off lights.

Carla would nag, "You girls are going to have to drop out of school and work in a coal mine to pay the electric bill." At one point she told them she was going to call the police. Charlie was ten when a friend told her that "lights on" wasn't a crime.

"This is the last time I say yes to doing this. I know I said that before, but this time, I mean it," Charlie said loudly, making sure she heard herself.

Charlie put the groceries down. As she felt her way along the wall looking for the switch, she tripped over something and fell. She crawled over to where she knew a lamp sat on a side table and turned it on. She saw what had tried to kill her; Rick's sweatshirt, jeans, and Nikes were clumped into a pile. It looked as if he'd been sucked up into an alien spaceship where clothing was discouraged. *Was he naked when he ran out of here?* The thought made Charlie snicker.

She headed to the kitchen, turning on every light she passed. She opened the bags and put the milk, the cottage cheese, and the rest of the groceries she'd bought into his refrigerator. Charlie stopped when she noticed the cream cheese, lettuce, blueberries, and an avocado she'd bought last time were moldy or turning brown.

"Are you kidding me?" she said, dropping the rotten food into the trash. Then she took a bite out of one of the apples she'd just bought him. "You don't deserve to sit here and go bad," she said to the apple.

She wiped down the shelves with a damp cloth. *I wish I had a cleaning fairy who would come to my house. Oh, yeah, there is one. Me.*

By the time Charlie was done, her T-shirt was stuck to her body and sweat clung to her skin. Rick barely used the air conditioner, no matter how hot it was outside. Charlie's place was always a comfortable seventy-one degrees, which was probably one of the reasons Rick liked spending their time together at her place--that and she never let her food look like it was creating its own civilization.

She finished the apple and tossed the core in the trash. Then she gathered the *Los Angeles Times* pages that were spread out all over the kitchen table and placed them in a neat pile. She picked up all of the clothes on the floor and dropped them in the hamper in his bathroom.

"Since this will be the last time I clean for him, I might as well finish the job," she said, then added, "Why am I talking to myself?"

As a reward for all her hard work, she laid down on his couch and opened a magazine. Before she knew it, she was asleep.

When she awoke there was a blanket over her, and the room was dark except for a red and white flashing light seeping through the blinds from the dry cleaners across the street. Charlie rubbed her eyes to focus. The digital clock on the mantel read 11:00 p.m. She tiptoed into Rick's room to find him tucked in bed, the comforter around him rising and falling rhythmically.

Charlie picked up the covers on her side of the bed, then thought, *If I stay tonight, I'll have to make breakfast in the morning and be late to the office.* She left Rick a note and went home.

Charlie spent the next day seeing clients and contacting others she had on her schedule for the following week. She let them know there had been a death in her family, and she would be gone for a short time. She gave them a referral for another therapist in case they needed to talk to someone before she got back. No matter how panicked a few of her clients seemed to be, she knew Rick would take her being gone again worse.

When Charlie got home late that afternoon, Rick was sitting on the couch waiting for her.

He jumped up and gave her a tight hug. "Why did you leave last night?" he asked, holding on to her a few seconds longer than usual.

Charlie recoiled as she took in the neediness that hung off him. "I had an early client," she said.

"I missed you."

"Well, we still have a few days together before I go back to my mom's house." She sucked in her breath, anticipating his response.

"Why are you going back?" he whined.

Charlie explained the plan that her sisters and she came up with to try to figure out her mom's motives for ending her own life.

"Isn't it obvious? Carla was depressed," Rick said.

"But she wasn't." Charlie turned away; she'd cried enough to him on the phone over the past week.

Rick shook his head. "Does it matter at this point? She's gone. Wouldn't it be better for you and your sisters to accept it so you can grieve and move on?"

Despite her best efforts, Charlie began sobbing. "I can't grieve until I know why she did it." She wasn't surprised that Rick didn't understand. He wasn't close to his parents; he only talked to them on birthdays and holidays.

Rick took her in his arms again. "Let it out. It's okay, I'm here for you." Charlie continued to cry into his chest, knowing she was probably staining his shirt with her mascara.

"So, you'll stay home?" he asked.

Charlie pulled away and looked at him. "Seriously?"

"What?" he said. "Most women would love it if their boyfriend missed them that much."

His attempt to make his clinginess a positive made her want to smack him. "I'll only be gone for a week," she said.

He doesn't need to know that I'm going to be away for however long it takes.

Realizing it was non-negotiable, Rick relented. "Okay, I can live without you for a week." He kissed her forehead. "I hope you and your sisters find the answers you're looking for." He kissed her one more time and then headed to the kitchen. Charlie followed him.

"Thank you for restocking my fridge last night," he said, taking out her milk and pouring himself a glass. "For the future, I've decided no more two percent milk, it's either skim or nothing. I need to get rid of this jiggly belly." He patted his six-pack abs beneath his shirt.

That evening, Rick took her out for dinner. As they talked about their day at work and a movie they both wanted to see, Charlie looked at him over the fake rose in the middle of the white tablecloth. She told herself that having him to talk to was better than being alone. She reached across the table and took his hand in hers.

"I love you a lot," he said, then lightly kissed her hand.

"I love you, too," she said, and right then, she needed to believe it.

After dinner they went back to Charlie's condo. Rick turned on CNN and played Angry Birds on his phone. Charlie headed to her bedroom.

She pulled out her largest suitcase and scanned her closet for what items she wanted to pack. She had a few more days to figure it out, but she'd rather pack than sit with Rick and listen to a bunch of correspondents contemplating why the world was falling apart when hers had already imploded.

Charlie took out several tops and pants in various colors. Even if she was in mourning, she didn't want to wear black every day she was there. She wished she was one of those women who bought every item in one or two colors so all the pieces would work together and she could stop overpacking.

I wonder if we should be sitting shiva, even though we aren't religious, she thought. Carla hadn't been a pious Jew, but she was a cultural one. She raised the girls according to Jewish traditions, lighting candles on Hanukkah and having a Passover seder in the spring. Charlie would also fast on Yom Kippur, although she would've had to admit that she mostly did it to jump-start a diet.

After packing enough and closing her suitcase, she suddenly remembered her favorite pink flowered dress. *Don't forget about me*, she imagined it saying. Charlie took the dress off its hanger; *I'll need it if we go somewhere nice.* She reopened her suitcase and neatly placed it inside.

But is it appropriate to go out when we're grieving? She pulled the dress out of the suitcase and held it in her arms. Her eyes darted around the room as if someone would give her a hard time for even considering going out. However, the only person who had ever made Charlie feel bad about anything besides Charlie herself was Morgan.

Charlie remembered the time when they were kids, and she and Morgan made peanut butter and jelly sandwiches. Not only did Morgan yell at Charlie for not spreading the preserves correctly, but she also blamed her for not paying attention to Abby, who had grabbed the olive oil out of the cabinet and spilled it all over the floor. Morgan made Charlie clean up the mess.

Another time, Morgan took Charlie to a parking lot so she could practice driving. When Charlie was working on parking, Morgan suddenly started screaming and flailing at a bee that had flown into the car. Charlie, startled, crashed into a post. Morgan told Charlie that she would never be a good driver, and for years, Charlie believed her.

Charlie looked at the flowered dress in her hand, then let it slip and fall gently into the suitcase. *It wants to come with me and doesn't care what Morgan would say.*

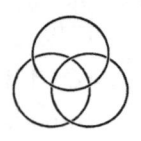

CHAPTER 11

Abby

When Abby left Carla's house, she had to make the two-hour drive to her home near San Diego, which took almost three and a half hours. When she walked through the front door, she didn't hear the usual hurricane of rambunctious activity that usually greeted her. *It's quiet--too quiet*, she thought, her maternal antennae quickly going up.

She tiptoed to the kids' playroom and peeked in. Her daughters, Addison and Emma, were sitting on two tiny chairs. Hudson and Levi were standing behind them, each holding scissors to one of their siblings' hair.

As Hudson and Levi counted down, "Four...three...two..." Abby raced in and, in one smooth motion, simultaneously grabbed the scissors out of both boys' hands before they reached "one."

"You cannot cut your sisters' hair." Abby's voice teetered on the precipice of yelling but didn't fall off.

"We weren't really going to do it," Hudson said, smiling impishly.

"Yes, we were," Levi said. "It was Hudson's idea."

"I was kidding," Hudson said.

"First of all, you're too young to use scissors without supervision," Abby said. "And second, I believe Levi." She looked at Hudson sternly, then to all of them. "Come with me."

Abby took the kids into the family room and told them to sit on the couch. Then she turned on the television to the latest sequel of *The Penguins of Madagascar*.

"Is this our punishment?" Levi asked.

Abby plopped down in a chair next to them. If one of them tried to escape, she was ready to pounce.

"No, this is so Mommy has a chance to catch her breath before she has an anxiety attack."

"What's an anxiety attack?" Levi asked.

"It's when Mommies curl up in a ball."

"You mean like a summersault?"

"Something like that."

"Cool," Levi said.

Ten minutes later, all four kids were sound asleep, lying half on each other like a litter of puppies. Abby couldn't help smiling; she loved when their eyes were closed. It was the one time she could remind herself that they wouldn't always be this age.

Alex came out of the bathroom, drying his hair with a towel. "Hi," he said. When he saw the sleeping brood, he whispered, "I jumped in the shower when I heard you drive up. I wanted to be clean before you saw me."

"You're so thoughtful," she said, kissing him. Abby debated whether to tell him about the scissors incident but decided not to since she was about to let him know that she'd be leaving for a week--that would be enough for him to handle.

Alex and Abby had the only traditional relationship of the Weiss sisters. Abby met Alex in middle school and married him the week after they graduated from college, neither of them having ever gone on a date with anyone else. Alex knew everything about her and accepted her no matter what she did. Like when she backed her car into the same fence three different times or when she threw out his Beastie Boys T-shirt. That last one she did on purpose, but he didn't get mad. He understood because she had so much on her plate.

Alex had all the qualities that were important to Abby. He was a steady presence in her life, someone who always had her back. The part of him she adored the most was how he could always make her laugh. He was her rock, a safe place, and the best father her kids could've had.

As evidenced by getting together with Alex so young, Abby didn't like change. Even as a kid, when she decided on something, she didn't waver. After performing as a tree in the school play in first grade, she announced that she was going to be an actress. Her only line had been, "Our leaves will be falling," which she practiced over and over. When it came time for her to say it, she said, "Our lives will be failing." The audience burst into laughter, and at the end of the show, Abby got a standing ovation. She knew immediately that joyful feeling was one she wanted to continue to experience.

She joined scene study, method acting, and cold reading classes in high school and college, winning the starring role in almost every production she auditioned for. She welcomed the praise people showered on her, but Alex was the only person who knew she was riddled with imposter syndrome. He talked her through her nerves before auditions and encouraged her to push through.

Determined not to let the fear take over, Abby signed up for showcases, hoping to see in herself what others did. Right after college graduation, a well-known Hollywood agent saw her and offered to represent her. The day before she was supposed to sign the contract, Abby found out she was pregnant.

She wouldn't admit it out loud, but relief wrapped around her like a warm coat in the dead of winter. The stress, anxiety, and fear that plagued her every time she auditioned or performed vanished when that extra line on the pregnancy test appeared. She no longer had to worry that people would discover that she was a talentless fraud.

Like her mother, Abby had all her kids in quick succession. She had two boys, then two girls quickly afterward, like a slightly smaller Brady Bunch. However, unlike Carol and Mike Brady, she and Alex felt overwhelmed by their mob. No matter how many parenting videos Abby watched on YouTube, her kids figured out she wasn't good at being consistent.

"Honey, can we talk for a minute?" Abby whispered to Alex.

"Sure, what's up?" he whispered back. The two of them sat at the far end of the sectional, careful not to touch the clump of arms and legs intermingled like a bunch of mannequins thrown into a garbage bin. He pulled her close, and she laid her head on his shoulder.

"I have to leave again in a few days," she said.

"Where are you going?" he asked, his voice rising slightly.

Abby put her finger to her lips and cocked her head at the sleeping brood. "Morgan, Charlie and I are going to stay at my mom's house and try to figure out why she…" The words 'killed herself' stuck in her throat.

He nodded. "Why do you have to stay there?"

"We need time to go through her things, and I can't drive three hours back and forth every day."

"Okay, but how will I go to work and watch the kids? My parents are going on vacation, so they won't be here to help this time."

"I'll find someone to watch them during the day."

"We've been through all the babysitters in a twenty-mile radius. Four little kids is a lot."

"There's still that one woman who said she'd come back."

"Who?"

"The one who used to volunteer at the juvenile detention center. She doesn't scare easily."

"We'll see about that," Alex grinned, and Abby laughed.

"It'll only be a week or so, and we'll pay her double."

Abby snuggled up even closer to him. She was asking a lot, but she also knew he would support whatever she needed. She gave him a slow, meaningful kiss and then carefully stood so as not to shake the couch and disturb her sleeping progeny.

She did five loads of laundry and paid the bills to lessen the upcoming burden on Alex. Then, she cleaned up the toys and prepared dinner while Alex bathed the kids. When she was folding the last of the laundry, Addison toddled into her room.

"Mommy..." Addison said, opening her tiny arms wide. Abby scooped her up and embraced her, peppering her with kisses. Addison giggled like a preteen girl with her first crush.

Abby took a whiff of Addison's freshly washed hair and remembered how much she loved babies. The day Emma was born, Alex confessed that he wanted six kids. Abby said she was happy with the four they had and didn't think they should have more. This caused a small rift between them until she relented and said she'd reconsider when Emma was four. When Emma turned one, Abby knew she wouldn't reconsider.

She carried Addison into the playroom and sat on the floor with the rest of her kids. Alex came in, and while Levi and Hudson colored together and raced cars, Emma and Levi played dress up. Abby and Alex let them stay up later than usual, as she would be gone again in a few days. Part of her felt guilty for looking forward to having no responsibilities for as long as she could before being sucked back into the chaotic universe that was her life.

CHAPTER 12

Carla

Carla never talked about her past; some things were too painful to revisit. During her childhood, she longed for someone to laugh at her jokes or wrap their arms around her when she was sad. Two things she never got from her parents.

Beverly didn't allow Carla to date until she was sixteen, and although her mother was rarely home to enforce that, Carla was a rule follower. She didn't go on her first date until she was a junior in high school. She dated four boys that year, but none of them flooded her brain with enough hormones to knock her off her platform shoes. That finally happened in 1988, when she met Brian in her sophomore year at Brooklyn College.

Carla had been going to the college library every day after school to study; it was better than being alone in her house. She had no idea until later that Brian had first noticed her outside that building. He told her that when he saw her, the wind was whipping her hair into her face, and it looked like she could barely see. She was weighed down by her denim backpack and trying to balance a purse, a jacket, and a can of coke. Something about Carla intrigued Brian, and he waited outside the library every day for a week, gathering up the courage to talk to her.

One day, as Carla walked home, she became aware that a guy had been following her for the last few blocks. She was slightly creeped out, so she walked faster and faster until she was almost jogging. When she developed a cramp, she stopped, bent over, and grabbed her side. The young man caught up to her, and she balled her fists just in case.

"Hi," he said.

Carla raised her head and looked him over. His jeans didn't have any holes, the color of his shirt was bright, as though it wasn't a hand-me-down that had gone through a washing machine hundreds of times, and he wore white tennis shoes without any scuff marks. He was either a regular guy or a well-dressed mugger.

"Hi," she said quietly. She ran her fingers through her hair.

"Do you mind if I walk with you?" he asked.

"It's a public street," Carla said, which might have sounded snotty, but her voice had a lilt to it that conveyed she didn't mind.

He walked alongside her for a moment before he spoke again. "I'm Brian. I just transferred to Brooklyn College, and I don't know anyone."

"I'm Carla." She put her hand out to shake his as if she were on a job interview.

"Nice to meet you, Carla," he said, taking her hand and shaking it lightly.

Carla smiled but wasn't sure what else to say. Her usual demeanor could be considered shy if one was being nice or standoffish if one wasn't. Her aura wasn't conducive to boys approaching her. She continued walking, and Brian kept in step with her.

Carla waited for him to speak again, which she quickly realized he excelled at. In a very short time, it became apparent that he could've had a conversation with a thumb tack.

"I love New York, don't you?" He didn't wait for her to answer. "I like the snow and that we have all the seasons. I'd never want to go to California; they have summer all year long. The only way I'd ever move away is if someday I had kids. Then, if my wife agreed, we might want to raise them in Connecticut or Massachusetts, but not Vermont or Maine, there's not enough to do there."

Carla listened to him go on about how he was raised in Mystic, a seaport town in Connecticut, and he loved movies, thin-crust pizza, and dogs. She enjoyed the fact that he talked so she didn't have to carry the entire conversation, which she had to do with other boys. And when he asked her a bunch of questions, he seemed genuinely interested in her answers.

Carla thought he was charming and felt a warmth and comfort she'd never felt around any other boys. Besides, they had a lot in common, from their love of U2's music to how many times they read 'Cider House Rules.'

After that first day, Brian waited for Carla in front of the giant elm tree on the corner of her street to walk with her to school every morning. And he'd show up at her last class every afternoon and walk her home. They got to know each other in bits and pieces, and by the end of that first month, Carla thought she must be in love. She hadn't fallen off her shoes, but her heart did a cartwheel whenever she knew she was about to see him.

When Brian invited her over to meet his parents, Carla felt it was a pivotal moment in their relationship. She put on her favorite slacks and shirt and ensured her nails were freshly manicured and her eyebrows perfectly shaped. When she drove to the address Brian gave her, he opened the door and, in a whisper, told her not to bring up that she didn't go to church. Carla knew he was Lutheran, but he'd never made a big deal about it before.

Dinner was lovely, and Carla thought his parents liked her until they asked—

"What's your last name?" his mother inquired.

"It's Christian," Carla said. Brian's mom smiled warmly until Carla continued. "Which is ironic because I'm Jewish."

"I see," his mom said, raising an eyebrow at Brian's father. Carla knew Brian wasn't going to be happy with her, but she'd never been embarrassed about being Jewish before, and she wasn't about to start.

The conversation became sporadic for the rest of the night. Carla tried to engage Brian's parents, but they had no more questions for her. She wondered if that would be the end of her and Brian's relationship, but Brian never said anything about the evening.

He was a year older than Carla, so when he graduated, he moved to the city for a job, but every weekend, he took the train to Brooklyn to spend time with her. A few days after Carla graduated, she and Brian went to city hall and got married. Carla wore a vintage dress she bought at a thrift shop and never felt more beautiful.

The ceremony consisted of her and Brian, the judge, and the judge's secretary as their witness. Beverly had taken a job out of town and missed both Carla's graduation and wedding. Mort had said he'd come to both but didn't show up at either. Brian's parents weren't there. They refused to speak to him because he was marrying a Jewish girl.

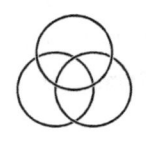

CHAPTER 13

Morgan

A little over a week after Carla's death, Morgan was the first of her sisters to arrive back at her mother's house. She put Albert in the backyard, where a squirrel taunted him from a low branch of a Sequoia. Albert looked as if he contemplated chasing it but then found a spot in the sun and collapsed like a mom after shopping with her teenage daughter.

Morgan went back inside and released Brigitta from her carrier. The cat walked around smelling the legs of the dining room table, looking under the couch, and then jumping on top of the media console and prancing around as if she owned it.

Morgan was making a grocery list when a loud knock rattled the front door. Brigitta leaped to the ground and ran down the hall. Morgan jumped as if she'd been watching a movie where a slasher had just popped up on the screen. She tried to remind herself that it wouldn't always be bad news when she heard someone knock.

She opened the door to find Charlie looking a little rattled. "Sorry, I forgot my key," Charlie said, dragging her suitcase behind her.

It was a marvel how whenever the Weiss sisters went anywhere together; they'd always show up in the order of their birth. Abby would be the last one to arrive, no matter where or when they were meeting. Once, Morgan and Charlie visited Abby for the weekend, and Abby got home twenty minutes after the babysitter had let them in.

Charlie pulled her arms out of the straps of her backpack and let it fall onto the couch. She pulled out a piece of paper.

"What's that?" Morgan asked.

"A list. I've been writing notes about where we should begin our search in the house."

"Abby isn't here yet," Morgan said, scanning the paper over Charlie's shoulder.

"If we wait for her, we won't start until her kids are old enough to help us," Charlie cracked.

Morgan took Charlie's list out of her hands and dropped it purposely on top of Charlie's backpack. Morgan stuck her hand in the pocket of her jeans and pulled out a crumpled piece of paper.

"This is my list," Morgan said, handing it to Charlie. "That's where we'll start."

"Why should you get to decide what we do?" Charlie asked.

"Because it was my idea to do all this...and I'm the oldest."

"You're barely a year and a half older than me and way more screwed up."

"Just because you hide it better doesn't mean you're less screwed up," Morgan said.

Abby opened the front door with her key.

"I have a master's degree in psychology and a successful therapy practice," Charlie said.

"And I'm just an addict, right?"

"Nope...well, yep," Charlie said.

"I've been sober for four years," Morgan said.

"Which is great, but you stopped maturing back when you started using, so you're like, thirteen now."

"Stop!" Abby yelled. "This is not the time; we need each other right now, so hug it out."

Neither Morgan nor Charlie moved.

"Do it! Love each other right now," Abby said forcefully.

"Fine, Pollyanna," Morgan said and opened her arms to Charlie. Charlie moved grudgingly into Morgan's arms, but instead of hugging, they patted each other on the back like two teenage boys.

"There's the love," Abby said, pulling her suitcase inside. "Now I need peace. My referee days are over for anyone who can cut their own food." She headed down the hall. "I'm putting my stuff in my old room."

"I've got dibs on my old room," Charlie said, following after Abby.

Morgan's old room had become Carla's office, so it no longer had a bed, and Morgan knew none of them wanted to sleep in their mother's bedroom.

"No worries—I love sleeping on couches," Morgan called after them. "That's what addicts do."

Fifteen minutes later, Charlie came back into the living room. Charlie and Morgan knew this was where their mother had been found, but the thought hung in the air like a ghost.

"What if Mom had a terminal disease and wanted to make sure we didn't have to take care of her," Charlie said, picking up her list from the couch. "I think we should go through the calendar on her desk and see if she had a lot of doctor's appointments."

"I told you, I'm leading this," Morgan said.

"Fine, what's on your list?"

"Number one, ransack the house like burglars and see what we find."

"That's how you lead?" Charlie asked.

Morgan gave her a sly smile; she enjoyed annoying Charlie. "Abby, we're waiting for you," Morgan called out. "What're you doing?"

"Resting," Abby called out from her room.

"We aren't on vacation," Morgan yelled back. "Can you please come in here?"

Abby, barefoot and with a blanket wrapped around her, trudged in and plopped down on the couch.

"I don't get why we have to start immediately," Abby said. "We just got here; can't we relax a little?"

Morgan had a twinkle in her eyes. "You should've relaxed at home."

"Hilarious," Abby said, then dropped her blanket onto the couch. "Well, you got me in here, so what's the plan?"

"Why don't we try breaking into Mom's computer," Morgan said, heading into Carla's office. Charlie and Abby followed her.

The office had bookshelves lining the walls, filled chiefly with historical fiction and memoirs of famous people. On the desk was a silver frame with two pictures side by side. The first was a picture of Morgan, Charlie, and Abby when they were eight, six, and four, and the second was a selfie of the four of them taken a few years ago at a restaurant on Carla's fifty-fifth birthday.

Morgan sat down at her mother's desk as Charlie flipped through Carla's calendar, which had a picture of a different national park on each page.

"Mom wasn't sick. Not a single doctor's appointment for the last six months," Charlie said, closing the calendar.

"We need to figure out her computer password," Morgan said. She sat quietly a moment thinking, then typed something in. Nothing happened. She tried again two more times, but still no luck.

"Try our birthdays," Charlie asked.

"I just did," Morgan said.

"Try her birthday," Abby said.

"Mom wouldn't be dumb enough to use her own birthday," Morgan said, then tried it anyway, but still nothing.

"Okay, so much for the second thing on your list, Morgan," Charlie said.

"Why don't we each take a room and tear it apart?" Abby asked.

"That makes sense," Charlie said.

"Hey, you thought it was stupid when I said that before," Morgan said, and Charlie shrugged.

"Which one of us is going to take Mom's room?" Abby asked.

They were silent. Then Charlie said, "None of us want to, but as adults, we can figure this out."

After three rounds of rock paper scissors, Morgan got the job.

"Why do I always lose?" Morgan said. "You guys must be cheating."

"How can you cheat at rock paper scissors?" Abby said.

Morgan struggled to find an answer, then conceded and went towards Carla's room. Charlie went into the family room and Abby tackled the junk drawer in the kitchen.

As Morgan passed the back door, she let Albert in. He followed as she moved down the hall at the pace of honey pouring into a cup of tea. She stood in front of the closed door to Carla's room.

Morgan gasped and couldn't breathe as she remembered being little, scared and unable to sleep until she was curled up on the bed next to her mom. *I can't hyperventilate,* she thought, abruptly turning and heading to the garage.

A little while later, she came back in carrying a shoebox that she placed under the kitchen table. The doorbell rang, and a delivery man held out a plastic bag to Morgan, and she thanked him.

"Who was at the door?" Charlie asked as she and Abby came into the room.

"Our lunch." Morgan took the food and put it on the kitchen table.

"We didn't order anything," Abby said.

"I know what you guys like," Morgan said.

Abby grabbed flatware and napkins, and they sat down at the kitchen table. Morgan pulled out three salads. She handed the beet salad to Abby and the cobb salad to Charlie and kept the chopped salad for herself.

"I don't like beets," Abby said, pushing her salad away from her.

"Yes, you do. You don't like avocados," Morgan said, grabbing plates from the cabinet.

"No, *I* don't like avocados," Charlie said. "They're too squishy. I'm the one who loves beets." Abby handed Charlie the beet salad and took the cobb for herself.

"Just say thank you," Morgan said.

"Thank you," Charlie and Abby said in unison.

They all dug into their food.

"So, did either of you find anything useful?" Abby asked, as she wiped avocado from her lips. "I found that Mom had a thing for Scotch Tape."

"I found my tambourine that Mom yelled at me for losing," Charlie said.

"You wouldn't stop shaking that stupid thing," Morgan said. "I hid it."

Charlie picked up a beet and looked like she was about to throw it at Morgan. Morgan stared her down, and Charlie put the beet in her mouth.

Morgan reached down, picked up the shoebox, and placed it in the middle of the table. "I found a box of photographs."

Charlie and Abby dipped their hands into the box, and each pulled out a handful of pictures.

Charlie held one up. "Here's one from Abby's second birthday," she said. "Only five kids came, and Morgan and I were two of them."

"I'm sure I had more friends than that," Abby said.

"You were young. You hadn't figured out the social thing yet," Charlie said. "You've improved a little."

Abby laughed, then held up a picture. "Here's one from that time Mom took us to Disneyland."

"She saved up for that day for over a year," Morgan said.

"It was so much fun," Charlie said.

"Until you *had* to go on Space Mountain and then threw up your chicken nuggets," Morgan said. "They shut the entire ride down for over an hour."

"And gave the people sitting behind you free passes," Abby said.

"At least I was brave enough to go on it," Charlie said, clucking at them like a chicken.

"There are so many pictures of you two and hardly any of me," Abby said, looking through the box. "Did the camera break when I was born?"

"Nope, you were just boring," Morgan said, and Abby playfully smacked her.

"I'm not letting that happen with my kids," Abby said. "I take a picture of everyone or no one."

"Then they better have a quadruple wedding," Charlie said.

"You can joke, but it will save me money on therapy. They'll never feel like they didn't matter."

Morgan put her arms around Abby. "You mattered to us," Morgan said.

"Hey, do either of you know who this is?" Charlie held up a picture of their mom with her arms around a man. Abby and Morgan stared at it.

"That was taken recently," Morgan said. "Mom's wearing the sweater I got her last Mothers' Day."

"She never mentioned she was dating anyone," Abby said.

"I would've thought she'd tell *me* if she was," Charlie said. "My clients pay me to be an expert on relationships."

Your relationship with Rick makes you the opposite of an expert, Morgan thought and struggled not to say out loud.

"I bet Mom's neighbor Esther would know who he is," Abby said. "She always seemed like the nosy type."

73

"I can't believe Esther's still alive," Charlie said. "She's been eighty since we were kids."

Morgan got up and looked out the window. "She's home. Her Dodge Dart's in the driveway."

"You two should go over and ask her," Charlie said.

"We're all going," Abby said.

"I need to get over the shock of her not being dead," Charlie said, taking another bite of her salad.

Abby grabbed Charlie's arms, pulling her out of her chair.

A few minutes later, the sisters walked up to Esther's front door. Her small, strangely narrow house had always unnerved them. The exterior color hadn't changed since they were kids: gun-metal gray paint with a jet-black door. Morgan thought it was far from the friendliest-looking house on the block.

Charlie knocked so lightly that no one inside could have heard her. "I guess she's not home," Charlie said, turning away. Abby grabbed Charlie's arm and held her there as she knocked loudly.

Esther appeared at the door in a pink housecoat covered in white and yellow daisies, fuzzy slippers, and her alabaster hair in a messy bun. An elderly cocker spaniel wobbled up behind her.

"Hi, Esther, remember us?" Morgan asked. "We're Carla's daughters."

Esther held up one finger, then walked away, leaving the door open. The cocker spaniel stood at the door, glaring at them and snarling with the one tooth it still had. The women took a step back as if it were a vicious pit bull.

Esther came back a moment later, fiddling with her ears. "I was charging my hearing aids," she said. The dog lunged at them and smacked into the wall.

"Poopsie is as blind as a bat," Esther said, then picked him up and put him back down facing the other direction. Poopsie wobbled off.

"You're Carla's daughters, right?" The women nodded. "I'm so sorry about your mother, the whole neighborhood is upset. She was such a nice lady. Do you know what happened?"

Morgan, Charlie, and Abby made eye contact with each other.

"They think it was a heart attack," Charlie blurted.

"How tragic, she was so young," Esther said.

Abby held up the picture of their mom and the unidentified man. "Do you know who this is?" Abby asked.

Esther took the picture and studied it as if she were trying to find a hidden number in an optical illusion. "He used to visit your mother a lot, I thought he was her boyfriend. He'd come over Tuesdays, Thursdays, and every other Friday and stay for about an hour, then one day he stopped coming. I figured they broke up." She handed the picture back to Abby.

"By any chance, do you know his name?" Morgan asked.

"Oh, no, I stay out of other people's business."

Esther rarely went outside, but somehow, she knew everything that happened in the neighborhood, and probably the surrounding ones. She slipped off one of her fuzzy slippers and scratched the top of her foot. The skin on her leg was crepey, and one blue vein on the top of her right toe stuck out prominently. "Do you girls want to come in? I could make you lunch."

Esther's loneliness radiated from her like steam rising from a cup of coffee. The sisters declined; Esther nodded sadly.

"How long had our mom been seeing the man?" Charlie asked.

"A little over two years," Esther said.

They thanked her for her help, then turned to leave. Poopsie trudged back in, barking as though they'd just appeared.

"Come back any time," Esther said. "Poopsie loves company. Don't you, Poopsie." She picked up the dog who bared his gums at the sisters.

The women thanked her and turned to walk home.

"If Poopsie would've been able to see us, we would've been goners," Abby said.

"That tooth did look sharp," Morgan said, and they all laughed.

When they arrived back at their mother's house, Albert greeted them happily.

Charlie bent down and kissed him on the head. "I can't believe Mom had been seeing that guy for two years and never said a word to any of us."

"Maybe he broke her heart, and she couldn't get past it," Morgan said.

"The mom we knew wouldn't have killed herself over a man," Charlie said.

"The mom we knew didn't have a boyfriend," Morgan said.

"Maybe we didn't know her at all," Abby said and began to cry. Morgan got a box of tissues and handed one to Abby, who sat back at the table.

"We have to figure out who that guy is," Morgan said.

"If we knew his name, we could google him," Abby said, blowing her nose.

"If we knew his name, we wouldn't have to google him," Charlie said.

"I meant to get is phone number," Abby said.

Frustrated, Morgan went back into Carla's office, her shoes stomping onto the floor. Albert trotted after her, with Abby and Charlie close behind.

Morgan pounded on the keyboard, trying to find the elusive password. Abby went through the papers on Carla's desk, finding a vet bill, an electric bill, and a phone bill. All of them were overdue. "Are we going to have to pay these ourselves?" Abby asked.

"Mom's estate will take care of them," Charlie said.

"Thank God. I have four kids."

"There we go," Charlie said.

"There we go, what?" Abby asked.

"You bring up your kids any time you want to get out of something," Charlie said.

"That's one of the reasons I had them," Abby said. Charlie looked at Morgan and crossed her eyes. Abby didn't notice and continued. "If you want to leave a party early, you say your kids are tired. If you need to get out of lunch with that one friend you have trouble saying no to, you say your kid is sick."

"Wait a minute," Morgan said. "When I was in San Diego, and we were supposed to meet for dinner, you flaked at the last minute, saying Hudson was sick." Morgan raised one eyebrow at Abby.

"And you said Emma was sick when I invited you to visit me." Charlie furrowed her brows.

"My kids get a lot of colds," Abby said.

"Right," Morgan said, then went back to the computer. After a few choice curse words, she rubbed her neck and gave up trying to break into the computer.

Morgan angrily grabbed a piece of paper that was sitting on the corner of the desk, looked at it, opened her hand, and let it fall to the floor. With that one paper gone, a file with the word 'Will' that had been underneath it was exposed. Charlie grabbed the file and opened it. She took their mother's will out of it and began turning pages.

"What is that?" Morgan asked.

"Mom's will," Charlie said.

"What does it say?" Abby asked.

"That we inherit everything," Charlie said.

"Who's the executor?" Morgan asked.

"All three of us," Charlie said.

"Finally, being a screw-up didn't hurt me," Morgan said, then noticed something stapled to the back page of the will. She grabbed it away from Charlie.

"There's a codicil here that had been notarized," Morgan said. "Mom left five thousand dollars to some guy named Mike Perez. And it was added three months ago."

"I bet that's the guy in the pictures," Abby said.

"Why would Mom leave him money?" Charlie asked.

"I don't know, but now we have his name and address," Morgan said.

Morgan got her own laptop out and searched the internet for Mike Perez in Las Vegas. "There's no phone number," Morgan said. "I guess we're going to Vegas."

"We're going to Vegas to talk to him?" Abby asked.

"Yes," Morgan said.

"What're we going to say when we get there?" Charlie asked.

"Hi, our mom killed herself because you broke her heart," Abby said.

"That would go over well," Morgan said. "We're going to ask him if he knows why Mom would leave him money," Morgan said.

"That's a good idea. We can assess whether he had any part in why she took her life," Charlie said.

"And if not, maybe he'll know something about her that we don't," Morgan said.

Abby clapped her hands together. "I love Vegas. I haven't been there in years," she said.

"Abby, did you forget that we're going because our mom died," Charlie said somberly.

"You're right. I'm a horrible person, aren't I?" Abby asked.

"No, you aren't. I just like making you feel bad." Charlie laughed.

Abby crossed her arms over her chest. "I hope you're proud of yourself," she said snidely and went to her room.

Morgan gazed off, remembering. "The last time I was in Vegas I got drunk at my hotel and crawled up on the craps table while people were playing. I'm sure that's been forgotten by now."

"Just in case your picture is up in their employee break room, which hotel did you desecrate?" Charlie asked.

Morgan shrugged her shoulders. "It had either a giant lion or a trapeze."

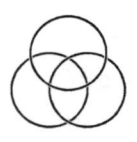

CHAPTER 14

Charlie

The next day, While Charlie and Abby waited on the porch with their suitcases, Morgan ran next door to drop Albert and Brigitta off with Esther. Abby didn't want to drive to Vegas as she'd already driven from Encinitas, and Charlie had rented a Mini Cooper, so when Morgan got back, the women piled their overnight bags into the trunk of her rented Nissan Altima.

"Shotgun!" Charlie called out as she hurled herself into the front passenger seat.

"That's poppycock!" Abby said grudgingly, as she crawled into the back.

"Poppycock?" Charlie said. "Are you a time traveler from the fifties?"

"I can't swear in front of the kids; they like that expression."

"Well, we don't," Morgan said.

"Okay, then it's bullshit that just because I'm the youngest, I never get to sit in the front. And just because I'm the smallest, even when one of us brought a friend home, I got stuck in the middle in the backseat."

"You have the entire back to yourself. It'll be great, you can stretch out," Charlie said.

"If you feel that way, then you sit back here."

"I already called shotgun," Charlie said, putting on her seat belt.

"I guess age does come before beauty," Abby said, preening in the rearview mirror.

"I haven't even pulled out of the driveway, and you two are going at it," Morgan said.

"It's her fault," Charlie and Abby said in unison.

Morgan turned around and looked at Abby. "When we're halfway there, I'll pull over, and you guys can switch seats."

"Works for me," Abby said, putting on her seatbelt.

"Okay, but don't wake me up if I fall asleep." Charlie smiled to herself.

Abby tapped her fingers on Charlie's head. "No worries, I won't let that happen."

Charlie realized that somehow, since their mother's death, she and her sisters had reverted to patterns that they had as children.

As Morgan began backing out of Carla's driveway, she suddenly slammed on her brakes so hard the car made a screeching noise, and Charlie jerked forward against her seatbelt.

"Geez," Charlie said. "What happened?" Charlie and Abby turned their heads to see what had made Morgan stop. A woman pushing a baby in a stroller was walking alongside a man carrying a toddler girl and holding another young girl's hand. After they walked past Morgan's car, Morgan backed out and headed down the street.

"Do you ever think about what it would've been like if our father had lived with us?" Morgan asked.

Charlie sat back stiffly, they usually avoided talking about him.

"I used to pretend my friends' dads were mine," Abby said.

Charlie relaxed her facial muscles. "When I was little, I'd go into Mom's closet, sit on the floor, and talk to him. I'd tell him about my day, who I had a crush on, and who was mean to me. Dad always took my side." A sad smile crept across Charlie's face.

"I wish he would've taken me to the father/daughter tea in elementary school," Morgan said, honking a little too aggressively at the car in front of her.

"I hated that day of the year. I used to tell Mom I had a stomachache and couldn't go to school," Abby said. "It wasn't a total lie."

"I played sick, too," Charlie said. "Mom knew, but she never said anything."

Charlie pulled a picture from her wallet that she had placed behind her driver's license. She turned to the back seat to show it to Abby. "This was one of the few pictures Mom had of me with my dad." It was a picture of their father holding Charlie when she was around two. "Mom didn't know I took it from her album."

"At least you and Morgan have memories of him," Abby said. "I was so young when he died."

Charlie put the picture back in her wallet. As much as she had fun teasing her younger sister, it hurt to see Abby upset.

"I wish Mom told us more about our father," Morgan said. "Whenever I'd ask, she'd get this faraway look and start crying, so I had to stop asking."

"Things are getting gloomy in here," Charlie said. She turned the radio on to a nineties station to liven things up.

Then, she sang loudly to Elton John's 'Candle in the Wind.'
"...pain was the price you paid even when you died..."

"Much better," Abby asked.

Charlie switched the station, and the song from *Friends*, "I'll Be There for You," by The Rembrandts, came on. The women sang at the top of their lungs. When they did the hand clap, Morgan let go of the wheel for a second, and the car lurched toward the next lane. Charlie grabbed the steering wheel and righted it.

"It might be safer to stick with ballads," Charlie said.

"Is there such a thing as an upbeat ballad?" Abby asked.

They sang almost every song that came on, and the two-and-a-half hours flew by.

"We're halfway there," Abby called out. "Time to switch seats, Charlie."

"Is anyone hungry, because I'm starving," Charlie ignored her.

"Why don't we stop for lunch, and then you kids can switch seats afterward," Morgan said.

Morgan got off the I-15 highway in Barstow while Abby found a Mexican restaurant nearby. The girls had always loved Mexican food. When they were kids, Carla would take them to El Torito Restaurant on their birthdays and let them order anything they wanted, including virgin banana daiquiris.

The scent of warm, fresh tortillas welcomed them as they entered the restaurant, Lola's Kitchen. In honor of their mother's favorite, they all ordered the same thing: *enchiladas suizas*.

From her seat at the window, Abby scanned the parking lot.

"What are you doing?" Charlie asked.

"Google said there's a lot of theft in Bakersfield, so I'm keeping an eye on our luggage," Abby said.

"No one wants your Yosemite Sam nightshirt and ratty old toothbrush," Charlie said, going to get a drink.

"You never know," Abby said.

They ordered at the counter and while waiting for the food to be brought over, Morgan got a Coke from the machine and sat across from Abby.

"How can you drink that poison?" Abby asked.

"They were out of Tequila." Morgan pointed at the machine. "Besides, I need the caffeine, I'm the one driving."

Charlie joined them, holding a big glass of water. "At least Charlie cares if all her teeth fall out," Abby said.

"I'm vain that way," Charlie said.

The worker brought their food over, and Charlie took a bite of her enchilada, reveling in the cheesy, saucy concoction.

"So, what are we going to do when we get to Vegas?" Abby asked.

"We're going to check into the hotel, then go directly to the guy's house," Morgan said.

"I have a better idea," Abby said, crunching on a tortilla chip. "I think first we should soak up some sun by the pool, then hit the slots."

"We aren't going to Vegas to have fun," Morgan said. "We're going to talk to Mom's mystery man."

"Can't we do both?" Abby pouted. "I haven't had a vacation since I had Hudson over a hundred years ago."

"Why don't we compromise," Charlie said. "We can go to the hotel, Abby can relax, and then we go to his house first thing tomorrow morning."

"That seems fair," Morgan said.

By the time they turned into the M Resort Hotel in Henderson, it was late afternoon. As Charlie got out she felt the oppressive heat from the sun radiating off the hood of the car.

"It's so hot here," Morgan said, fanning her face with the ticket the valet handed her.

When Charlie pulled open the heavy glass door to the hotel, she luxuriated in the blast of cold air that greeted her as if Jack Frost had sneezed in her face. The women checked in and then headed through the maze of gambling tables to find the elevators to their room.

Abby froze at the sight of a Wheel of Fortune slot machine. "Can you take this to the room with you?" she said, pushing her suitcase over to Charlie. "I need to do one thing first." She all but skipped away.

"Stop once you lose twenty!" Morgan called after her. "You have to pay a third of the hotel bill."

"I'm going to win because Mama's kids need a new pair of shoes." Abby chuckled.

Charlie shook her head and muttered a soft 'ugh', as she and Morgan dragged the three suitcases into the elevator.

Abby joined them ten minutes later and thirty dollars poorer. "I was so sure I'd win. I'm good at Wheel of Fortune on TV," Abby said. "I guess my kids are going to keep getting hand-me-downs."

Abby looked out the floor-to-ceiling window that spanned the entire length of the back wall. Charlie noticed how the natural light coming in lit up the highlights in Abby's hair.

"Where's the Vegas strip?" Abby asked. "All I see is miles and miles of dirt out there." She continued staring out at the view of a never-ending desert.

"The strip is twenty minutes away," Charlie said. "We're in Henderson."

"Why are we in Henderson when we could be in Vegas?" Abby scrunched up her eyebrows.

"One, the hotel is cheaper," Morgan said, "Two, this is where Mike lives, and three, I'm not allowed anywhere near the strip."

"You could have told me that before I got all excited about being in Vegas," Abby said, falling onto the bed.

"I could have, but your excitement makes your disappointment so much funnier," Morgan grinned, and Abby couldn't control a laugh.

"We're at a nice resort with a pool," Charlie said. "Abby, why don't you put on your bikini and go downstairs and lie in the sun."

"Good idea. When's the last time you got to do that?" Morgan added.

"You're right, I almost forgot I'm childless!" Abby jumped off the bed. "No one will splash me, or scream at me to watch them, or cry because their brother bonked them on the head with a pool noodle. It will be someone else's kids doing all that, and I get to comment on how they can't control their kids." Abby said.

"That's the spirit," Charlie said.

"You guys have no idea how hard it is lifting an infant out of the water wearing a soggy swim diaper that weighs more than you do."

"I'd rather have my nose hairs pulled out one at a time while having gum surgery," Morgan said.

CHAPTER 15

Abby

The next morning, the sisters ate a quick breakfast, and then Abby called downstairs for the car. Even though it had been parked in an underground lot, it had still absorbed the 110-degree heat, and the women had to be careful not to burn their butts on the leather seats. Morgan put the mystery man's address into her phone's navigation.

Fifteen minutes later, they pulled up in front of a small house on a street where every structure looked alike. The tract homes were painted 'Builders Beige' with brick-colored tile roofs and garages the color of dirt that matched the brown desert landscape. In the driveway sat an older Honda Civic in pristine condition.

Morgan parked at the curb across the street. Abby opened the passenger door and got out, then saw Morgan wasn't moving.

"What's wrong?" Abby asked, sitting back down and closing the door to keep the cool air inside.

"I'm nervous," Morgan said, tapping her hands on the steering wheel. "We're going to grill some guy that Mom purposely kept a secret from us. What if there's something about their relationship that she didn't want us to know?"

"Maybe he was blackmailing her," Abby said.

"That's a little dramatic, don't you think?" Charlie asked.

"It happens. You see it all the time on those police shows," Abby said.

"We could be walking into a trap," Morgan said.

"You're coming up with this now?" Charlie asked.

"It just hit me," Morgan said.

"We drove four and a half hours, you had lots of time for it to *hit* you," Charlie said.

Morgan shrugged and nodded. "You're right." She turned off the engine and got out. "No matter how nervous we are, we have to know why Mom left some strange man money in her will."

"I'll take the lead here," Charlie said. "It's my job to get people to open up to me." Morgan and Abby agreed.

When the sisters got to the front porch, Abby rang the bell. A high-pitched bark reverberated through the door. Abby recognized the man who came to the door as the same one in the picture with their mother. He had black hair, scruff on his chin, and squinty eyes, although, to be fair, his eyes might've been squinting because of the blinding sun that was breaking through his dark entryway. He wore baggy sweats, and his T-shirt was inside out, so either he'd just woken up or he had no sense of fashion.

"Can I help you?" he asked, his voice deeper than Abby had expected for his slight build and short stature. His white, fluffy dog ran in circles around them, yapping incessantly.

"Are you Mike Perez?" Morgan asked, cutting Charlie off as she opened her mouth to speak.

"Yes," he stared at them.

Charlie stepped in front of Morgan and Abby. "We're Carla Weiss's daughters."

"Oh, hi…" he said, his voice trailing off.

Abby could tell by the way Mike's eyes began to dart back and forth between her and her sisters that his mind was racing.

"Our mom died…" Abby's voice cracked, and she stopped mid-sentence.

"Oh, no, I'm so sorry. Please come in." Mike picked up his dog and moved away from the door so they could enter. Deciding he didn't seem like a serial killer, Abby nodded at her sisters, and they all walked inside.

Mike led them into a small but cozy living room. On a tufted rug sat a well-worn couch, two chairs, and a coffee table, probably from IKEA, as it had a drawer that stuck out and didn't quite fit.

When the women sat down, the sofa made a subtle woosh as their bodies settled into the leather. The room was warmer than Abby expected, and the ceiling fan wasn't helping as it pushed the warm air around her. Abby wiped away the sweat that was breaking out on her brow.

"This is Pillow," Mike said, putting the dog on the ground. Mike sat in the La-Z-Boy chair across from them while Pillow jumped up next to Abby.

"I'm shocked about Carla. The last time I saw her, she was fine."

"When was that?" Charlie asked.

"A little over a month ago when we finalized the divorce."

"You were married to our mom?" Abby said, practically jumping out of her seat.

"She didn't tell us she got married," Morgan said.

"Or divorced," Charlie exclaimed.

"It's not what you think," Mike said. "It wasn't a real marriage. We worked together at the real estate agency and became good friends. When she found out my visa had run out and I would have to go back to Guatemala, she suggested we get married," Mike said.

"Why would she do that? Were you holding something over her?" Abby asked.

"No, your mom was just a caring woman," Mike said.

Abby choked up. "She was."

An awkward silence hung in the room until it was broken by Pillow, who had fallen asleep on Abby with his head on her thigh and seemed to be having a bad dream. He was whimpering and shaking his legs. Abby wiped her tears away with one hand while gently stroking the dog with her other hand until his nightmare passed.

Mike stood up, rubbing his chin. "Can I get any of you something to drink?"

The sisters shrugged; they were in too much shock to form words.

Mike returned from the kitchen with three bottles of water and placed them on the coffee table. No one reached for them.

"I can't believe Carla's gone," Mike said, putting his hands up to his temples and rubbing them as if doing so would help him make sense of things. "What happened?"

The sisters exchanged a long look, and then Abby blurted out, "She took her own life."

"Oh my God, why would she do that?" Mike asked. Although he turned his head away, Abby could see him wipe away a tear.

"That's what we're trying to find out," Morgan said.

"We were hoping you could help us," Charlie said.

Abby began hurling questions at Mike like darts shooting balloons at a carnival. Before he could answer one question, she'd fire off another one.

"Did you take advantage of our mother's kind heart?" Abby asked. "Did she take the divorce hard?" "Did she tell you she had three daughters?"

"Carla talked about all three of you a lot," Mike said. "She was so proud of her daughters." Now, it was Charlie's turn to cry. "I didn't mean to upset you," he said.

He stood up as though to comfort Charlie, then quickly sat back down. He grabbed the box of tissues next to him and pushed them toward the women. When Abby stopped petting Pillow to grab a tissue, Pillow raised his head and licked her hand. She picked him up and held him to her chest.

"If she never told you about us, how did you find me?" Mike asked.

Morgan told Mike how they had found a picture of him with their mom. "Then we saw that she left you money in her will, so we googled you," Morgan said.

"She left me money?" Mike said. "Why would she do that?"

Abby watched him to see if he was genuinely as surprised as he appeared. "Is it possible that our mom fell in love with you?" she asked.

"I highly doubt it. We never even dated; we were just friends. As soon as we'd been married long enough that I could safely stay in the United States, I moved here, and we filed for divorce. When I returned to Los Angeles to sign the papers, she seemed happy and excited that she was on the partner track at the agency."

Realizing there was nothing else they would discover here, Abby moved off the couch. Pillow jumped onto the floor as Morgan stood up; then Charlie followed suit.

"When we get home, we'll make sure you get the money our mom left you," Morgan said.

"You all keep it. Carla did more than enough for me."

"Thank you for talking to us. We're sorry to have barged in on you like this," Charlie said.

"I'm glad I finally got to meet all of you, but I wish it were under better circumstances." Mike led them to the front door with Pillow skittering behind him. As they were about to cross the threshold, Mike stopped them. "Wait, I just remembered something your mother gave me. You should have it."

A moment later, he came back holding a refrigerator magnet shaped like the state of New York with the words 'The Only Pizza in Town' written on top of a picture of a slice of pizza. Abby glanced at her sisters quizzically. "Your mother gave this to me when we signed the divorce papers. She thought I'd get a kick out of it because every Friday night after work, we'd order pizza, and I'd once mentioned that going to New York was on my bucket list," he said.

"Why would Mom have a magnet from New York?" Abby asked.

Charlie shrugged her shoulders. "I don't know, she hated that place."

"One year, I suggested we all visit New York City, and she said she never wanted to go there because the rats ran rampant, and everyone who lives there is a mugger," Morgan said.

"I don't know where she got the magnet," Mike said, holding it out to them. "But I'm sure she would've wanted me to give it to you."

Abby took it, bounced it from one hand to the other, then turned it over to study it.

"I'll always be grateful to your mother for what she did for me," Mike said.

The women thanked him and left.

"Well, that was a waste of time," Charlie said as they got back in the car.

"No, it wasn't. We now know that Mom had secrets," Morgan said.

"And we did get a consolation prize," Abby said, holding up the magnet.

"I wonder what else she was hiding from us," Morgan said, hitting the gas and pulling away from the curb so quickly that Abby almost dropped the magnet.

CHAPTER 16

Carla

Carla didn't share much with her daughters about her marriage to their father. When they asked how they met or about their relationship, she gave vague answers or changed the subject. She didn't want to lie to them, but her and Brian's story wasn't one she wanted to discuss.

When Carla met Brian, they had an instant connection. When she wasn't with him, she thought about him and even dreamed about him. She didn't care that they didn't have the same goals in life. At the time, her fascination with his athletic prowess was more important and exciting.

Brian had been the best player on the baseball team through most of college. During Carla's junior year, she went to all his games and was proud to tell anyone who would listen that he was her boyfriend. She was enamored that Brian was on track to attain his lifelong dream of getting recruited to pitch in the major leagues. That is until the first game of his senior year when he threw a fastball, and with the crack of the opposing team's bat came a crack in his arm and excruciating pain. The dream ended faster than Brian could stand up.

Brian was never the same after that. At the end of that year, he graduated and joined an accounting firm in New York. "This wasn't the way my life was supposed to be," he would complain to Carla. "I should've been traveling with my team and making more money than we could possibly spend in a lifetime."

Carla worried that he wouldn't be able to move on from his disappointment, but right after she graduated, they got married, and she convinced herself that he was past it. They rented their first apartment, and she took classes to get her real estate license. She hoped knowing the ropes would give them an advantage when they could afford to buy their first house. Unfortunately, right before Carla got her first job as a real estate agent, she found out she was pregnant.

Morgan was born when Carla was twenty-four, and a year and a half later, Charlie came into the world. Before she and Brian could catch their breath, they were a family of four.

Carla got bored staying at home, so even though Morgan was barely three and Charlie one, she would take them to museums and movies. Afterward, they'd visit her favorite pizza place in Brooklyn for lunch. Anthony, the owner's son, was a close friend of Carla's from high school, so he'd give her a discount.

Brian was barely around, and when he was, he seemed distant and stressed. Carla could tell something was going on with him, but whenever she tried to talk about it, he would dismiss her concerns and pick a fight.

Things got worse and worse until Carla filed for divorce before Brian could find out she was pregnant with their third child. She was done with him, even if he wasn't aware of how unhappy she was.

Being a single mother wasn't that different from what she already had been doing. As the girls grew, she avoided talking about what led to her and Brian's split. The only thing she told the girls was that their father hadn't been a good guy, and he walked out on them and never looked back.

Carla never wanted to be raising three young kids alone, but she ended up thriving in the role. She could decide how to raise them without anyone criticizing her, and she made sure that she was always there for them--the complete opposite of the way her parents raised her.

They ate dinner as a family every night, she attended every school event, and she helped them with their math homework up until she realized she couldn't figure out how to divide decimals. The most important thing to her was that her children knew they were loved, cared for, and never lonely.

While the girls were young, Carla refused to bring another man into their lives, and by the time they were all adults, she had no desire to date. She never wanted a man to lie to her or hurt her again. Morgan, Charlie, and Abby were not only her family, but her whole life, and being with them made her happier than she could have imagined.

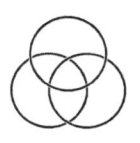

CHAPTER 17

Morgan

Morgan spent most the four-and-a-half-hour drive back to Los Angeles trying to understand why Carla would keep her green card marriage a secret from them. It's not like they would have turned their mother and her "husband" into immigration. Didn't she have faith her daughters would understand wanting to help a friend?

Charlie spent the time sending emails to health insurance companies on her clients' behalf, and Abby had a running text chain with her babysitter to figure out the best way to get peanut butter out of her dog's ear. Morgan knew all this because she could hear her sisters periodically yelling into and at their phones.

By the time she pulled into Carla's driveway, Morgan's stomach was growling like a police dog excited to catch a predator. The moment they walked into the house, Charlie went to call Rick, and Abby plopped down on the couch with an audible sigh.

"That was exhausting, Abby said, closing her eyes.

"Yeah, sitting in the backseat doing nothing is tough," Morgan mumbled.

As Abby drifted off to sleep, Morgan grabbed an apple from the kitchen and headed to Carla's office. The room was exactly how they'd left it when they went to Vegas. Papers on the floor and all over Carla's desk. A small piece of her expected her mother to have straightened up while they were gone.

Morgan sat in the desk chair with such purpose that it shot backward so quickly that she almost fell off. After she righted herself, she pursed her lips and cracked her knuckles as if she were about to play a piano concerto. She wanted the device to know that she was serious about finding the password, and this time, she wouldn't take no for an answer. Her muscles tightened in readiness, then she put her fingers on the keys and typed.

Morgan started by trying Carla's favorite things: coconut, Seinfeld, coffee ice cream, and Baby Yoda. Each time a password didn't work she banged on the keyboard harder. After one particularly hard jab, the 'A' key popped out and landed in her lap. "None of you are leaving until I get past this screen," she said to the other letters on the keyboard.

She picked up the 'A' key and pushed it back into the keyboard until she heard it click back into its slot. *Thank goodness,* she thought. Otherwise, when she wanted to curse someone out, she'd have to write 'sshole,' which wouldn't have the same effect.

"I need a glass of wine," Charlie called out from the other room. "Where is the bottle?"

"I hid it," Morgan called back. "You'll have to get another alcoholic to find it for you,"

"I need wine," Charlie said again.

When Morgan heard Charlie opening and closing cabinets, she marched into the kitchen.

"Now *I* need wine," Morgan said. Charlie stared at her. "I didn't say I was going to have any. I just said I needed some." Morgan grabbed the wine out of a cabinet above the refrigerator and handed it to Charlie. "Sometimes you're a real 'sshole," Morgan said, going back into the living room.

"What did you say?" Charlie asked, following her.

"Nothing," Morgan said.

"Hey, you woke me up," Abby said.

"How can you fall asleep in the middle of the day?" Charlie asked.

"It's a gift," Abby said, sitting up and stretching her arms above her head.

Charlie opened the bottle, poured Abby a glass and filled her own glass almost to the top.

"I'm guessing your call with Rick didn't go so well," Morgan said, eyeing Charlie's glass.

"Instead of asking me how I was doing, he spent most of the time trying to convince me to come home," Charlie said. "He hasn't had time to go to the market or wash his sheets." Morgan crossed her arms in judgment. "I know I have to break up with him," Charlie said, rubbing her temples.

"Needy is not sexy," Abby said, taking the wine glass from Charlie. "Hey, I should sell T-shirts with that on it."

"Charlie, you can't keep saying you're going to end it with Rick and do nothing. Just pull the plug and let it slip away," Morgan said.

"It's not that easy," Charlie said.

"Yes, it is. Remember, I told you I'm great at break-ups," Morgan said.

"That's because you aren't good at relationships," Abby said.

"It's a gift," Morgan said.

Charlie drained her glass of wine and poured herself more. "Just when the words, 'Rick, we're done,' are about to come out of my mouth, he says something sweet or brings me roses."

"You don't like roses," Morgan said.

Charlie shrugged and nodded at the same time, looking like a bobblehead. "What if I end it, and he immediately finds someone else."

"Then he'll be that woman's problem," Morgan said.

"True, but what if *I* never find someone else?"

"I was lucky I found my soulmate right away," Abby said.

"How do you know Alex is your soulmate?" Morgan asked. "You've never dated anyone else."

"I dated George Clooney in some of my dreams, but it didn't work out," Abby said to Morgan. "He was always away on a movie, so we didn't get enough time together." Abby turned to Charlie. "I'm sure you'd find someone else. You're still relatively pretty."

"I'm still *very* pretty," Charlie said. "But men seem to have an easier time finding their next relationship. You'll see when Alex gets tired of you." Charlie toasted Abby then drained her glass and began coughing.

"Ha! The wine is trying to kill you for being mean," Abby said, putting her glass on the coffee table and closing her eyes again. "Alcohol makes me sleepy."

Morgan went back into Carla's office. Charlie grabbed her wine glass and the bottle and followed her. Morgan sat on the floor in front of the desk, opened a file drawer, and pulled out a bunch of folders.

"What are you looking for?" Charlie asked.

"Anything that explains why mom killed herself," Morgan said. As she looked through the papers inside, she fed them into the paper shredder, which munched on them purposefully.

"Are you sure none of those are important?" Charlie asked.

"Not unless you want to keep Albert's diploma from obedience school. He failed the first two times." Morgan dropped the paper into the shredder; the sound of it being destroyed somehow comforted her. She held a piece of paper out toward Charlie. "Do you need your vaccination record to enter elementary school?"

Charlie dropped the paper into the shredder and then sat in the chair facing the computer. She picked up her glass and took a drink. "Does it bother you that I drink in front of you?"

"I had to get used to that a long time ago."

Charlie nodded. "Hey, why is the 'A' trying to escape from the keyboard?" she asked.

"I couldn't figure out the password for Mom's computer," Morgan said as if that was explanation enough.

Twenty minutes later, Abby walked in, yawning.

"Thanks for joining us, Sleeping Beauty," Morgan said.

"Give me a break. I never get to nap. I feel like a lady of leisure," Abby said.

"Well, lady of leisure, it's your turn to try breaking into the computer," Charlie said, standing up and offering the chair to Abby. "Morgan and I haven't made any headway."

"What passwords have you already tried?" Abby asked.

"Too many to count," Charlie said.

"I tried all of mom's favorite things," Morgan said.

"What about her most favorite thing of all?" Morgan and Charlie looked at her expectantly. "A-B-B-Y." Abby's fingers dashed across the keyboard. "Damn." She slumped down in the chair.

"You overestimate your importance," Charlie chuckled.

Abby tried a few more words, then shook her head, and got out of the chair.

"We haven't found anything in here," Morgan said. "I think it's time to search Mom's bedroom."

"I'm worried that if we go in there, we'll lose it," Abby said.

"Then how about we open the door but not go in right away," Morgan said. "That way, we can get used to seeing it first."

Charlie and Abby agreed. "Which one of us is going to open it?" Charlie asked.

"You're the oldest, Morgan, you should do it," Abby said.

The three of them walked toward the room, but Charlie and Abby stopped at the end of the hall.

"Hey, you guys come here, I'm not going in alone," Morgan said.

Charlie and Abby joined her outside the bedroom.

"Ready to go in?" Morgan asked, as she put her hand on the knob.

"No," Abby said.

Morgan opened the door slowly, and the three women held hands and walked inside. As soon as they crossed the threshold, Morgan began to mist up.

"Don't you dare cry," Charlie said, bursting into tears. Albert ran past them joyfully, jumped on the bed, stretched out, and immediately began snoring.

Morgan picked up a library book with a bookmark tucked three-quarters in. "Mom didn't even get to find out how the book ended," she said, a tear rolling down her cheek. *I hope the library doesn't fine her*, Morgan thought then realized how stupid that was.

Their mom's bed was neatly made, and every throw pillow perfectly placed. On the nightstand, was a picture of Carla with the three of them from Charlie's college graduation, and another from right before the first and only time the three of them went kayaking. They had to be rescued by the junior lifeguards after getting stuck on the rocks.

Morgan looked over at her sisters. She had always thought that she and Charlie looked the most alike. Charlie had strawberry-blonde curls; Morgan's hair was the same color, but straighter. Charlie was five feet three inches tall, and Morgan was half an inch taller. The biggest difference between them was that Charlie's fair skin had very few wrinkles, while Morgan had the face of someone twenty years older. Eighteen years of drugs and alcohol did that to a person.

Although Abby looked a lot like Carla, Morgan thought Abby was also the perfect blend of her and Charlie. She was five feet two inches tall, with the same golden-brown waves that her mom had. The sisters shared blue eyes and little button noses.

When Morgan was in fourth grade, she had asked Carla if any of them resembled their father. Carla didn't answer, but the look on her face made Morgan sorry she'd asked.

As if they were out-of-sync jack-in-the-boxes, the sisters popped up off the bed one by one and began searching the room.

Abby opened the dresser drawers while Charlie looked in the bathroom. When Morgan went into the walk-in closet, she bathed in the faint scent of her mother's perfume. Dolce &

Gabbana's Light Blue hung in the air like the fog over the Santa Monica mountains. Morgan took her mother's winter coat off a hanger, wrapped her arms around it, and imagined Carla inside. She felt as if she'd been pulled out of icy water and enveloped in the warmth of a blanket just pulled from the dryer.

"Hey, what's this?" Charlie said, interrupting Morgan's fantasy. Morgan turned around to find Charlie in the closet with her. She was pulling out a wad of cash from the toe of Carla's Stuart Weitzman pumps. The only shoes their mom had ever paid more than a hundred dollars for. It was Carla's gift to herself after she sold her first high-priced house.

"How much is there?" Morgan asked.

Charlie counted it. "A thousand dollars."

Abby barged into the closet, shoulder to shoulder with her sisters in the cramped space.

"You don't think Mom was selling drugs, do you?" Abby asked. Morgan shook her head at Abby, who shrugged.

"Maybe she thought if they had an earthquake, she wouldn't be able to get money out of an ATM?" Charlie wondered out loud.

"At least I have one sister with all her brain cells," Morgan cracked.

Abby turned around, "accidentally" knocking Morgan into the shoe rack. Morgan then "accidentally" shoved Abby back.

Suddenly, they were all rifling through the pockets of Carla's jeans, jackets, and boots.

Slowly, they pulled out more and more cash, all wrapped in stacks held together by rubber bands. When they were done going through the whole closet, Charlie counted the money. There was more than three thousand dollars, mostly in one-hundred-dollar bills.

"This is far more than Mom would've kept out of the bank in case of a disaster," Morgan said as she stacked the money in neat piles on the dresser.

"Then what was she hiding it for?" Abby asked.

Charlie left the closet, got down on her knees, and looked under the bed. She slid out two big suitcases and stood each one upright. "Why are these so heavy?" she asked.

Charlie unzipped the first suitcase, which was packed neatly with winter clothes. Abby unzipped the second suitcase, which was packed with summer clothes, toiletries, and their mother's passport.

"What the hell…" Morgan said.

"Was Mom going on a trip?" Charlie asked.

"Not that I knew of," Morgan said. "And where would she go that she'd need both warm- and cold-weather clothes?"

"And her passport," Charlie said.

"It's like she didn't think she'd be coming back," Abby said.

"And she didn't," Morgan said solemnly.

"Was she running away from something?" Charlie asked.

"Or someone?" Morgan said, staring at the suitcases as if the clothes would answer all their questions.

Morgan pulled out her phone and started typing while Charlie and Abby continued to look through their mom's suitcases.

"I texted Mom's friend Ginny to see we could come over to talk to her," Morgan said. "Maybe she knows where Mom was planning on going."

"Good idea," Charlie said.

"She invited us for brunch tomorrow," Morgan said.

"That's nice of her," Abby said.

"Speaking of food, I'm starving," Charlie said.

"That's because we haven't eaten since lunch," Morgan said.

Abby volunteered to make dinner with the groceries she'd bought before they went to Vegas. Forty-five minutes later, the women sat down to chicken tenders, macaroni and cheese, and apples cut into chunks—foods of the toddler gods.

After dinner, each sister took on the job Carla had assigned to them when they were children: Morgan washed the dishes, Charlie dried them, and Abby put them away. When the kitchen was clean, Morgan dished out bowls of mint chip ice cream, which was their mother's favorite, and they sat down to watch a sappy TV movie. Albert cuddled up with Abby, Morgan held Brigitta on her lap, and Charlie grabbed a throw pillow and held it against her chest.

When the credits rolled, Abby yawned. "I'm going to bed."

Morgan turned off the TV, and Charlie and Abby went to their bedrooms. Morgan pulled a sheet and blanket out of the linen closet and made up the couch. After she got comfortable, she suddenly jumped up, knocking her pillow to the floor. They had forgotten to close their mom's bedroom door. If Morgan had to use the bathroom in the middle of the night, she couldn't bear to see Carla's bed without her in it. Morgan went into the dark hall and closed the door.

The following day, the sisters parked on a quiet street in Hancock Park across from a stately Victorian mansion. The four-story cream-and-white house, designed by a famous architect, looked as if it had been put together with pieces from different puzzles. It had a mixture of bay and arched windows, and the roof was steeply pitched with a turret and multiple cantilevered gables. The archway above the large double wood doors was brick, as was the walkway and the five stairs leading up to the front door.

Morgan had gone to the house with Carla the year before, but Abby and Charlie had never been here. The expression on her sisters' faces were the same ones Morgan had the first time she saw the house: wide eyes and open mouths.

"It's wild, isn't it?" Morgan said. Abby and Charlie nodded; Morgan continued, "Mom told me that the house was built in the early nineteen hundreds, but four years ago, Ginny restored it. Wait until you see the gorgeous view of the Hollywood sign."

"I can't believe a friend of Mom's lives here," Abby said.

"Ginny's father was a famous sports announcer and left the house to her in his will."

"Wow, I wish we had a father like that," Abby said.

"I wish we had *any* father," Charlie said.

They walked up to the oversized pine doors with beveled glass in the center. Morgan raised her hand to knock, but the door opened before her hand met the wood. Ginny threw her arms around Morgan, who stepped happily into them. The hug was warm, tight and loving. Morgan looked up at the sky. *Mom, thank you for at least leaving us Ginny. She's not you, but she's here for us, and that helps.*

"I'm so glad to see you all again," Ginny said, hugging Charlie and Abby. "Please come in."

Even with its stately columns and twelve-foot-high ceilings, the interior of Ginny's house felt cozy. She led them into the dining room.

"Please sit," Ginny said, pointing to the long glass table, which could have seated a small village. The table was adorned with bagels, and cream cheese, deviled eggs, and a platter of potato pancakes.

Morgan caught a whiff of the scent of garlic bagels, which took her back to her childhood and a special time that she and her sisters had shared with her mother. Every New Year's Day, Carla would set up four TV trays and pass around bagels, cream cheese, and deviled eggs. Then they'd watch the Rose Parade while they ate. After each of the girls turned twelve, Carla would pour a tiny bit of champagne into their orange juice glass, and they'd toast to the new year.

When Abby turned twelve and had her first mimosa, she acted drunk and wouldn't stop giggling. It wasn't until years later that Carla confessed that she had never actually given them champagne. It was only sparkling apple cider.

"It's so nice of you to have us over," Charlie said to Ginny then pointed to the table. "You didn't have to go to all this trouble."

"It's nothing. I'd do anything for you three."

"Thank you, we're happy to be here," Morgan said.

"I know how hard this has been for you guys and how much you miss your mom. I miss her so much, too," Ginny said, then stood back up. "Oh, I forgot the orange juice." Ginny ran off to the kitchen, where Morgan saw her grab a tissue and wipe her eyes.

When Ginny came back in, her mascara had slightly smudged. She poured orange juice into each of their glasses.

"Morgan said you have some questions for me," Ginny said, "but as close as your mother and I were, there were a lot of things she wouldn't talk to me about."

"Is one of them our father?" Abby asked.

"Yes, the only thing she told me about him was how they met," Ginny said.

"That's pretty much the only thing she ever told us, too," Abby said.

"Did you know she got married again?" Morgan asked.

"That wasn't a real marriage. I met him once. He's a nice guy," Ginny said.

"We just met him, too," Abby said.

"Carla told you about him? She told me she didn't want you all to find out; she thought you would think he took advantage of her," Ginny said.

"She didn't tell us. We found his name in her will," Charlie said.

"I'm not surprised, Carla was always generous."

Morgan reached across the table for the water pitcher and poured herself a glass. "Was my mom depressed about anything?" Morgan asked, taking a sip.

"Not that I could tell. And I talked to her a few days before she…she…" Ginny's voice trailed off, and her hand began to shake. Morgan put her hand on top of Ginny's. Ginny took a breath, then continued. "Your mom seemed fine other than being stressed that the video of her saving her neighbor was all over the internet. She couldn't stand that the media had camped out in front of her house."

"There's no way she'd kill herself because she didn't want to go outside for a few days," Abby said, looking at her sisters.

"I know," Ginny said. "Carla had to know the attention would be over as quickly as it started," Ginny said, then stood up again. "Oh, now I forgot the coffee. Where is my mind today?" She went back into the kitchen.

Morgan called out toward the kitchen. "Was our mom about to go on a trip somewhere?"

"Not that I know of. Why?" Ginny asked, pouring coffee into all the mugs.

Morgan blew on the steam that was rising from her cup. She told Ginny about the money they found in Carla's closet, how the suitcases were packed, and how her passport was inside.

"That's strange," Ginny said, wrinkling her forehead. "Maybe she thought she'd go somewhere to get away from all the attention."

"Why wouldn't she have told us?" Morgan said.

"It could've been a spur-of-the-moment decision," Ginny said.

"I guess, but where would she have gone that she'd take both winter and summer clothes?" Charlie asked.

"I have no idea—she could've been stopping in New York on her way to someplace warm," Ginny said, her eyebrows scrunched together like two caterpillars head-butting each other.

"Mom hated New York," Morgan said more passionately than she intended.

"But that's where she grew up," Ginny said.

Morgan, Charlie, and Abby stared at Ginny as if she had two heads and had turned into a dragon.

"Mom grew up in Los Angeles," Abby said.

"No, she didn't. Your mom was born in New York. After she graduated high school, she went to Brooklyn College," Ginny said.

"That can't be right. She told us she'd only been to New York once and hated it," Charlie said.

"I didn't get the feeling she had a great childhood there, but Brooklyn is also where she met your father," Ginny said. "Carla didn't move to Los Angeles until she filed for divorce from your dad."

"I lived in New York?" Morgan said. She felt nauseous and pushed her plate away from her. She couldn't grasp this information any more than she could have held on to a tiny fluttering butterfly.

"You and Charlie lived there when you were first born," she said to Morgan. "Abby was born in Los Angeles."

"But Mom told us she went to UCLA. She took us on a tour of the school and said how proud she was to have graduated from such a renowned university," Charlie said.

"And remember how she pointed out that older man with the long, scraggly beard who was walking toward Royce Hall?" Morgan said. "She said he was her Microeconomics professor and almost failed her."

"How could she have known how good the hot chocolate was at the coffeehouse on campus," Abby said.

"Well, now we know why she said she'd thrown out her diploma after 'accidentally' spilling red wine all over it," Morgan said.

"This is crazy," Charlie said.

"Why would Mom lie about all that?" Abby asked.

"I don't know." Ginny rubbed her hands together and shook her head.

The day had barely started, yet Morgan's world had been shaken up even more. When they got back to Carla's house, Morgan pulled out her list of AA meetings, grabbed her keys, and headed out the door.

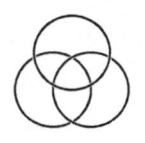

CHAPTER 18

Charlie

Charlie prided herself on her ability to fall asleep easily. Every night in the past, she could be in dreamland in a matter of minutes and fully rested by seven a.m. Over the last few weeks, that had been far from the case. Four-thirty a.m. had become her new normal.

Since her mom had passed away, before Charlie even opened her eyes, her brain was on overdrive. Since she couldn't come up with obvious answers for her mother's actions, she began analyzing Carla's life. Had Carla been happy, or was she an expert on pretending? Did she fulfill any of her dreams or live vicariously through her children? As Charlie contemplated these things, it hit her. *Am I living the life I wanted for myself?*

Charlie's reason for becoming a psychotherapist stemmed from her childhood. She had her sisters and her mother, but some of her friends had almost no support system. Charlie had been the person everyone went to for advice, so she knew exactly what she wanted to pursue when she went to college.

As her therapy practice grew, Charlie loved the feeling of being able to help her clients deal with life's most challenging situations. But what if she hadn't made a different? Had she been fooling herself and hadn't had an impact on anyone? Could it be possible to be a completely different person professionally than she'd been personally?

When Charlie was younger, she considered herself a feminist. She couldn't imagine any man walking all over her. So, where did that strong woman disappear to, leaving this weak one who couldn't end a relationship she didn't want anymore? She looked up at the poster of Ruth Bader Ginsburg, which still hung above her childhood bed.

"Ruth, you'd never agree to pick up your boyfriend's mother from the airport because he didn't want to miss his favorite TV show," she said. "You would tell him to take a hike. Maybe if I wore a lace collar, I would be that woman who stood up for herself again."

Carla's death had prompted Charlie to start dealing with the things she had compartmentalized to get through each day. She realized that the effort it took to hide from her life was way more exhausting now.

Unfortunately, today and most other days, it didn't matter how tired she felt; she couldn't fall back to sleep or nap. Her ability to stay awake during the day when she hadn't slept for many nights before had been an attribute she wore like a badge of honor--a superhero of fatigue.

Charlie's bladder let her know it wouldn't wait any longer for her to get up. She headed to the bathroom, tripping on a shoe she'd left on the floor. She grabbed the bedpost to keep herself from falling and she tried to adjust her eyes to the darkness to find the other shoe before she also tripped on that one. Her shoes seemed to hide in places waiting to kill her.

When she made her way into the kitchen to make coffee, she found Morgan had already made a pot and was staring down at the crevices in the wood of the kitchen table.

"You couldn't sleep either," Charlie said, not sure Morgan heard her come in.

"Huh?" Morgan said without looking up.

"Sleep? You couldn't sleep," Charlie said.

"Is that something we're supposed to do?" Morgan rubbed the dark circles under her eyes, which seemed more prominent than usual.

After grabbing a mug and pouring herself a cup of coffee, Charlie joined Morgan at the table. Charlie was silent as she scrolled through her phone.

"Why aren't you talking?" Morgan asked.

"I know you're not a morning person," Charlie said. "When we shared a room, if I spoke to you before seven-thirty, you'd throw your alarm clock at me."

"Well, I'm an adult now. Besides there aren't any alarm clocks in the kitchen. Although that spatula is looking pretty good."

"You're losing your touch. The wooden spoon would do more damage."

"Don't give me ideas."

Morgan got up and handed Charlie a blueberry muffin from a plate on the counter.

"Where did these come from?" Charlie asked.

"I made them this morning. Or it could've been last night. I can't remember."

"What time did you get up?"

"Which time?" Morgan took a muffin for herself.

Charlie enjoyed her first bite. "These are good. When did you take up baking?" Charlie asked.

"When I stopped drinking, I needed a substitute, and sugar was the next best thing."

Abby came into the kitchen, yawning. "What're you doing up?" Morgan asked her.

"Emma has woken up every morning at four-fifty-five since she was born. My body now thinks that's a normal time to rise and shine, skipping the shine." She poured herself coffee and joined them at the table. "Don't have kids. Or if you do…don't." Abby smiled.

"We know you love them," Charlie said.

"I do, during regular work hours," Abby smirked.

The clock in the living room chimed. "Oh, shut up," Charlie called out to the clock.

"I hate it, too, but mom loved that clock, so I haven't had the heart to stop it. Every hour, when it plays music, it reminds me of her," Morgan said.

"I don't know how she didn't go crazy listening to that. The first thing I'd do when I visited was stop the pendulum," Charlie said. "Mom pretended not to notice, but every time right before I left, she would smile at me and push the pendulum to move again."

"I miss her laugh," Abby said.

"I'd miss it too if I weren't so angry at her," Morgan said. "She lied to us about so many things."

"Why would it matter to us that she was raised in New York," Charlie said.

"Or that she graduated from Brooklyn College and not UCLA," Abby added.

"What happened to her in New York that she didn't want us to know?" Charlie asked.

"I think we need to go there," Morgan said.

"How will going to New York help us figure out why she died?" Abby asked.

"I'm not sure, but something in my gut tells me that we need to go back to the place that made her want to run and not look back," Morgan said.

"Morgan's right. We might be able to put some pieces together if we know more about her past," Charlie said.

"It feels weird talking about our mother like she's a stranger," Abby said.

"Because she was," Charlie said.

Morgan stood up. "I'm going to check on flights out of LA leaving in a few days."

"I want to go home and see Alex and the kids first before we go that far," Abby said. "Also, I didn't bring warm enough clothes for New York."

"You could wear something from Mom's suitcase. I think we can safely say she won't be needing it," Morgan said.

"Nice," Abby said.

"Too soon?" Morgan said.

"I'm going to see if Rick can come for the weekend and bring me my coat and some sweaters," Charlie said.

"That's great. Then you can break up with him," Morgan said.

"I can't break up with him when he'd be flying out here as a favor to me," Charlie said.

"Good point. It's much better to wait until you're walking down the aisle," Morgan said.

The next day, Abby left to go back to Encinitas, and Rick was on a plane heading for Los Angeles. Morgan came in carrying an overnight bag, with Brigitta in the cat carrier.

"You don't have to leave just because Rick will be here," Charlie said.

"Yes, I do. Otherwise, watching your dynamic with him will make me want to drive to Abby's and babysit her kids."

"We can stay out of your way."

"Not far enough; I'm going to stay at my friend Suzanne's house. I'll be back Sunday night."

"Okay, have fun."

"I'd say the same to you, but I'm hoping you two have a horrible relationship-ending fight." Morgan took her suitcase, backpack, and Brigitta and left.

Charlie enjoyed the sudden quiet in the house. She took advantage of it by reading a book until she remembered she needed to change the sheets, do laundry, and vacuum. She hadn't realized how late it had gotten until she looked out the window at a sky that had turned the color of black shoe polish.

A few minutes later, a car parked behind Charlie's in the driveway. Rick, wearing his hunter-green T-shirt, Charlie's favorite, pulled a suitcase from his trunk. As he walked up the path, the reflection from the porchlight made his hazel eyes glow.

Charlie didn't feel even a hint of a smile cross her lips. *Shouldn't I be more excited to see him?*

When she opened the door, Rick grabbed her, dipped her backward, and kissed her passionately. Charlie imagined they looked like the old photograph of the sailor and the nurse kissing in Times Square, although the nurse appeared to be enjoying it. Charlie used to love Rick's grand gestures, but lately, more often than not, she felt herself just going along with them.

The first few years she and Rick dated, every time she thought of him, she felt a kaleidoscope of beautiful colors waltzing inside her. The first time they met was at her friend Louisa's twenty-first birthday party. He was wearing a beige sweater and black jeans. Charlie was surprised at how good he looked in a V-neck since she was not fond of that neckline on men.

The party was going strong when she came in—loud music, drinking, and wild dancing. Charlie liked to dance but wasn't comfortable asking a random stranger, so she kicked off her platform boots and pulled Louisa onto the dance floor. They jumped around in an odd freestyle, combining hip-hop and The Running Man.

Rick came up behind Louisa and tapped her. "Hey, is there any more beer?" he asked, yelling over the loud music.

Louisa nodded, and when she crossed toward the kitchen, Rick remained next to Charlie. He reached out, took her hand, and twirled her around. She laughed as the beer and a half she had drunk swirled in her brain making her slightly dizzy. Rick caught her in his arms when her stocking feet slid out from under her. Charlie wasn't sure if she'd accidentally slipped or done it on purpose. Either way, she was in a cute guy's arms. She may have been in college, but her maturity level with boys was that of a twelve-year-old.

"I'm surprised I never noticed you before," Rick said.

"I fly under the radar," Charlie had said.

"Not anymore." He stared at Charlie, and she wasn't sure if he liked what he saw or was trying to figure out if she was his type.

"I'm Rick," he said.

"Charlie."

When Charlie saw Louisa coming back with a beer, she jumped away from Rick as if she'd been caught by her parents having sex with a stranger. Louisa handed Rick the beer and took Charlie's hand.

"There's someone I want you to meet," Louisa said to Charlie.

As Louisa and Charlie began to walk away, Rick called after.

"Aren't you going to give me your number?" he asked.

Before Charlie could answer, he said, "Never mind; I'll give you mine." He reached into her pocket, pulled out her phone, and typed his number into it.

"Call me," he said.

"And what if I don't?" Charlie said.

"Oh, I think you will." Rick grinned at her and walked away.

Charlie couldn't believe the nerve of the guy, yet she felt her heart palpitating to the beat of Taylor Swift's "Shake It Off." The last time she had felt this odd was when she was twelve at her cousin's bar mitzvah and a fourteen-year-old boy told Carla that he was going to marry her daughter in ten years.

Now, eleven years after that party, Rick was curled up on the couch next to Charlie.

"I've missed you," Rick said.

"Me, too," Charlie said—how could she not say that back?

Rick rubbed her arm up and down as if strumming a guitar. "I hate when you're not around. I count on you a lot."

Charlie looked him in the eyes. "Which honestly is not great."

"It's what couples who love each other do."

"It's too much. Our relationship isn't equal," Charlie said. "I'm not getting some of my own stuff done, because I'm constantly taking care of you."

"I thought you loved me," Rick said, turning on his best smile.

"I'm being serious. I need to start prioritizing myself, so you have to stop relying on me so much."

"Okay, you're right. I get it, more equal. You got it."

"Thanks." Charlie breathed a sigh of relief. *Maybe this can work.* "When you go home, can you water the orchids in my apartment? I don't want them to die before I get back."

"Didn't we just decide to prioritize ourselves more?" Rick asked. "Since I've been spending so much time doing all my errands lately, I need to have time to get to the gym."

Charlie slowly counted to five in her head. "Do you want to watch TV?" she asked.

"Sure, I heard there's a new Dahmer documentary on Netflix."

"I can't watch serial killers at night."

"This one will be different."

"No, it won't." She looked at the menu for another show to watch. "What about a show about Joan Rivers' rise to fame."

"Boring." They sat for a minute in silence. Then Rick continued, "I know what we can do." A flirtatious smirk spread across his face; Charlie knew his expression well.

"I'm kind of tired," she said. "I haven't been sleeping well." She saw the disappointed look on Rick's face. "Cuddling would be nice, though."

"Okay, and then tomorrow night you'll have more energy."

After Rick fell asleep, Charlie tossed and turned for quite a while, trying to figure out how she had ended up being so strong in some parts of her life and so weak in others.

She must have finally drifted off when she found herself having the same dream she'd had many times before. She and Rick were at a fancy restaurant. He was talking incessantly about some video game he'd been trying to beat. Suddenly, he clutched his chest, fell off his chair and dropped to the ground. The lamb chop in his hand skittered across the black and white tile floor, landing beside the cowboy boot of a woman at the next table. Charlie looked down into Rick's wide-open eyes as their normal iridescent color lost its light. She knew he was already gone.

Commotion reverberated in the restaurant, but Charlie was paralyzed and couldn't stand up. A man at the next table called out that he was a doctor and ran over. He began CPR while his wife called 911. The doctor continued compressions on Rick's chest, and his wife kept her finger on Rick's pulse until the paramedics rushed in. Charlie stared at her plate where the congealed linguine had transformed into a bunch of live worms. Rick was put on a stretcher, and a sheet was placed over him. This was the always the part of the dream where Charlie woke up.

When she first started having the dream, Charlie told her therapist about it.

"Do you notice that Rick is the one to leave you?" the therapist said. "Is it possible your subconscious is telling you it's time to end that relationship?"

"Probably. But I'm scared of being alone," Charlie told him.

"Aren't you alone now?" the therapist asked.

Charlie knew it was wrong to lie to another therapist, but she couldn't let him see that she didn't have the energy to change anything. During the subsequent few sessions, she told her therapist that Rick had an epiphany and realized that he'd been taking her for granted. Charlie said he was now devoted to making her needs his top priority, and they were heading toward an engagement. After a few weeks, Charlie left therapy instead of revealing the truth. Besides, she didn't have enough to talk about if she couldn't complain about Rick.

While Rick snored quietly, Charlie stared at the clock and clenched her jaw, *Mom, I'm glad you aren't here to see me not taking control or standing up for myself.*

A day later, when Rick left for the airport, Charlie leaned on the closed door, letting her head rest gently against the cool wood. Then she crossed her arms and gave herself a much-needed hug. An hour later, she'd never been happier to see Morgan come home.

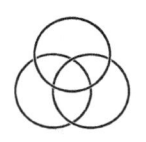

CHAPTER 19

Abby

The moment Abby walked through her front door three of her four kids attached themselves to her like koala bears hanging onto a tree branch. Abby couldn't distinguish what they were saying because they were all talking at once, but she knew it didn't matter. They just wanted her to love them, which she did with lots of hugs and kisses.

"Guys, give your mom some breathing room," Alex said, gently removing the tiny beings from her as if they were crazed teens at a Taylor Swift concert.

"It's okay; I missed them so much," Abby said.

"Well, I want my turn, too." Alex pulled Abby into his arms and kissed her. The two boys giggled and covered their eyes.

When Alex and Abby moved apart, the kids fought over who their mom had missed the most.

"Hey," Alex said. "Mom missed you all the same amount."

"I really did," Abby said, leaning down to hug them again.

"You can't miss everyone the same," Levi protested. "You have to have your favorite."

"Her favorite is Daddy because none of you would be here without me," Alex said. "Why don't you all go to the playroom and draw Mom pictures of all the things that have happened since she's been gone."

The three kids jumped up and scampered off. "And Hudson, no more pictures of dinosaurs eating your siblings!" Alex called after them.

"Then I have nothing to draw," Hudson called back.

"We're missing one kid," Abby said, after the others were gone.

"I sold Emma to the highest bidder. We got a lot for her. Thank God she's still cute, and her new mom hasn't seen how much she eats."

"You're adorable," Abby said, kissing him.

"I won't argue with that."

Abby looked up at Alex's tall, lanky frame, which dwarfed her. She hooked her hand in his belt loop, the way she'd been doing since they were teenagers. "Seriously, where's Emma?" she asked.

"She got so overtired that she broke down, so I put her to bed. I didn't think you needed to come home to any extra crying."

"You're a good husband."

"I was hoping to give you a peaceful night, although I'm not sure that will be possible."

Alex took her hand and led her to the couch, then got her a Diet Coke and sat beside her. He put his arm around her, and she melted into his chest, feeling his heartbeat against her back.

She had loved Alex from the time they were thirteen, and although their lives mainly consisted of going to the park, attending birthday parties, and finding new ways to entertain their kids, she knew he was still in the trenches with her. He'd never walk away the way her father had.

"Do you want me to empty your suitcase into the washing machine and start a load?" Alex asked.

"I'll do it tomorrow. Right now, I'd rather sit here quietly with you."

Six little but thunderous feet pounded into the room, running after the dog like Miss Piggy chasing Kermit the frog.

"Please leave Walter alone; he's going to collapse," Abby said, scooping the dog up in her arms.

"Walter loves it," Levi said.

Walter panted in Abby's arms and nuzzled his head into her chest. "Walter needs a nap. Or a nursing home," Abby whispered to Alex.

"Why don't you guys go back to the playroom and torture each other," Alex said.

"Okay!" Hudson and Levi said, and they all ran off again.

"That was a joke!" Alex called after them.

Alex stood up. "I'll be right back. I want to make sure they *went* into the playroom." He followed behind them.

Abby put Walter down on the floor. "Go to your crate and lock the door," she said. He skittered away as if he understood.

Abby pushed aside the action figures, stuffed animals, and Lego blocks that littered the coffee table and grabbed the television remote. Her house used to be decorated with scented candles, plants, and a lovely bride-and-groom figurine that had been a wedding gift. Now, all of that was in a box in the garage, and her décor matched Target's toy department.

Thinking about which reality show she wanted to watch—*Married at First Sight, Love Island, Temptation Island, Love Is Blind?*—Abby couldn't help but wonder why she had such a thing for dating shows. Could it be because the only person she'd ever been on a date with was Alex. *Could I have missed out on an important part of life? Then again, who else would be understanding when I lose my passport or forget to pay the mortgage? And what other man would find it cute when I mix up metaphors?* When Abby said things like 'the light at the end of the rainbow,' 'eyes are the windows to your head,' or 'no skin off my toes,' Alex would look at her with amusement and so much love.

Alex returned to the room looking slightly more haggard than when he'd left.

"I know me being gone has put a lot on you," Abby said. "But I appreciate you taking care of everything."

"I love you," Alex said.

"I love you, too." Abby turned so she could gaze into his eyes. "I'll come home as soon as I can."

"Don't worry about us, we're fine."

"I promise, I'll make it up to you."

"Can you start tonight?" Alex asked.

Abby grinned. "Give me fifteen minutes to put them all to bed."

"Fifteen minutes? That's ambitious."

"I'm fast." Abby stood up.

"Don't expect me to be fast," Alex flirted.

Abby bent down and kissed him long and hard. Alex stood up, and as she turned to leave, he grabbed her butt.

"I'll hurry," Abby said, then called out. "So, which one of my three adorable children will be able to get in bed and fall asleep the fastest?"

A chorus of "me-me-me" rang out as three little beings raced to their rooms.

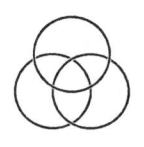

CHAPTER 20

Carla

Carla loved New York and would never have considered moving away. She loved the smell of hot dogs wafting through the air, picnics in Central Park, the marquees in the theater district, and the way that Statue of Liberty was lit up for every holiday. These were just some of the things that made the city exciting all year long.

When Morgan and Charlie were born, Carla couldn't wait for them to get old enough to introduce them to everything the city had to offer, musicals, art museums, the Empire State Building, and Serendipity for hot chocolate. But she didn't experience most of those things with them because Brian's actions ruined New York for her so badly she had to move.

When Carla decided to leave, she felt she had to get as far away from Brian as possible. Los Angeles was across the country, and it was so different from New York that it would never remind her of how wonderful things had been with him when they first got married. She only hoped the girls were young enough to forget they ever lived in New York. The thought of them bringing it up brought a shiver to her bones.

Carla felt sure she was making the right decision by leaving Brian. When she told the girls that their father wasn't joining them, Morgan, not even six, seemed to be the only one who understood. One night, Carla overheard Morgan explaining her father's absence to her stuffed elephant. She wasn't crying, only slightly sniffling, so Carla told herself Morgan would move on quickly.

As the girls got older and they pushed for details about their father, Carla made it clear she wasn't going to go there, and they finally stopped asking. Over the years, Carla experienced moments of guilt, wondering whether her daughters would eventually be affected by growing up without a father. If at any point Carla had given any thought to the relationships her daughters had with men, she would have had to admit the truth, but she didn't allow herself to go there.

Carla didn't know anyone in Los Angeles, but she didn't mind because she had her daughters, and they were all she needed. She found a two-bedroom apartment in a quiet neighborhood in the San Fernando Valley. She put sheets over the bedroom windows because drapes were not in her budget. She cooked a lot of Hamburger Helper and chicken nuggets. She couldn't afford to take the girls to the Natural History Museum, amusement parks, or the zoo, but at least the city parks and beaches were free.

Brian had never been great at saving money, which was why Carla kept the small amount she'd inherited from her grandparents a secret. That money served to keep her and the girls afloat while she worked to pass the test for her real estate license in California.

After two years and a lot of hard work, Carla could finally afford a small house on a street near the girls' elementary school in Studio City, a small suburb of Los Angeles. The eighteen-hundred square foot four-bedroom house sat between two mansions that towered over it like a short person at a standing-room-only concert.

During those first years in Los Angeles, Carla's social life revolved around her daughters.

That is until the day she met Ginny. Carla had made an appointment with a new client interested in buying a house. From the moment Ginny Baxter walked into Carla's office, Carla knew she'd found a good friend. It wasn't that they had a lot in common; it was that they admired each other.

Carla was a single, working woman taking care of three daughters, while Ginny, who was married, used to be a high-powered attorney but quit when she inherited money from her father. That gave her the ability to relax and travel the world. Carla envied Ginny's close relationship with her parents, while Ginny envied Carla's relationship with her daughters, as she had been unable to have children.

Not only did Carla find Ginny the perfect house, but the two of them spent many afternoons there drinking wine and chatting about their lives. Carla avoided talking a lot about the past, but because she trusted Ginny, she did reveal a few things about her life in New York.

When Carla's daughters eventually moved away, she turned to Ginny for comfort. Charlie was the first one to go. She attended the University of Arizona for graduate school and opened her therapy practice in Scottsdale. A year later, Morgan took off for Oregon to distance herself from the friends she used to drink with, and Abby moved to San Diego when Alex got promoted and transferred. Carla missed them but wanted them to be happy and enjoy their lives wherever they were.

After her last daughter left, Carla joined a book club and tried to make a few new friends, but her social life remained small. She didn't go out that often and continued to make a point of being private, so she panicked when her face was suddenly plastered all over the internet. People from her past would know where she was.

I'm going to lose my mind if I have to live like this, she thought, until she stopped living altogether.

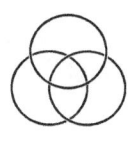

CHAPTER 21

Morgan

Morgan boarded the plane to New York first, leaving Charlie and Abby racing to catch up to her. When she got to her row, she put her purse on the seat, then bent deeply at the knees trying to pick up her weighty carry-on.

"You're holding everyone up," Charlie piped up, gesturing to the line of people behind her.

With a grunt, Morgan lifted the overnight bag over her head and shoved it in. She moved into the window seat, stretching her back and grimacing.

Charlie tossed her suitcase into the overhead compartment as easily as if she'd only packed a down pillow inside, then she sat in the aisle seat.

Abby stood looking at them, tapping her foot. "Why do I have to take the middle seat?" she asked Charlie. "You're the middle child."

The passengers waiting behind her began to grumble.

"Abby, just sit," Morgan said.

Charlie pulled her legs up to her butt, and Abby crawled over her. Abby sat and expelled a powerful breath of air through her nose like a killer whale through its blowhole.

Charlie sniffed. "I can smell the peanut butter you had for breakfast."

"And I can smell the spinsterhood on your breath," Abby said.

"Okay," Morgan said. "We're all a little tense. Some of us more than others." She put her hand on both her sisters' knees. "Why don't we hold off the snotty insults and try to enjoy each other on this long plane ride."

"When did you become the therapist here?" Charlie said, grinning.

"I have my moments," Morgan said.

When the plane left the gate, the scream of the engines filled the cabin as it picked up speed along the runway. Abby grabbed her sisters' hands as the front wheels lifted off the ground. Morgan had forgotten that Abby had a fear of flying.

"If we all go down, does Albert inherit Mom's estate?" Abby asked, clenching her teeth and not letting go of her sisters until the plane leveled off.

The flight was smooth, but the six hours went by excruciatingly slow for Morgan. She spent most of the time with her eyes closed, wishing she could fall asleep, but questions ping-ponged around her brain as she wondered what else they might discover about Carla's life. The only clues they had so far were a magnet from New York, suitcases filled with stacks of money, and that their mother had lied to them about where she'd grown up. None of which answered the question as to why Carla would have wanted to die.

When the plane landed and pulled up to gate 44 at JFK airport, the flight attendant turned off the seatbelt sign. When that familiar ding reverberated throughout the cabin, Abby jumped up, pulled her suitcase from the overhead bin, and tried to race off the plane ahead of other passengers.

"Abby, you have to wait your turn," Morgan said, holding her back.

"I need to get out of here," Abby said, seemingly unable to keep it together a second longer.

Morgan gestured to the couple in front of them, who were each over six feet with two suitcases and two backpacks blocking the aisle. "Unless you're planning to fly over them, you aren't going anywhere," Morgan whispered to Abby.

The driver who picked them up at the taxi stand had a thick and unidentifiable accent. His red beard, peppered with gray, grew below his chin to a point like an upside-down triangle. Morgan got into the back of the cab and sat directly behind the driver. Abby made a mad dash around to the other door and sat behind the front passenger seat, leaving Charlie to crawl into the middle seat. Morgan glanced over at Abby and saw the satisfied smile on her sister's lips.

"Can you take us to the William Vale Hotel," Morgan asked.

As the driver hit the gas, he asked, "Brooklyn?" somehow making the one word seem like a judgment.

"Yes," Morgan said.

"We aren't staying in the city?" Abby wailed.

"No," Morgan said.

"First, I got all excited about going to Vegas, only we were in Henderson. And then I was thrilled to be traveling to New York City, but we're staying in Brooklyn," Abby said. "Is this a mean joke on the person who never travels anywhere that doesn't have a water park?"

"We're staying near where Mom grew up," Charlie said.

"If we have time, we'll go into Manhattan," Morgan said.

"Just so you know, these trips aren't living up to their hype," Abby pouted.

The cabbie drove like he was in a road rage with another automobile. He sped around cars, buses, and pedestrians in crosswalks. Every time he slammed on the brakes, Charlie held on to the seat in front of her to avoid being thrown into one of her sisters' laps.

"At least the taxi rides are crazy and dangerous no matter what borough you're in," Charlie whispered in Abby's ear, who didn't appear to find the comment funny.

When the cab pulled up to the William Vale Hotel, Morgan felt slightly dizzy and nauseated. While she paid the driver, Abby and Charlie got their luggage out of the trunk.

Their hotel room was small, with two double beds and not much else. The same argument the sisters had when they were kids—about who got their own bed and which two had to sleep together—started: "You hog the covers." "Well, *you* snore." "And *you* take up the whole bed."

Since they would have the room for three nights, Morgan suggested that each of them should have a bed to herself for one of the nights. That perfect solution satisfied both Charlie and Abby.

When they had unpacked, Morgan fell back on the bed and relaxed into the comfy mattress. Charlie put her feet on an ottoman as she sat in a small club chair in the corner of the room. She read the news on her phone.

"Don't get comfortable; I'm starving," Abby said, putting on her coat and wrapping her scarf around her neck. Morgan and Charlie grabbed their coats and headed back to the hotel elevators.

"There's a seafood restaurant down the street," Morgan said. "I did some research before we got here, and it got a good rating on Yelp."

Five minutes later, they approached a warehouse with a small sign that they would've completely missed if they hadn't been looking for it.

"Wow, I've always wanted to go to Costco for dinner," Charlie quipped.

"Me, too," Abby said. "Will they have people in the aisles giving samples?" Abby and Charlie high five.

"Ha ha," Morgan said. "It's hard being the only hip sister among us."

The inside of the restaurant was a complete contrast to the exterior of the building. The walls were lined with red velvet wallpaper, mini crystal chandeliers hung over the tables, and the servers dressed in black and wore white gloves.

"Still think we're in Costco?" Morgan asked.

As soon as they were seated, Charlie and Abby ordered cocktails, and Morgan ordered a mocktail. The waiter was so quick to bring the drinks over that Morgan wondered if her sisters appeared to need a buzz.

"I want one of everything," Charlie said as she read through the menu.

"I'm so hungry I could eat a small child," Abby said. "Not one of mine, of course, but someone else's that has more meat on their bones."

"Order whatever you want. It's on Mom, and I doubt she'll complain," Morgan said.

Charlie and Abby looked at each other and then at Morgan.

"That's kind of morbid," Abby said.

"But true. I took a stack of those hundred-dollar bills from her suitcase. I think she would've wanted us to enjoy ourselves while we were here," Morgan said.

"Here's to Mom," Charlie said, lifting her cocktail glass.

"Thanks for the expensive fish, too, Mom," Abby said, her eyes raised toward the sky.

"And thank you, Morgan, for stealing her money," Charlie said.

The women clinked glasses.

Morgan took a sip of her drink. "Don't let anyone tell you this is the same without the vodka," she said, swallowing.

The sisters discussed what should be the first thing they do in the morning. Morgan didn't divulge that she had no idea what their endgame would be in Brooklyn. The most important thing was to find out why their mother lied about living in New York.

The waiter brought over their meals.

"I can't believe Mom would put us through this," Abby said, taking a bite of her halibut.

"Most people who get to the point of suicide are in such a dark place they don't think about what or who they're leaving behind," Charlie said.

"Are you saying she never thought of any of us? Or her grandkids?" Abby asked. "How could she not have realized we'd be devastated?"

"It wasn't about us," Charlie said. "Mom probably had tunnel vision and could only see things from her perspective. I know from clients I've had that when someone gets to that point, they don't see another way out."

Morgan cleared her throat, then gazed down at the table for a moment. "Four years ago, I thought about killing myself," she said. "If I hadn't gone to AA, I would have done it."

"Seriously?" Charlie asked.

Morgan nodded.

"I had no idea," Abby said.

"You needed us, and we weren't there for you," Charlie said.

"You couldn't have known; I didn't tell anyone how I felt." Morgan met their eyes. "At first, it was a fleeting thought that would come and go, then I considered it more often, and then it became all I could focus on. When alcohol didn't solve my problems, I thought disappearing would. I couldn't handle disappointing you all anymore."

"I wish you'd come to us," Charlie said.

"I was sure you'd all be better off with me gone, and I didn't want to be guilted out of it," Morgan said. "I knew Mom was always worrying about me, and I thought I could end that for her. It's ironic, that I'm still here, and she's not."

The silence that floated between them told Morgan her sisters must be thinking about what would've happened if Morgan had gone through with it, and how their mother must've felt as she made that final decision.

Abby put her hands up to the gold butterfly around her neck. "I always wondered why you gave me this expensive necklace you said you didn't want anymore."

"I forgot about that," Morgan said. "Since I'm not dead, you need to give it back."

"Me and my big mouth," Abby said under her breath.

Morgan reflected on how different she was back then. "It seems so long ago that I was in that place. Being sober and going to AA made me see that just because my father didn't want me, I'm still worth having around. And now, I have a community of people in AA who understand and help me stay in the right head space."

"And you have us," Charlie said.

"We need to watch out for each other," Abby said. "Now that Mom's gone, we're all the family we have."

Morgan slumped as the weight of that sunk in. She had been to the funeral, and she'd stayed in her mom's house without Carla there, but hearing Abby say those words out loud hit her harder than a fly ball coming at her head at eighty miles an hour.

"Because of everything you went through, does that give you a better understanding of how Mom might've been feeling?" Charlie asked Morgan.

"No. You all knew I was struggling, but Mom didn't show any signs that she was in trouble. It seemed like she had everything together," Morgan said.

"I think whatever it was that made her do it happened quickly," Charlie said.

"I agree. I'm hoping we find something here that gives us answers and some closure," Morgan said.

Abby sighed. "So, where do we start?"

They agreed to begin with the most straightforward clue: the pizza place listed on the magnet that Carla had given Michael.

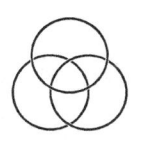

CHAPTER 22

Charlie

When Charlie awoke the following morning and rolled out of bed, she wrapped her arms tightly around her body in the frigid room. She couldn't stop trembling as she pulled a sweatshirt over her pajamas and turned the thermostat from sixty-five degrees to seventy-one. She looked out the window and saw a dusting of snow on the pavement below that resembled powdered sugar.

She touched the window with her fingertips, the raw, icy glass numbing her skin. Charlie had never liked cold weather. That was part of the reason she lived in Arizona—year-round sun.

Charlie stepped in the shower before her sisters got up. When she finished, Morgan was lying in bed looking at her phone, and Abby was still asleep. Charlie turned on all the lights in the room, and Abby groaned. Morgan smiled without taking her eyes off her phone.

As much as Charlie enjoyed giving her sisters a hard time, she wouldn't have wanted to live without them for anything.

Morgan and Abby were a part of her, and she of them, and with their mother gone, she wanted to hold on to them tightly.

"Time to get up," Charlie announced. "I'm ready to go."

"I'm moving," Abby said, without opening her eyes.

"I'll take the next shower, Sleeping Beauty," Morgan said to Abby who nodded and rolled over.

By the time they were ready to go, it was noon. Charlie turned the DO NOT DISTURB sign on the door so that it read, PLEASE MAKE UP THIS ROOM. She looked down the hall and saw three hotel maids standing around their carts, talking.

"I hope they haven't been waiting to clean our room." Charlie gestured toward the maid.

"I doubt it," Morgan said.

Charlie looked at her watch. "How do you know? What if one of them missed her lunch because you two took so long?"

As far back as Charlie could remember, if she thought she had disappointed someone, including a maid she'd never met, she perseverated on it for hours. All the therapy she'd had hadn't succeeded in eliminating that guilt within her. After pressing the down button on the elevator, Charlie turned and, as inconspicuously as possible, looked over her shoulder down the hall. The maids still hadn't moved.

Why did it matter if the maid judged her? What if Charlie wanted to stay in her room all day and night? Why couldn't she do what she wanted and screw everyone else?

The maid was an example of a far more significant issue within Charlie. Why was it okay that Rick put himself first during their entire relationship, but she wouldn't make her needs known? *I'm thirty-two, and I can't remember the last time someone took care of me. Rick is never going to be that person. It's time to end it. I hope I'll be able to do it.*

It was a half mile walk to the pizza parlor, but because of the falling snow and chill, the women hurried and got to the restaurant in under ten minutes. When Morgan opened the door, the heat from inside rushed out to greet them. For a moment, Charlie let her face absorb it like rays of sunshine upon her. She shook her head to disperse the snowflakes that remained on her. The freezing temperatures were why she reminded herself to stay away from the East Coast during winter.

There wasn't anyone behind the hostess desk, only a sign taped to the front that read, PLEASE SEAT YOURSELF. The tables all had the same black, red, and white plaid tablecloth that seemed to be required in every pizza joint in America.

As the sisters looked for a place to sit, they passed a woman with three very young daughters sitting at a table. The infant cheerfully grabbed every piece of silverware and dropped it on the floor, the toddler was crying, and the oldest daughter had a tantrum about how long the food had been taking. The mom's ponytail had become loose, and strands of hair had fallen out, draping her face. The woman reached down and picked up the silverware with one hand while, with her other hand, brushed her fingers through the toddler's hair. Then she spoke to her soothingly. When the waiter approached the table with their food, she thanked him as if he'd saved her from falling through the ice on a frozen lake.

Charlie imagined that was what it had been like for her mother when she was out with the three of them. She wondered if Carla had looked as harried as this woman did.

The sisters found a booth toward the back, removed their coats and hats, and placed them on a hook.

Morgan looked around. "So, this is the place," she said as they sat.

"It looks like any other pizza joint to me," Abby said.

"Why do you think Mom kept the magnet?" Charlie said.

"I don't know," Morgan said, taking a whiff. "But it smells good in here."

"What do you guys want? I'll go up and order," Charlie said.

"Get a large pizza, half pepperoni and half olives and mushrooms," Abby said.

A boy with shaggy light brown hair sticking out from a tan beanie slumped behind the counter, an adolescent in hibernation. The faint odor of marijuana came off him, mixing with the scent of garlic wafting from the kitchen. Charlie wondered if he had smoked in the back alley before his shift started. Teenage girls would have found him cute if it wasn't for the large pimple that had made a home on his nose, resembling a mountain with a snowy white peak. The boy turned to hide his face when Charlie placed their order.

When Charlie returned to the table, Abby looked uneasy, shifting in her chair, crossing and uncrossing her legs.

"What's wrong?" Charlie asked.

"That old man near the kitchen is staring at me," Abby said, holding her menu up so he wouldn't notice her pointing at him.

Charlie looked in that direction. She saw a man in his fifties. He had an egg-shaped face, dark, bushy eyebrows, and wore a white apron covered with tomato sauce stains. His eyes were intently fixed on them as if he were trying to figure out the latest Wordle with only one correct letter.

"Maybe he's staring at me," Morgan said.

"No, he's definitely staring at Abby," Charlie said.

"You're both delusional," Morgan said.

"Do you think he's interested in me or just a creep?" Abby said.

"At his age, if he's interested, then he's definitely a creep," Morgan said.

The man untied his apron and hung it on a hook near the kitchen door. Then he smoothed his hand through his hair, and walked toward them, not breaking his gaze.

"He's coming over," Abby said.

"Excuse me," the man said as he approached their table. "I'm so sorry to be staring at you." He looked directly at Abby.

"See, he *was* looking at her," Charlie whispered to Morgan.

"It's just I'm a little taken aback at how much you look like a woman I went to high school with," he said, not letting his eyes off her.

"Okay..." Abby said.

A light went off in Charlie's head. "What was her name?" Charlie asked.

"Carla," he said.

"Was she about five feet three with dark eyes and a dumb penguin tattoo?" Charlie asked.

"On her right wrist," the man said.

"Yes! Carla was our mom," Morgan said.

"Oh my God, you're her daughters," he said looking, like he had just been handed a box of his favorite candy. "I'm Antonio."

The women introduced themselves by name and birth order, and he reached out to shake each of their hands.

"You said *was* your mom. Did something happen to her?" he asked.

"She recently passed away," Charlie said.

"Oh no, she was so young. I'm so sorry for your loss," Antonio said. The women thanked him, and he continued. "Is it just a crazy coincidence that you came in here today?"

"No," Abby said, reaching into her purse and pulling out the magnet. "This was hers." Abby held it up.

Antonio took the magnet out of Abby's hand. He turned it around and around. "I haven't seen one of these in years. I gave it to Carla a long time ago. I can't believe she kept it."

"It must've meant a lot to her," Charlie said.

"Carla meant a lot to me," Antonio said.

"We're discovering things about our mother's past we didn't know. We came to Brooklyn to find out more," Morgan said.

Antonio gestured to their table. "Do you mind if I sit? My legs get tired from standing back there all day," he said, hooking a thumb toward the kitchen.

The women gestured to him to join them, so Antonio grabbed a chair from another table and pulled it up to theirs.

"Dylan, bring these ladies some garlic rolls," Antonio called over to the one-zit wonder. Dylan nodded and went into the kitchen.

"Did you know our mom well?" Morgan asked.

"We grew up down the street from each other but didn't start hanging out until high school. My dad owned this restaurant, so Carla and I would come here after school to do homework and goof off."

"Were you her boyfriend?" Abby asked.

"No, we were just good friends."

"Did you know our dad, too?" Morgan asked.

"Not really. Carla didn't meet him until college; and she only brought him here once. Then, the next time I saw her was a year later, and she was married and pregnant with you," he said to Morgan. After you were born, Carla would come here every other Friday, and then it wasn't long before she became pregnant with you." He gestured toward Charlie. "And I wasn't even aware that Carla had a third child," he told Abby.

"Yep, I'm the one nobody seems to know about," Abby said.

Dylan placed rolls and three small plates in front of them.

"These look good," Charlie said, taking a bite, then grabbing her napkin and wiping off the little bit of butter that had dripped onto her chin.

"When you were two, Morgan, garlic rolls were your favorite. You'd keep eating them until you got a stomachache," Antonio said.

"I guess things never change," Morgan said, taking another bite.

"What was our mother like when you knew her?" Charlie asked, leaning in.

"Outgoing, sarcastic, funny."

"Qualities we all inherited," Abby said with a smirk.

"And she was adorable," Antonio added. "Everyone loved her. She had so many friends; we used to call her the social butterfly because she flew from group to group."

'That's not the mom we knew, she rarely went out," Charlie said. *What could've happened that changed her entire personality?* Charlie wondered scrunching her forehead, knowing she was creating wrinkles where there hadn't been any.

"Do you remember our mom's old address?" Morgan asked.

"Of course. It wasn't far from here. Give me a second."

Antonio went up to the counter and came back with their pizza and a pad of paper. He wrote down an address and handed it to Morgan.

Even after devouring one and a half rolls, Charlie was still starving. She grabbed a piece of pizza almost before the metal platter hit the table. She took a bite and then began fanning her hand in front of her mouth to wave away the heat. She grabbed her water and chugged it.

"Sorry, I should've warned you that it just came out of the oven," Antonio said.

"It's delicious," Charlie said, moving her tongue along the roof of her mouth, hoping she still had some skin left up there.

Abby offered Antonio a piece of pizza, but he shook his head. "Thank you, but I've had my fill of pizza…at least for today." He patted his rotund belly, which poked out under his grayish-white T-shirt.

Morgan blew on her slice and took a bite. "Did you know our grandparents?" she asked after swallowing.

"Not really. They weren't around much. I heard they both died a long time ago."

"At least that's one thing Mom told us that was true," Charlie whispered to Abby.

"Do you remember the last time you saw our mom?" Abby asked.

Antonio put his hand up to his forehead and rubbed it as if summoning a genie out of a bottle. "I think it was when Charlie was almost two. Carla came in one day, and I could tell something was off. I asked if she was okay, and she wouldn't give me a straight answer. That was the last time I saw her. At first, I thought she had gone on vacation, or one of you was sick. But after a few weeks, I called her, and her phone had been disconnected."

"That's weird," Morgan said.

"I know," Antonio said. "About six months later, I ran into one of our mutual friends who hadn't heard from her either. After a while, I figured if Carla wanted to talk to me, she knew where I was." Antonio had a far-off look. "I'm so sad to find out she died but meeting you all tells me that at least she did okay for herself."

"Can you tell us anything about her life when she lived here?" Charlie asked.

"It doesn't matter if it's good or bad," Abby added.

"I remember the first time your mom and I tried pot," he said, chuckling. "Oh, I shouldn't be telling you this story."

Morgan laughed. "We're all adults, we can handle it."

"We had no idea what we were doing," he said. "We got a joint from some kid in school and drove to the parking lot of an ice cream parlor. Every time we tried to light it, we'd get nervous, so nervous that the match would go out. Finally, we took a puff and coughed a lot. We both pretended to be high so we could stop. Then, just as we got in the car to leave, we realized the police station was across the parking lot on the street behind us. We convinced ourselves we were high, even though we'd only taken one puff, and we laughed the entire drive home."

"If you want to get high now, you could go smell Dylan's T-shirt," Abby said, and everyone laughed.

"Let me think, what else I can tell you," Antonio said, then after a minute, he went on. "Did you know your mom had impressive math skills? I only passed geometry because she let me copy her homework and helped me cheat on the tests."

"I wish she were here so we could hold that over her head," Morgan said. "She would've killed us if she found out we were cheating."

"What about boyfriends? Did she date a lot?" Charlie asked.

"Not much, and at first, I couldn't figure out why. A lot of guys liked her, but Carla had a wall up, probably because of her childhood."

"What do you mean?" Abby asked.

"Carla didn't talk about her parents much, but I got a little out of her, he said. "Her mother had a lot of rules about dating, so I was surprised when Carla married your father and shocked when I heard they ended it. She told me if she ever married, she'd never split up because of how her parents' divorce affected her."

Charlie enjoyed hearing stories about their mom, but Antonio didn't tell them anything that helped them understand her better. *I hope coming to Brooklyn wasn't a waste of time,* Charlie thought.

Antonio went on to tell them about how Carla enjoyed taking Morgan to a neighborhood park to play—the same park where, in high school, Carla, Antonio and their friends had gone to drink beer and feel like rebels.

"It used to be just a big expanse of grass and woods, but after we graduated, the town put in swings and a jungle gym, and it became the place where moms took their kids," Antonio said.

"What's the name of the park?" Morgan asked.

Antonio pulled a pen from his pocket and wrote down the name on the same paper he had given them with Carla's old address. Morgan took out cash to pay for the food, but Antonio wouldn't accept the money. He made them promise they would let him know if they found out why Carla left New York so suddenly.

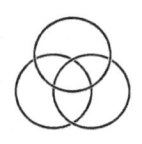

CHAPTER 23

Abby

As Abby, Morgan, and Charlie headed to their mother's childhood home, Abby concentrated on breathing in the fresh air and enjoying the tiny bit of sun peeking through the dark clouds.

Brooklyn had turned out to be much better than Abby expected. It had beautiful brownstones, cool boutiques, and hipster restaurants, although, she thought the best part was the art galleries. Abby felt a tinge of sadness as she remembered how she and her mom shared a love of art.

When Abby was thirteen, Carla took her and her sisters to the Getty Museum. Morgan and Charlie spent the afternoon complaining about how bored they were and how much their feet hurt, but Abby was entranced. After that, Carla created 'Art Day', where she and Abby spent special time together at least twice a year discovering new artists. Each gallery that Abby passed created a deep longing for her mother and a realization they'd never again go to the Getty together.

Abby loved those days with Carla, and no matter how many new artists she learned about, Picasso had been her favorite---especially his Cubism-style paintings. Abby could have stood for hours marveling at Picasso's ability to show multiple perspectives in one picture. As she grew older and wiser, she became an expert at interpreting his work as joyful and, at other times, tumultuous, kind of the way she viewed her own life.

Abby's relationship with Alex had been steady for more years than she could remember, but at times, she'd wondered if having no experiences with other men had stifled her. Picasso had so many lovers; did those relationships help make him the creative he became?

The sisters crossed the street and turned down the next block. Abby stopped suddenly in front of a stylish boutique, staring at a dress in the window. Morgan and Charlie stopped to see what had caught her eye.

"If it looks that good on the mannequin, it will look even better on me since I at least have a head," Abby exclaimed.

"First of all, that dress looks very expensive," Morgan said. "And second if Alex saw you in it nine months later, you'd be pushing out your fifth child."

"Good point. I'm hard to resist in sweatpants, can you imagine me in a black halter dress?" Abby said.

"At least your ego's intact," Charlie said.

Abby had been insecure about not keeping up with current events or reading books on the New York Times best-sellers list. But before kids, she was at least confident that her peachy complexion, glossy hair, and toned figure would garner male attention wherever she went. She would often use her looks to her advantage. At times, she felt almost guilty that she could get a man to stop on the freeway and change a tire for her or buy her drinks in a bar, even after she told him she wasn't interested. Once, in a raging rainstorm, a man had given her his umbrella when she stupidly left hers in the car.

The rewards of being a mother were great, but Abby had been inundated with the needs of her family for so long that she'd lost sight of who she was as a woman. She couldn't remember the last time she had done anything for herself. Flying off to Brooklyn with her sisters seemed decadent, even though the reason broke her heart.

Morgan looked at Google Maps and directed them to turn the corner, where they found themselves in front of a bakery. The aromatic scent of fresh java seeped from under the door. A line of people waited outside and down the street, and Abby couldn't understand why any customers would be willing to stand in the frigid weather. *I wonder if no one is speaking because their lips are frozen shut.*

"That bakery must be amazing," Abby said, then realized she was talking to herself as her sisters had continued down the street. She rushed to catch up with them. Did they notice she wasn't following behind them?

"Now I understand why so many Manhattanites have moved out to Brooklyn," Charlie said, looking around. "It has this cool vibe."

"Yep, unlike you," Morgan said.

"That's coming from the person who still thinks shoulder pads are hip," Charlie said.

"At least I'm not wearing a purple sweater with a pink panda on it," Morgan said, pointing to Abby's top.

"My kids gave me this," Abby said.

"And you wear it out of the house?" Morgan laughed. "You're a good mom."

Abby wasn't sure if Morgan was being sarcastic, but she decided to take it as a compliment.

A few minutes later, the women walked up to a charming two-story home the same color as a tin can. The house was guarded by a white wooden fence with a trellis on top and a gate in the middle. Morgan, Charlie, and Abby stopped outside the fence.

"This is Mom's old house?" Abby asked.

"Seems to be," Morgan said, checking the address against the numbers attached to the front of the exterior.

"Wow, this is where she grew up," Charlie said.

Abby blinked a few times, then examined the house. "If our grandparents still lived here, I wonder if they'd be happy to see us."

"I'd like to think so, but we know so little about them," Morgan said.

Abby knew next to nothing about the kind of childhood her grandparents provided for her mother, but she assumed it wasn't a good one. Otherwise, when the subject came up, Carla would have talked about her past and not remembered something she had "forgotten" to do in another room.

Abby nudged her sisters when she saw a woman staring down at them from the second floor. "Hello, can I help you?" the woman asked from the open window.

"We don't want to bother you; we used to know someone who lived here," Morgan said.

"Give me a minute," the woman said, then closed the window and disappeared.

"Do you think she's getting her guard dog?" Abby asked.

"Right, because we look like your average burglars," Charlie said.

The woman walked out the front door and up to the gate that separated them, but she didn't open it. The deep voice they had heard came out of a petite four-foot-eleven-inch woman. She had beautiful coal-black hair that cascaded to her shoulders and a full but perfectly proportioned figure. Her crimson dress was tailored to fit her every curve, and her style reflected her smile, which was warm and vibrant.

"I'm Maria," she said.

"Hi, I'm Morgan, and these are my sisters, Charlie and Abby."

"It's nice to meet you. You said you knew someone who used to live here?" Maria said.

"Our mother grew up in your house," Charlie said.

"It's not ours, my husband and I rent it. Does your mom still live in Brooklyn?" Maria asked.

"No," Charlie said. "She passed away."

"Oh, you poor girls," Maria said, even though she looked to be only in her mid-twenties. "Did you want to see inside?"

"If it wouldn't be too much trouble," Morgan said.

"Not at all. Give me a few minutes to straighten up." Maria turned and jogged as fast as those little legs would go back inside.

Not even five minutes later, Maria opened the front door and welcomed them in. Abby's nose did a happy dance when she took a whiff of the scent of peppers, onions, and garlic that wafted through the house.

"Whatever you're cooking smells amazing," Abby said, breathing in deeply to take in the flavorful aroma.

"*Pollo guisado*," Maria said.

Abby rubbed her chin and glanced at her sisters; they looked as puzzled as she was.

"It's a chicken stew," Maria said.

"I bet it tastes as good as it smells," Abby said.

"It's my husband's favorite," Maria said.

Maria walked them through the house with her head raised high and a big smile as if it were a ten-million-dollar estate. In the living room, there was a Puerto Rican flag on the wall, which contrasted with the furniture's rustic American farmhouse theme. There was a denim couch with a red, white, and blue quilt across it and a pine wood coffee table, like the one that Abby and Alex had in their house.

Maria then led them into the kitchen. The kitchen didn't look as if it had been updated. The cabinets were scratched and worn, indicating that many people had lived there. Could they be the same cabinets their mother opened to get cereal out? Carla told them her mother wouldn't allow her to eat cereal when she was a kid, but whenever Beverly was gone for work, Carla would buy five boxes of Frosted Flakes and eat them for breakfast, lunch, and dinner.

"You're welcome to look around," Maria said. "I need to add a few things to my stew." She pointed toward the stairs. "The bedrooms are on the second floor."

The sisters headed up the stairs alone and began exploring. They looked into the bedrooms and bathrooms.

"This feels weird," Morgan said. "We're not going to find anything in a house our mother moved out of many years ago."

"Maybe, maybe not. Look," Charlie exclaimed an octave higher than her normal voice. She pointed to the door frame at the stairs to the basement. It had pencil marks. They all stopped to take a closer look. The writing was almost illegible, but next to one pencil mark, it looked like a capital C, and on another, a capital R.

"The C has to be for Carla and the R for Roy!" Abby said.

"Wow, is that whose growth chart that is?" Maria asked as she came up behind them. "My husband and I wondered who C and R were. We had fun making up our own stories."

"Carla was our mom, and Roy was her brother," Morgan said.

"How wonderful that you found this," Maria said. "I doubt there's anything else in the house, but I can show you the backyard."

An old tool shed sat in the corner of the yard. The grass was an inch taller than it should have been and looked wild.

Maria's face took on a rosy glow, and she let out a tiny giggle and didn't make eye contact with them. "My husband promised to mow the lawn every afternoon for the last few weeks. I'm embarrassed that you have to see it looking like this."

"I live in the desert, so any grass is beautiful to me," Charlie said, pulling her coat around her tightly to ward off the chill.

Maria smiled and seemed to relax. "I wish there was more from your mother here, but it was empty when we moved in," she said.

"How long have you lived here?" Abby asked.

"About two years. The man we rent from bought it fifteen years ago from a charity. He said the woman who owned the home for over fifty years died, and since she had no heirs, she left it to some suicide prevention organization."

"That must've been our grandmother," Charlie said.

"Maria, you've been more than kind allowing us to come into your house," Morgan said.

"We appreciate it," Abby said.

"It was my pleasure. I wish I could've been more help."

The women said goodbye, and the sisters walked back down the path.

"Isn't it strange that our grandmother left her house to some charity to help prevent suicide years before her daughter took her own life?" Morgan said, holding the gate for Charlie and Abby to walk through.

"It's eerie," Charlie said. "And Mom was alive when her mother died, so why wouldn't our grandmother leave the house to her?"

"Maybe they had a fight," Abby said, then wondered what happened in that house that Carla wouldn't talk about and Beverly disowned her?

"Now what?" Charlie asked as they headed back down the street.

"That park Antonio told us about is local, which means it has to be near here," Morgan said. "Let's check it out."

Although it hadn't snowed much, not many people were out that day, which made sense because McGorlick Park was covered with a thin, treacherous layer of ice. Abby took each step carefully; the last thing she wanted was to fall and end up in a hospital in New York.

A woman being dragged by her Mastiff flew past them, yelling, "Barney, stop." The dog had found its soulmate in a French Bulldog wearing a green and white polka-dotted sweater. Barney was drawn to her like the magnetic balls in Newton's Cradle. It was love at first sniff.

The sisters walked farther into the park and found the kids' play area that Antonio had described. A lone boy swaddled in a puffy down jacket, scarf, mittens, and a beanie that almost covered his eyes slid down the slide. As Abby heard his joyful laughter, her chin dipped toward her chest, and her lips quivered. *I wonder what my four are doing right now. I hope they miss me as much as I miss them.*

The boy's au pair, wearing a trench coat and two braids in her hair, stood near him, talking animatedly on the phone in French. Abby's high school French had mostly vanished to the recesses of her brain, although she did recognize the words boss and cheating.

When Morgan stopped suddenly, Charlie almost crashed into her, and Abby almost crashed into Charlie. Morgan seemed captivated by the swings, even though they were the same as every other swing at any park in the United States.

"What's wrong?" Abby asked.

"Either I'm having déjà vu, or I've been here before," Morgan said.

"Are you sure? It's not like we haven't been to a million parks in our lives," Charlie said.

Morgan walked over to the swings, put her hand on the rope, and then pulled it off as if electricity had passed through her arm.

"Are you okay?" Abby asked.

"Our father and I came here," Morgan said as she began pushing the swing back and forth.

"Are you sure?" Charlie asked.

"Yes. He'd lift me onto these swings and sing 'You Are My Sunshine.' I remember him wearing a Yankees sweatshirt and a Mets baseball hat, although maybe that was in a dream." Morgan looked like she was having an out-of-body experience as she kept pushing on the swing. "I can still see his smile," she said.

"That doesn't add up with what we were told," Abby said. "Do you think Mom lied, and he wasn't the bad guy she said he was?"

"Why would she hurt us like that?" Charlie said.

"Is it possible your mind is playing tricks on you, Morgan? Abby asked.

Morgan shook her head back and forth. "No."

"I wish I had even one memory of him," Abby said. "You two are lucky."

How could my father not want to get to know me? Abby thought. Envy that her sisters had memories of him crept inside her and took up residence like a squatter in an abandoned house. *Why would he abandon me when I was just a baby? Had he ever thought about me after he left?*

"I really missed having a father," Charlie said.

"Me, too," Abby said. "My friends got to have their dad walk them down the aisle and do the traditional father/daughter dance. When I hired the DJ for my wedding, I told him to skip it. I remember his pitiful look when I told him why. It was embarrassing."

"You had nothing to be embarrassed about," Charlie said. "You didn't have anything to do with our father abandoning us."

"Didn't I? Mom said he left because he couldn't handle all of us," Abby said, her eyes misting up. "He stayed until right after I was born. What does that say about how much he loved me?"

"It says he was selfish. You were a cute baby; he would've been lucky to have you--- or any of us," Morgan said.

Abby wanted to respond, but the words got stuck deep inside her.

While Morgan continued to push the empty swing back and forth, the other three swings were now populated by happy kids. A girl with springy blond hair bounced on her toes as she and her mom approached Morgan.

"Excuse me, are you done pushing your friend?" the little girl asked, pointing to the empty swing.

Morgan smiled at her and her mom. "Yes, my friend is tired," Morgan said, moving away from the swing. The sisters walked over to a nearby bench and sat.

"Did Mom tell either of you where Dad was buried?" Abby asked.

"No," Morgan and Charlie said.

"Don't you think that's odd?" Abby asked, then pulled her phone out of her purse and googled obituaries for Brian Weiss in New York. A ton of results came up. Of the ones that had died, either they weren't from New York, or they weren't the right age.

"That's the problem with having a common Jewish last name," Morgan said.

"And we don't know where he moved to after he left us," Charlie said. "He could've gone anywhere in the world."

"I don't think we're going to find anything else here in Brooklyn," Morgan said.

"Since we don't leave until tomorrow night, can we spend some time in the city?" Abby asked.

"Sure," Morgan said. "Why don't we stop at the pizza place tonight and say goodbye to Antonio? He's been nice and helpful."

When the three of them got back to the hotel, Morgan and Charlie got on the elevator to return to their room, but Abby wanted some time alone. She waited for their elevator to leave, then pushed the button again to go up to the rooftop bar.

The space was upscale and sophisticated, with subdued lighting and floor-to-ceiling windows featuring sweeping views of Brooklyn and Manhattan. Abby sat at the bar, hoping the bartender would stop flirting with the gorgeous woman with full lips and hair pulled back to reveal high cheekbones.

A man in a leather jacket and distressed jeans sat down, leaving one empty seat between him and Abby.

The man looked around her age, with tawny hair shaped in an "Ivy League" haircut, with sides and back cut shorter than the top. The dimples in his cheeks remained visible even when he wasn't smiling. He had the kind of boyish face that Abby found adorable.

Abby managed to notice all these details without looking directly at him. *I don't want him to think I want to talk to him, even though I do.*

"Do you think the bartender knows we're here?" the man asked Abby.

"I doubt it. He still hasn't figured out that woman is out of his league," she said, turning to him. She noticed that his eyes were so blue they almost had a purplish tint, and his posture conveyed self-confidence but not cockiness.

"You got that right," the man said. He began to mimic what the bartender might be saying to the pretty woman. "You're the most beautiful thing I've ever seen. How could you possibly be here alone?"

Abby followed suit, pretending to be the woman. "Please, I am not that beautiful."

"Oh, but you are," the man added.

Abby let out a mock sigh, then as the woman, "You're right. Does that mean I get free drinks?"

They both watched as the woman got up and left, leaving the dejected-looking bartender—behind.

"He must've said no to the free drinks," Abby said.

The man laughed, then called out to the bartender. "Excuse me, you have customers over here."

"What can I get you?" the bartender asked, walking over to them.

"What would you like?" the man asked Abby. "It's on me."

"You don't have to do that," Abby said.

"It's a business expense," he said, putting the word 'business' in quotes. "The sky's the limit."

"Well, then I'll have a vodka tonic," Abby told the bartender.

"I'll have the same," the man said.

As the bartender walked away, the man slid over to the seat next to Abby and put his hand out.

"I'm Greg," he said.

Abby shook his hand. "Kelsey," she said, thinking, *I can be anyone I want to be.* She dropped her left hand into her lap, quickly slid off her wedding ring, and then slipped it into a pocket in her purse.

As they continued talking, Greg told Abby about his job as a Wall Street Trader in the city. They discussed their favorite movies and reality TV shows, a shared guilty pleasure. Abby led Greg to believe she was single and worked as a caregiver for the elderly. At least that last part was true, she reasoned—she did take care of her whole family as they aged.

When the bartender brought their second drink, Abby proposed a toast.

"To expense accounts," she said, and they clinked glasses. When her fingers inadvertently brushed Greg's hand, Abby felt anticipatory goose bumps rising on her arms.

Greg seemed to lean in a little closer and lightly touched her arm while she told a story about her 'caretaking.' and how one of her patients kept forgetting the days of the week. *So, I left out that this is my two-year-old. Greg doesn't need every detail.*

After an hour, a text popped up from Morgan asking if Abby was okay. Abby told Greg that her sisters were waiting for her and that she should go.

"I'm sorry you have to go, Kelsey; I've enjoyed talking to you," he said.

Abby picked up her purse and stood up. Greg stood up also.

"I have a business dinner to go to, but would you be up to meeting back here when I'm done?" he asked.

Abby felt herself flush. "Sure," she said before she had time to think about the fact that she had just accepted a date.

"Great. I'm looking forward to seeing you again." He asked for her phone number and said he'd text her when he finished his meeting.

Abby nodded. As she headed to the elevators, she felt lighter and bouncier. She turned to look at Greg to make sure she hadn't been dreaming. When the elevator closed, and she was alone inside, she caught her reflection in the doors. She noticed how peachy her skin looked, and her eyes sparkled as if her face enjoyed flirting with someone new as much as her mind did.

That was fun! I haven't felt like this since… Hmm, it's been so long I can't even remember. Her heart felt like it was beating to the rhythm of her favorite dance song. *He's so cute, and he gets me. What if he's the guy I was supposed to spend my life with, and I'm only meeting him now in a bar far from home?*

Abby ran her right hand along her naked ring finger on her left hand while continuing to fantasize about Greg, *I'm so glad Kelsey isn't married.*

In a daze, Abby exited the elevator and walked down the hall to her room. Before she went in, she put her wedding ring back on. Morgan and Charlie looked up as soon as Abby opened the door.

"You've been gone a long time. We were beginning to worry about you," Morgan said.

"I'm fine. I just had a drink at the bar…by myself." Abby didn't want to look at them, fearing that her expression would give something away.

Her phone began ringing. Even before seeing the caller ID, she knew it was Alex. They spoke every day while the kids were napping.

"I'll be right back," she said, going into the bathroom and closing the door.

"Hey," she said.

"Hey," Alex said. "I wanted to check on my gorgeous wife. I miss you."

Abby smiled. "I miss you, too."

"How is everything?"

"About the same, nothing new." *At least, nothing I want to tell you about*, she thought, then added, "I feel bad for saying this, but I can't come home yet. We need to look into a few more things when we get back to Los Angeles."

"Take all the time you need."

"Thank you!" *And I hope you don't mind if I start dating again.* Abby continued, "I appreciate it."

"I know you do. I don't mind holding down the fort for a while."

Emma began to cry, so they had to hang up. Abby looked at Greg's phone number in her contacts.

If Alex never knows, what harm would it do to see Greg tonight? I'll be back home in no time, and it'll all be forgotten. Abby took another shower and put on more makeup.

When the sisters entered the pizza parlor that evening, it was packed and lively. Families, groups of women drinking and chatting, and two men who looked madly in love enjoyed their dinner.

Dylan pointed out the only empty table. Unfortunately, it was close to the front door. The women sat down but kept their jackets on. The temperature outside had dropped to sixteen degrees. Whenever a customer opened the door, the frosty air hit Abby like she had gotten trapped inside the walk-in freezer at a meat processing plant.

Dylan had finally washed his hair and left the beanie at home. This time, instead of pot, he smelled of Calvin Klein Obsession. Abby recognized the scent, as she had bought it for Alex as an anniversary gift. The pimple on Dylan's nose was barely visible under the concealer he must have used to cover it up. Abby wondered if he had a date after work, too.

"Dylan, is Antonio here?" Morgan asked when he brought food to the table next to them. "We wanted to say goodbye before we went back home tomorrow."

"He'll be back soon. He had to run to the market because we ran out of milk. Lots of kids here tonight." Dylan went into the kitchen.

An older man leaning on a walker made his way slowly over to their table. The top of his head was completely bald, but little tufts of white hair surrounded the lower part of his scalp. He wore wireframe glasses and had on a sweater vest and khakis. He looked as if he belonged at a nursing home.

"Are you Carla's daughters?" the man asked.

Abby brightened. "Yes," Abby said. "How did you know?"

"Antonio described you all; I'm his father, Antonio Sr."

The women introduced themselves by name and shook his hand.

"This used to be my restaurant until I had my knee replaced, and I couldn't stand for long periods anymore," he said, then patted his knee as if to prove what he'd told them. "I do miss running this place, though."

"When did you open it?' Abby asked.

"Over forty years ago. My first restaurant was in New Jersey, but my wife and I moved to Brooklyn when Antonio was in elementary school."

Antonio Sr. pushed his walker against the wall a few feet away, then put his hands on their table to steady himself. Even though he was old, his muscles were taut against his shirt. He leaned in toward them.

"Did Carla really die?" he asked in almost a whisper.

What a strange question, Abby thought. Then a shiver ran through her. "Um, yes…" she said.

"You wouldn't lie about that, would you?" he asked.

"No…" Charlie said. "Why would we lie?"

"My son said your dad passed away, too. That's too bad," Antonio Sr. said. Abby noticed he didn't seem sorry.

"He died a long time ago," Morgan said.

Antonio Sr. got in Abby's face. "You must be her youngest. You look exactly like Carla." His voice had a deep, menacing quality.

"Uh huh," Abby said, her hands rubbing her legs and a sheen of sweat appearing on her forehead.

"Your mother's lucky she's not here," Antonio Sr. said so quietly that Abby wasn't sure she heard him right.

"What did you say?" Abby asked, trying to keep her voice from quivering. The man was old and had a bum knee, but Abby was still worried that he was going to grab one of them.

Antonio Jr. walked into the restaurant carrying two grocery bags. He saw the women and immediately walked over. Antonio Sr. stood up, reaching for his walker.

"You guys are back," Antonio Jr. said to the women, then looked at his father. "Dad, I didn't know you were coming tonight."

"I was just leaving; your mother needs me home. Goodbye, ladies, come back anytime," Antonio Sr. said in a voice suddenly as cheery as SpongeBob's. "It's been nice talking to you."

"Bye, Dad, see you tomorrow," Antonio Jr waved.

Abby looked at Morgan and Charlie, sure they were all thinking the same thing. It was clear that Antonio Jr. was utterly unaware of what had just happened.

"I'd love for you three to try a new pizza I'm thinking of putting on the menu," Antonio Jr. said.

"Thank you, but we were about to leave," Morgan said, and all three women stood up so quickly the table shook. "We just wanted to say goodbye to you before we fly home."

"Thank you for talking to us yesterday," Charlie said.

"It was great hearing what our mother was like when you knew her," Abby said.

"My pleasure. Our conversation brought back wonderful memories. If any of you are in Brooklyn again, please come by," Antonio Jr. said.

Abby nodded but knew none of them would ever step foot into that restaurant again.

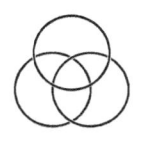

CHAPTER 24

Carla

The loss that Beverly felt when Roy died permeated the house so intensely that to Carla, it no longer felt like home. To make matters worse, Carla was sure that her mother blamed her for her brother's death. If only Carla could've talked Roy into staying home with her that night, her family would still be whole. At least that's what Carla's young brain told her.

Beverly was away a lot before Roy's death, but afterward, she became more of a visitor than a resident. Even when she was in town, Carla would have no idea where her mother was. Beverly left early in the morning before Carla woke up and came home after she was asleep. Carla stayed out of the house as much as possible, only coming home in time for dinner--a dinner she had to buy the groceries for and cook.

No one was around to ensure that Carla went to school or did her homework. Luckily, she was smart enough and cared enough not to let herself slip through the cracks. She had a great friend group of thoughtful, ambitious teens who got good grades but also liked to have fun. On weekends, they'd all meet at McGorlick Park, drink beer, and smoke pot, but when Monday rolled around, they were back on track.

Antonio was her closest friend through high school. They met freshman year when seated near each other in four of their seven classes. When they were assigned as lab partners in chemistry, they realized they had a lot in common. Since there didn't seem to be any romantic interest in each other, they didn't have to deal with any sexual tension. Occasionally, Carla would look at Antonio and wish she was attracted to him because he was a nice guy who treated her well, but sparks never ignited.

Antonio worked in his father's restaurant. Most days after school, Carla would meet him there, and they would do homework while eating free pizza.

Antonio's father knew Carla's situation, so he'd send her home with extra food, and occasionally, he'd tell her he found a ten-dollar bill on the ground and give it to her. There were whispers he was in the Mob, but Carla didn't believe it. Antonio Sr. seemed like a good husband and father who cared about his community. Carla thought it was a ridiculous stereotype that anyone with an Italian accent who had ever lived in New Jersey was a gangster.

However, one day, during Carla's senior year of high school, her image of Antonio Sr. shattered. She was supposed to meet Antonio Jr. at the restaurant, but his track practice ran late. When Carla got to the pizza place, the door was unlocked, and the lights were dim, but the place was quiet. Carla savored the scent of garlic and onions and figured the prep cook was in the kitchen preparing for the dinner rush.

She dropped her backpack on a chair at the table she and Antonio Jr. always took and headed to the restroom. She was startled by a loud *thu*mp as she ran her hands under the warm water and lathered them with soap. It sounded as if someone had dropped a heavy barbell on the floor. Her instincts told her to stay put, but curiosity got the best of her, and she pushed the bathroom door open a crack and peeked out. A man was on his back on the floor as Antonio Sr. stood over him, like an immense black cloud that took pleasure in repelling sunlight. The man covered his nose with his hand and turned his head, but Carla could see blood running down his chin.

"You get me my money by tomorrow, or you better move to another planet. And if you move to another planet, I'll still find you," Antonio Sr. said.

"Please, I just need a little more time."

"You know my policy; I don't give more time."

The man reached into his pocket and pulled out some cash. "Here, I have half of it," he said, dropping bills on the floor.

Antonio Sr. ignored the money, and his voice got as loud as a bullhorn. "I am not in the business of covering your bets," he said, then kicked the man in the ribs.

The man screamed, and Carla jumped back as if she'd been the one hit.

"Either you bring me my money tomorrow, or I'll be visiting that wife of yours to plan your funeral," Antonio Sr. said. "Now, get up and get out of here!"

The man hobbled out of the restaurant, one hand on his nose, the other on his ribs. Antonio Sr. marched back into the kitchen with a satisfied smile.

When Carla was sure he was gone, she quietly crept out of the bathroom and headed to her table. She picked up her backpack, and while debating how to get out of there without

Antonio Sr. seeing her, she heard a rattle as the front door opened. Carla spun around so quickly that she got dizzy.

"Hey," Antonio Jr. said.

"Hi," she said, her voice vibrating in her throat.

"You okay?" he asked.

"Uh, yeah," Carla wasn't about to tell him what she had witnessed. Antonio idolized his father. He talked about his parents reverently, as if they were one step away from godly.

"You don't look good," he said, taking her in.

"I'm just hungry; I skipped lunch."

"Sit."

She sat down, and he gave her some water. Then he went into the kitchen to get garlic rolls. Antonio Sr. came out of the kitchen with his son.

"Hi, Carla," Antonio Sr. said as if he hadn't just pummeled a man. "Nice to see you."

Carla tried to smile, but her face wasn't cooperating. She hoped he couldn't tell anything was wrong.

That was the last time Carla went inside the restaurant without Antonio Jr. being there. She never told him about what happened that day. She figured either he already knew who his father was, or he didn't, and if he didn't, he might not have believed her anyway.

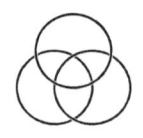

CHAPTER 25

Morgan

The Weiss sisters' flight back to Los Angeles had been delayed in New York. They couldn't get on the plane until the airline could locate a new flight crew. After three hours, they were finally allowed to board.

"They're lying to us," Abby said. "Something's wrong with this plane," Morgan had to practically carry her down the aisle to their seats. Charlie stayed far behind, acting as if she didn't know them.

"My kids are going to be left without a mother," Abby said. Morgan tried to calm her down, as the other passengers stared at Abby as if she knew something they didn't.

When they finally got back to Carla's house late that night, and Abby and Charlie had gone to bed, Morgan looked at the couch. She bit down hard on her lip, knowing there was only one way she would get a good night's sleep.

The following day, she woke up in Carla's bed with her arms wrapped around Albert. Her stomach clenched as she looked around the room, knowing her mother would never sleep in that bed again. She pushed that thought out of her mind and pulled a happy memory into its place.

Growing up, the three girls would get into bed with Carla while she read them stories from Winnie-the-Pooh. As Morgan got older, she couldn't admit she'd aged out of having her mom read to her. She didn't want to give up listening to Carla's rendition of Eeyore. Even at thirty-four, Morgan could still imagine Carla pursing her lips together, producing a nasally tenor to her voice and sounding exactly like the cartoon character.

Morgan fluffed the pillows behind her back and sat up straighter, waking Albert. He licked her face repeatedly; he missed Carla as much as she did.

Morgan listened for any sounds coming from the kitchen. She didn't smell fresh coffee, bacon, or burned bread. Although Abby kept telling her it was terrible for her, Charlie liked her toast charred.

"I guess we're the only ones awake, Albert."

Albert crawled beside her, put his head on her pillow, and fell fast asleep.

"Fine, *I'm* the only one awake," Morgan said, nuzzling Albert, who blasted her with a wet dream snort. She wiped her cheek with the edge of the sheet and laid back down.

The moment she closed her eyes again, the thoughts plaguing her for days returned with a vengeance, like a game of Tetris where none of the shapes fit in their correct spots. Going to Las Vegas hadn't given them answers, and they had found very little in Brooklyn. Morgan didn't want to give up, although all the signs pointed to them never knowing why her mother did what she did.

Since Morgan couldn't drink alcohol, she needed a different kind of distraction. She padded off to the kitchen to make oatmeal with blueberries. As the water began to boil, another thought pushed to the surface. *What could Mom have done to Antonio Sr. for him to hate her?*

Morgan turned the burner off and headed into her mother's office. She tried three more times to figure out the computer password. When those didn't work, she slammed her hands on the desk. *Look what you're doing to me, Mom!* She yanked one of the desk drawers out in frustration and dropped it onto the floor with a bang. Charlie and Abby ran into the room.

"What's going on in here?" Charlie said. "It sounded like you lost it." There were pens, paper clips, rubber bands, and Post-its littering the floor. "And…I was right."

Morgan pulled another drawer out and dropped it on the ground alongside its sibling. Printer cartridges, return address labels, and thumbtacks were scattered on the ground with the other office supplies.

"This isn't going to help anything," Abby said.

"I can't take it anymore," Morgan cried. "We're fighting a losing battle."

"Then let's fight it together," Charlie said, copying Morgan by yanking out another desk drawer and sending it flying.

"Not you, too," Abby said to Charlie. She got under the desk to clean up the mess. "Hey, look!" Abby yanked off a few papers that were taped to the wood under the desk.

"What is that?" Charlie asked.

As Abby stood up, Morgan took the papers out of Abby's hands and looked at them. "They're our birth certificates," Morgan said.

"They can't be. Mine's in my safety deposit box back home," Charlie said.

Morgan handed Charlie and Abby theirs. The women stood so close together that their arms were almost intertwined, like strands of a braided challah.

"Why would Mom hide copies of our birth certificates under her desk?" Abby asked.

Charlie stared at the one she was holding. "These aren't right; they must be fake."

"They don't look fake," Abby said. "They have that raised stamp from the hospital."

Morgan's body went limp. "Why would Mom hide these if they weren't our real ones."

"So, you think the ones we have at home are phony?" Charlie asked.

"None of this makes sense," Abby said. "Were we even born?"

"You're right. We don't exist," Morgan said to Abby, then interlaced her fingers to stop herself from cracking her knuckles. "I need to sit down," she said. She worried her legs might crumple beneath her.

Morgan made her way down to the floor, and Charlie and Abby sat next to her. Each had a far-off, cloudy gaze. Morgan tapped her fist against her lips as if she wanted something to come out of her mouth that would be a reasonable explanation.

Abby pointed to the document she was holding. "This says I was born in January, not March, and my last name isn't Weiss; it's Brenner."

"All of these say our last name is Brenner," Morgan said.

"If those are our real birth certificates, then who are we?" Charlie said.

"Where does yours say you were born?" Abby asked Charlie.

Charlie looked at both her and Morgan's papers. "Morgan and I were born at Maimonides Medical Center in Brooklyn," Charlie said.

"Mine says I was born at Providence St. Joseph's Medical Center in Burbank, California. I thought Mom left our father *after* I was born," Abby said.

"Mom told us a lot of things that are not true. She had to have moved to Los Angeles when she was still pregnant with you," Morgan said to Abby.

"So, if these *are* real, our dad's last name is Brenner, not Weiss," Charlie said.

"Yes, Brian Brenner," Morgan said.

"That's why we couldn't find his obituary on the internet," Abby said. "We had the wrong name."

Morgan jumped up and sat down at Carla's computer. Charlie and Abby got up and stood on each side of Morgan. Morgan typed in the password Brenner4, and the computer brought up Carla's app screen.

"You're in," Abby said.

"How did you figure out the password?" Charlie asked.

"It hit me when I saw our real last names. I just added Mom's favorite number," Morgan said.

Abby nodded vigorously. "Mom used to say we were the four musketeers."

Morgan signed into her mother's email as Abby and Charlie hovered nearby like children waiting for their parents to open the Fruit Loops-decorated frame they'd made at school. Morgan clicked on every email, going back as far as she could.

"There's nothing here," Morgan said.

"We've hit another dead end," Charlie said.

"Maybe not," Abby said. "I have an idea."

Morgan got out of the chair so Abby could sit. Abby searched obituaries for Brian Brenner in the tri-state area. There were two, and both men had died in the last four years and were over the age of seventy when they passed away. "There's no obituary," Abby said.

"What if he's not dead?" Charlie asked.

Abby picked up a pencil and started tapping it on the desktop. "What if Mom knew he was alive and kept it from us."

Morgan couldn't concentrate because of the rhythmic noise Abby was making. She reached over, took the pencil from Abby's hand, and dropped it on the floor with the other office supplies.

"Mom wouldn't do that. She knew how hard it was for us growing up without him," Morgan said.

"Mom also told us our last name was Weiss," Abby said.

Abby typed in Brian Brenner in New York; nothing came up. Then, she tried the name in all the states bordering New York. There were several Brian Brenners in New Jersey, Connecticut, Massachusetts, and one in Rhode Island.

"We can call these men and see if they are our father," Abby said.

"But what if we find him, and he hangs up on us? Mom said he didn't want to be a father," Charlie said.

"If we don't call, we'll never know the truth," Abby said.

"And we won't be able to move on," Morgan asked.

They looked at each other. There was nothing else to say.

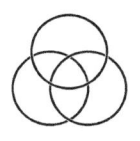

CHAPTER 26

Charlie

Whenever Charlie had a problem, her favorite place to think—or not think—was the bathtub. If she couldn't figure something out, she'd turn on the water and throw in a few capfuls of bubble bath. This morning was no exception. After a half hour of soaking, when the water had gotten cold enough to be uncomfortable, Charlie got out, wrapping a towel around herself. At least the muscles in her back felt a little less tight, although she still hadn't decided if it was a good idea to call those men.

Could their father have been alive all this time? And if so, no matter how her mother felt about him, they should've been allowed to decide if they wanted to get to know him. *Mom, you've shattered our lives in countless ways. How can I grieve you when all I feel right now is anger?*

After Charlie had gotten dressed and put on her Fitbit watch, she wandered through the house. If she wasn't going to get answers, she might as well get her steps in. She found Abby watching a cooking show in the living room. Charlie marched in place while she scrutinized contestants vying for $100,000 as they sabotaged their competitors' soufflés by making as much noise as possible.

"It's addictive, isn't it?" Abby said.

"Unfortunately," Charlie said. "Where's Morgan?"

"In Mom's office. I have no idea what she's doing, but she said not to interrupt her."

Charlie barged into Carla's office. Every book from the bookcase had been stacked on the floor like a tower of Lincoln Logs. The closet door stood open. A broom, wrapping paper, an extra-long extension cord, a mouse trap, and a vacuum were strewn across the floor. Morgan sat in the middle of the mess with her head in her hands.

"Didn't Abby tell you I didn't want to be interrupted," she said, her voice muffled by her fingers.

"Yep, but I never listen to her. It looks like you're planning to strangle a mouse, then gift wrap it after you clean up the mess."

Morgan raised her head. "Either help or get out."

"I'd help if I knew what you were looking for."

Abby marched in. "If Charlie's coming in, so am I," she said.

"I see you've both learned boundaries," Morgan said.

"Our boundaries are lost amongst all this junk," Abby said.

Morgan stood up, kicked some junk out of her way, and headed out the door. Charlie gestured with her head to Abby to follow her.

"Morgan, you can't leave all this stuff here," Charlie called after her.

"Mom left us with a mess. Why can't I leave her with one," Morgan said over her shoulder.

"You know she's dead, right?" Charlie said as they all arrived in the kitchen.

"She'd better be," Abby said. "If she's not, she's going to get mad that you left her office like that."

Morgan began to chuckle, and then Charlie and Abby followed suit. The chuckling turned into guffaws, which turned into hysterics, and then uncontrollable tears of laughter ran down their cheeks.

"We've gone over the edge, haven't we?" Morgan said.

"Yes, we're in this together," Charlie said.

"You know, I wouldn't have made it through the last few weeks without you both," Abby said.

"Me either," Charlie said, and Morgan agreed.

"I'm starving," Morgan said. "We can clean that mess up later."

"You mean *you* can clean it up later," Charlie said.

"I thought we were in this together," Morgan said.

"Hey, we're not attached at the hip," Charlie said.

"I'll make some waffles," Abby said, heading to the kitchen.

"I have to call Rick; he's been texting me since last night," Charlie said.

"We'll call you when breakfast is ready," Abby said, getting eggs, milk, and the batter out of the refrigerator. "Wait, where's the waffle iron?"

"I'll get it," Morgan said, reaching into a cabinet above the refrigerator.

Charlie picked up her phone and went into her bedroom.

"Hi," Rick said. "Why haven't you texted me back?"

"I was asleep," Charlie got on her bed and leaned against the headboard.

"I want to talk to you about something," he said.

"Okay…"

Charlie could hear him take a breath. "While you've been gone, it's given me a lot of time to think about our relationship," he said. "Things haven't been as good as they used to be."

Charlie got up and began pacing around the room. She wondered if he was about to break up with her. "Do you agree?" Rick asked.

She started to cough as though a bug had blown into her throat. "Uh, uh…I guess so," she finally got a few words out.

"Good, then we're on the same page," Rick said.

Charlie felt dampness spreading across the back of her neck, and she put her hand up to her heart, which felt like it was skipping beats. *If anyone's going to break up, it should be me,* she thought. *I need to beat him to the punch.*

"I've been trying to understand where things went wrong," Rick said. "All I can figure out is the excitement is gone."

Speak, Charlie, damn it! Break up with him before he does it. Get the upper hand.

"So, I've decided we need to get married," Rick said as if he was ordering a plain turkey sandwich from a deli counter.

Charlie stopped pacing. *What?* she screamed, then realized she had only said it in her head.

"I know you're surprised, but I think it's the only thing that'll save our relationship," he said. "We can find a ring at some point, and we don't even have to set a date. We can just be engaged to be engaged. Okay, I've got to run to a meeting. I'll talk to you later." He hung up.

What have I done? Charlie kicked the bedpost, then ground her teeth so hard her jaw hurt.

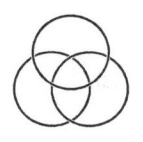

CHAPTER 27

Abby

The night Abby met Greg again, he smelled musky and floral at the same time. They sat at a table in the back of the bar, had another drink, and continued their conversation where they had left off earlier.

Abby could tell he wanted to kiss her; he'd lean in so close that his lips almost brushed her cheek. She had never kissed anyone other than Alex, so when she thought about kissing Greg, she felt a surge of adrenaline rushing through her, causing her heart to beat as though it was trying to escape her chest and run to him. At the same time, the rest of her body tightened up as if she were a frozen waterfall. The water wanted to move; it just couldn't. To be safe, she told him she was getting over a cold. She didn't want him to think she wasn't interested, but she knew there would be no turning back if she started kissing him.

Since Abby had returned to Los Angeles, she had decided to only allow herself to think about Greg right after waking up or right before she fell asleep—as well as when he texted or they talked--so, in essence, most of the time. She had been sleeping with her phone under her pillow so she wouldn't miss any time he contacted her.

Even though they had met a couple of days before and lived in different states, he'd been pursuing her in the exact way she'd want if she were single. Every time her phone vibrated, her heart fluttered like a string caught in a fan. And when he called, just hearing him say hello in that smooth, sexy voice made her brain become simultaneously focused and cloudy. She was living in a romantic fantasy that she couldn't bear to put an end to. Greg was the exciting secret she kept all to herself---or that is, Kelsey kept to herself.

For the fourth time since she woke up that morning, Abby read the last text Greg had sent.

I miss you, he wrote, *which says a lot since I barely know you.*

Abby was grinning when she joined her sisters on the back porch. Charlie was drinking coffee, and Morgan nursed a cup of tea.

The air was crisper and cooler than usual for Los Angeles, and the dew glistened on the grass. Although Charlie had a blanket across her knees, and Morgan had a scarf around her neck, Abby was perfectly comfortable in just her long PJ shirt.

"How are the kids?" Morgan asked.

Abby figured Morgan noticed her goofy smile while holding her phone and assumed Alex had relayed some funny tidbits about the kids.

"They're fine, surviving without me," Abby said. She wanted to change the subject before her sisters saw her fair complexion turn crimson. They knew her well and would wonder what was causing her to blush.

"So, what's the plan for today?" Abby asked to distract them.

Morgan blew on her tea, the steam mixing with the cool morning fog. "I guess we should try to call all the Brian Brenners you found."

"There are twelve, so we can each take four," Abby said.

Abby divvied up the list, and Charlie went into her bedroom to call the men she was given. Morgan walked into Carla's office to make her phone calls. Abby stayed in the living room.

After fifteen minutes, Morgan and Charlie returned to the living room, where Abby had just ended one of her calls.

"None of the Brian Brenners I called were *our* Brian Brenner," Charlie said.

"Same here," Morgan said.

"I still have one more call to make," Abby said. "But on the positive side, one of the Brian Branners was fifteen, and he thought I sounded cute."

"Is that who you've been talking to all this time?" Morgan asked.

"He was such a nerd, I didn't have the heart to hang up on him," Abby said.

"Was that heart or ego?" Charlie asked.

Abby called the final phone number on her list for the Brian Brenner in Connecticut. She put the call on speaker so her sisters could listen.

"Hello," a man said.

"Is this Brian Brenner?" Abby asked.

"Yes."

"This might sound crazy, but I'm looking for a Brian Brenner who could possibly be my father." Abby anticipated the answer would be no, so she had her finger ready to hang up.

"Who is this?" Brian Brenner asked.

"Abby Weiss."

"How old are you?" he asked.

"Thirty." A long silence followed, so Abby continued, "I'm sure you aren't used to somebody calling you out of the blue and asking you if you're her father."

"It's not that. I don't have a thirty-year-old daughter."

"Okay, then thank you," Abby said, disappointed.

She was about to hang up when Brian added, "But I did have two daughters I haven't seen since they were small."

"What were their names?" Abby asked.

"Morgan and Charlotte." The man sounded choked up.

Morgan and Charlie were stunned.

"Morgan and Charlie are my sisters," Abby said. "They're here too."

"Hello, this is Morgan," she said quietly.

"How old are you?" he asked.

"If you're my father, then you tell me," Morgan said.

"My Morgan would be thirty-four. And Charlotte would be thirty-two," he said, his voice cracking.

Abby put the phone down on the coffee table. Morgan's hands shook as she moved closer to the speaker.

"Where were we born?" Morgan asked.

"Maimonides Hospital in Brooklyn, New York."

"Yes!" Charlie yelled as if she'd been picked as a contestant on a game show.

"Is that Charlotte?" Brian asked.

"I go by Charlie now."

"I can't believe this," Brian said, sounding both elated and shocked. "I've been looking for you two since Carla disappeared."

Abby moved toward the phone. "What about me?" Abby asked.

"I'm sorry, Carla wasn't pregnant when she left me. Are you sure you're mine?"

Abby didn't say anything. She walked away and let Morgan and Charlie continue to talk to him. Morgan told Brian that Carla had passed away, and he said he was sorry to hear that.

"How did she die?"

"She committed suicide," Morgan said.

"I can't believe Carla would do something like that. She was destroyed when her brother killed himself," Brian said.

Morgan couldn't stop blinking. "We had no idea," Morgan said. "We knew her brother had died when she was young, but she never told us how."

"I wonder if that's why she thought it was a valid way out," Charlie said.

"Well, it wasn't. It only left us with unanswered questions," Morgan said.

As Morgan and Charlie continued their conversation with Brian, Abby stared out the window at the house across the street. The fire had eaten the exterior, and most of the front windows were broken or warped from the heat. The archway at the front door had collapsed, and soot and grime were on the walkway and the grass.

I feel like that house, Abby thought. *Abandoned, forgotten, no one wants me.* Abby shuddered; her insides felt singed and burned. *Oh, Mom, I could really use you right now.* Abby stayed at the window and silently cried for all the things she might never have.

CHAPTER 28

Carla

Brian had been obsessed with money. His excuse for gambling was that he wanted the best for his family, but he was an addict. Before Carla decided to leave, she tried to get him to admit the harm he was bringing to all of them. He kept assuring her that the people he owed money to wouldn't come after her—only him.

But one day, three men showed up at Morgan and Charlie's Gymboree class to threaten her.

"Carla, you're making too much of this," Brian said later that night when the girls were asleep. "I told you those men aren't going to hurt you or the girls. They're just trying to intimidate you."

"Well, it's working. You're supposed to protect us, not put us in the middle of your mess."

"It's all going to be fine. I have a bet on a game this weekend, and I'm going to win big. I'll get the money I owe them, and things will go back to normal."

"And what if you lose?" Carla asked.

"I won't. It's a sure thing."

Carla didn't want to argue, so she nodded and walked away. Then those same men showed up at the park the following week.

"Your deadbeat husband now owes us thirty thousand dollars, and if he doesn't pay, one of your girls could "accidentally" go missing," a man with broad shoulders and arms bigger than Carla's thighs said.

"You know, accidents can happen," the other man said.

Carla was shaking so much she didn't know if she could drive them home.

"I have to get out of here, I have to get out of here," Carla repeated as she paced in the family room. Morgan, a little over four years old, and Charlie, two and a half, were clapping their hands with glee over the contraption they'd built with their Legos. The front of it resembled a dune buggy crossed with a front-end loader. The back was part castle and part sphinx. On the top of their creation was an umbrella, a beach chair, and a knight standing guard.

The girls' innocent joy made Carla happy—they were her only priority, and she knew she was doing the right thing. Suddenly, nausea overtook her, and she ran to the bathroom. After Carla had emptied everything in her stomach, she steadied herself by holding onto the bathroom wall. As she returned to the girls, she unconsciously rested her hands on her stomach. She had to leave New York soon; it wouldn't be much longer before her belly would no longer be flat, and Brian would realize she was pregnant again.

She put the girls in front of a *Lion King* DVD and wrote down a list of everything she needed to do. She'd been saving money from the groceries, twenty dollars here, forty dollars there. She also emptied her secret bank account. She knew even before the last week that Brian was in trouble, but she didn't realize how much. When he told her about his upcoming business trip to Philadelphia, she dropped the girls off with a sitter and went to the airport to buy them plane tickets to Los Angeles. She needed to pay cash, or he'd be able to find out where she'd taken his daughters.

Carla didn't want to leave anything open-ended, so she hired a lawyer to serve Brian with divorce papers as soon as he came home from Philadelphia. By that time, she and the girls would be across the country.

Carla would miss all her friends, especially Antonio. They had a strong bond; he had been the one person she went to when she had a problem, but not this time. As much as she trusted him, she didn't want to put him in a position to lie if Brian contacted him looking for them.

The day Brian left for his trip, Carla woke up before their alarm and watched him sleep. As he snored ever so softly, she thought, *why couldn't you have died?* As soon as that thought came into her head, she turned away. *How can I say that about the only man I'd ever loved—and still love.* It would have been easier if he disappeared because deciding to leave her home and life in New York had almost broken her.

The alarm went off, and Carla, her eyes wide, sat up quickly.

"What's wrong?" Brian asked, suddenly awake, staring at her.

She imagined she had a sign across her forehead that read, 'Ask me why I'm guilt-ridden.'

"Nothing," she said. "I just realized that before you go today, I need a little extra money. Morgan and Charlie have birthdays coming up, and I want to start buying them gifts and planning their parties."

"Of course, anything for my girls," Brian said.

She knew he meant it, but his actions didn't support it. Carla turned away as he grabbed his wallet and handed her most of his cash. "I'll go to the bank before I get on the train today," he said.

When Brian picked up his overnight bag to leave, Carla grabbed him and hugged him tightly, then gazed into his eyes and kissed him.

"I'm not joining a cult; I'll only be gone for a few days." Brian laughed, then suddenly stopped when he saw Carla's expression. "Are you okay?" he asked.

"I'll just miss you," she said, her voice tearful.

"Now, I can't wait to come home," he said, grabbing her. "I'll see you all in a few days."

"Daddy..." Morgan and Charlotte yelled as they ran into the room and enthusiastically jumped into his arms; Carla couldn't bear to watch.

"Goodbye, my sweet girls. I'll see you soon," he kissed each of them on the forehead.

As Carla stood in the driveway watching Brian's car disappear down the street, for a split second, she considered trashing her plans. Then she told herself she was doing the right thing. Brian had lied to her, lost most of their money, and put his children's lives in danger. The only way for Carla to take the kids away from their father was to convince herself that he was so self-destructive and selfish that he'd eventually forget about them and move on with his life.

Carla walked through each room of the house, a house she treasured. As soon as she saw the MLS listing, she knew it would be the perfect place to raise their kids. She spent days picking out the paint colors and even longer choosing the furniture. Tears streamed down her face as she realized she was sadder about leaving her home than she was about leaving her husband.

She needed to stay busy; otherwise, she might've reverted to an old habit that started in middle school. When Carla felt anxious over an upcoming test, she'd pull hairs from her eyebrows. Starting a new life with no eyebrows would not make the best impression.

Carla got out three suitcases and packed them full of the girl's clothes and her own. She selected very few sweaters because they wouldn't need them in Los Angeles.

After Carla had packed as much as would fit in the suitcases, she took the girls to her mom's house. Beverly had breast cancer, and her prognosis wasn't good, so Carla knew that she'd never see her mother alive again. Although they had never been close, Carla still wanted to say goodbye, even if Beverly didn't know that's what was happening.

"Grammy," the girls yelled as they ran toward Beverly who sat in a recliner chair watching a soap opera on TV. The sound was loud and intrusive, causing everyone to shout.

"Remember, girls, it's not Grammy, it's Glammy," Beverly said, reaching for her oxygen tank and attaching the tube under her nose. Any word that sounded like Grandma was a curse word to her.

She wore a scarf around her head and a housecoat that seemed to be two sizes too big. Beverly held her arms stiffly at her sides, and then, as the girls got close to her, she turned away as if they had a swarm of killer bees attached to their shirts. Carla was amazed that the girls greeted Beverly with such affection even though it wasn't returned.

"Cookies, Glammy?" Morgan asked.

"There's some on the counter in the kitchen, but don't eat them all." Morgan and Charlie ran to the kitchen. Beverly turned to Carla. "Those girls are going to get fat if all they care about is sweets."

Carla had learned to ignore her mother's snide comments. "How're you feeling, Mom?" Carla asked, sitting down on the couch next to her.

"I have cancer. What do you think?" Beverly said. "You don't bring those girls to see me much."

"You're dealing with a lot; I wouldn't want to overwhelm you."

"Good point. Besides, I'm no fun anymore," Beverly said.

Were you ever? Carla thought.

Carla listened to Beverly describe every detail of her treatment. Morgan and Charlie returned, each chomping on one cookie and holding another one.

"Girls, we're going to get lunch soon," Carla said.

"We'll be hungry," Morgan said.

"We love to eat," Charlie said.

Beverly raised her eyebrows at Carla, who pretended not to notice.

"Mom, we don't have a lot of time today. We're going to have to get going," Carla said.

"I get it; no one likes to be around someone in pain."

Morgan and Charlie ran to the front door, waving as they left. Carla hugged her mother goodbye, which felt as warm as holding a concrete slab.

Next, Carla took the girls to the pizza parlor to see Antonio. He had always been able to read her even better than Brian could, so she needed to make sure he couldn't see how painful this goodbye would be for her.

During the past couple of years, she'd confided in Antonio that Brian had some issues, and at times, she feared for her family's safety. Antonio stewed in anger over what she had told him. He respected her enough not to get involved when she asked him not to. The only time she'd introduced him to Brian, she had sensed that Antonio wanted to hit him, so she had suggested they take their pizza to go.

Today, she did her best to smile and be her happier self. She thought she had been doing a good job until Antonio asked her if she was okay. She said she was fine, just fighting a cold. That was the first lie she'd ever told him.

While Carla and Antonio visited, the girls stuffed themselves with garlic rolls and pizza. Carla held back her tears when she said goodbye to him until she got in the car. The moment she sat behind the wheel, the immenseness of everything flooded her like a dam breaking.

"What's wrong, Mommy? You're crying," Morgan said.

"Did you get a boo-boo?" Charlie asked.

"Yes," Carla said. "My heart is hurting right now."

"Then you should put a Band-Aid on it," Morgan said.

"That's a great idea," Carla said through her tears.

The following morning, after Carla had placed all their suitcases in her trunk, she woke the girls and announced they were going on an adventure.

"What about school?" Morgan asked.

"It's a holiday," Carla said. "It's 'Mommy takes her kids on their first airplane' day."

"Yay," Charlie said.

Charlie and Morgan leaped out of bed. Carla handed Morgan clothes to put on, then helped Charlie get dressed. After breakfast, she drove them to the airport, leaving her car in a corner of the long-term parking lot. She hoped it would be a while before anyone found it. The girls had never been on a plane, so the thrill of flying kept them from asking why their father wasn't with them.

After the six-hour flight and a lot of adrenaline, both girls were exhausted. Carla gave the taxi driver the address of an apartment building in the San Fernando Valley that she had researched to ensure it was in a safe neighborhood.

Carla felt the tension in her spine lessen when they pulled up to a newer building on a quiet block. The building was a charming brick structure, four stories tall, with a row of purple and pink Lantana flowers surrounding a large Crepe Myrtle tree in the middle of a verdant green lawn.

The best part was the tenants were mainly elderly and were excited to see young kids moving in. The first person they met was Julia, a widow who lived in the apartment next door. Julia had an abundance of white hair that she wore in a bun, and when she let it down, it cascaded down to her waist. She seemed ten years younger than her age of eighty-one.

The first time Julia met Carla and the girls, her eyes sparkled with a warmth that almost made Carla fall apart. Carla felt that Julia was sent from above to be the mother she never had. And when she offered to babysit the girls, Carla was sure of it. Julia missed her grandchildren, who had recently moved with their parents to a foreign country while their father had been deployed.

One of the first things Carla did after she got settled in was change her last name from Brenner to her mother's maiden name, Weiss. Then she discovered someone who forged birth certificates and she changed the girls' last names, too. Carla was intent on making sure that no one would ever find them.

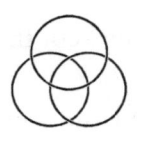

CHAPTER 29

Morgan

Morgan hated taking anything to sleep, but after hearing her father's voice, she knew she would be up all night.

When she woke up the next morning, she gasped, realizing she had slept for ten hours. She got out of bed slowly, her head fuzzy and her eyes taking a moment to focus. The only thing that would completely wake her up was strong coffee.

She left the house without telling Charlie or Abby where she was going. She wanted to surprise them with their favorite vanilla lattes.

Morgan didn't turn on the radio. She soaked in the silence until thoughts of her father barged in like an uninvited houseguest. *Brian seems nice, but for all I know, he could be a serial killer. Mom could have run away so she wouldn't have to turn him in.*

As Morgan's tears drenched the steering wheel, she fell deeper down a well of despair. She pulled over to the side of the road. "Did he hit you? Did he hit us? What didn't you tell us and why?" she said, towards the car's roof.

When Morgan had composed herself, she noticed she was in a dingy part of town, in front of a run-down building with a sign that said, 'Way Pen.' She knew it meant 'Always Open,' even though the neon letters for A, L, S, and O were out. Morgan could spot a dive bar from a mile away. The building's exterior was black or a very dirty shade of brown. Whatever the color, it seemed bleak, which matched Morgan's mood.

As she pulled into the parking lot, she considered what going into a dive bar would mean: that she had sunk to a low she'd never thought she would return to.

A trail of tents lined the sidewalk, and men with scraggly facial hair huddled together. Morgan should have been nervous, but instead, a wave of nostalgia washed over her. A familiar calmness overtook her, and she heard a warm voice beckoning her inside.

If finding out my mother lied to me about my father isn't a good reason to have a drink, I don't know what is. She looked up at the sky. "I promise to stop at one," she said, but another voice told her she might be lying.

Morgan heard a creak when she shoved open the door to the bar. Before she walked in, she rubbed her palms together to get rid of the lead paint that came off in her hand. When she was a full-blown alcoholic, Morgan would find little neighborhood dives like this one that would open early in the morning. She hadn't wanted to run into anyone she knew, and if she did, she'd pretend she didn't see them, and they'd do the same in return.

I shouldn't be here, she thought, yet still moved forward. It was so dark inside that she couldn't make out if people were there. She wanted to wait for her eyes to adjust, but needing a drink outweighed her temporary blindness. As she moved across the sticky tile floor, she put her hands out like Frankenstein, hoping she wouldn't crash into anything. Morgan rested her elbows on the wood and waited for the bartender to notice her. She didn't call him over even though she was desperate for alcohol.

When the bartender finally headed toward her, she decided he had been a pirate in a former life or possibly still was one. He had a bandana wrapped over his shoulder-length shaggy hair and wore one silver medium-sized hoop earring in his left ear. She expected him to greet her with, 'Argh matey,' except he wasn't that friendly.

"What do you want?" the bartender asked, wiping a small wet spot on the wood in front of her.

"Bourbon on the rocks," Morgan said.

As the bartender reached for a bottle on the shelf behind him, a man, probably in his late fifties, wobbled up to her. He had a whiskey in one hand and a beer in the other.

"Hey, lady, are you for sale?" he asked.

"What?" Morgan said.

"How much?"

Morgan had no makeup on and couldn't have looked less sexy in her navy sweats and gray dingy t-shirt. "If you were even half as attractive as a one-eyed toad, I might consider it," she said.

"That's not very nice." The man frowned.

"But accurate."

He ordered another whiskey, which the bartender poured into a clean glass. The man poured what was left of his first whiskey into the new one and then walked away.

"That's our councilman you just insulted," the bartender said, putting a glass of bourbon in front of her.

"You must be so proud," she said.

Morgan picked up the glass and inhaled the spicy aroma of whiskey, feeling like an old friend had come to visit. She considered what she was about to do and put the glass back down. After a moment, she picked it back up, and as she brought it to her lips, her phone rang. She saw Charlie's picture come up. She didn't plan on answering but didn't want her sisters to worry.

"Hey," Charlie said. "Where are you?"

"I'm just driving around," Morgan said.

A woman sauntered up next to her. "Hey, bartender," the woman yelled. "My glass is empty. How did that happen?"

"Morgan, are you in a bar?" Charlie asked so loudly that the woman turned toward the phone.

"Yep, she is in a fine establishment," the woman called out, although she slurred the word, so it came out as 'estabullshit.'

"Abby!" Morgan heard Charlie yell out. "Come quick."

Morgan could tell Charlie had put the phone on speaker. "You need to leave that bar right now," Charlie said.

"Don't drink!" Abby said. "Where are you? We're coming!"

"I'm fine," Morgan said.

"No, you're not; you're in a bar," Charlie said.

"Give us the name," Abby said.

Morgan looked at the glass of bourbon for a long moment. She could still drink it before they got there.

"It's someplace in Van Nuys called 'Always Open,'" she said.

"Sounds lovely," Abby said. "Stay there, we're on our way."

They hung up, and Morgan pushed her glass toward the tipsy woman. "Here, it's yours," Morgan said.

The woman downed it in one swallow. "Thank you so much. You're an angel from heaven," the woman said.

"If I were, I would've dumped it out," Morgan said.

Morgan went outside and stood next to her car. The air was scented with vomit and urine. *Next time I decide to throw away four years of sobriety, I'm doing it at a high-class hotel.*

Ten minutes later, Charlie's car skidded into the parking lot. Charlie, still in her pajamas, rolled down the window. "Did you drink?" she asked.

"No, but I would have if I hadn't answered the phone."

Charlie and Abby jumped out of the car, leaving the engine running. They hugged Morgan, relief written all over them.

"You need to go to a meeting right now," Abby said, putting her hand firmly on Morgan's shoulder as if she were going to drag her there.

"We'll go with you," Charlie said.

"It's okay, I'll go," Morgan said.

"You promise?" Abby said.

"Yes."

"Right now?" Charlie said.

"Yes. You did your job. You can go home," Morgan said.

Morgan got in her car. She noticed that Abby and Charlie didn't move until she had pulled out of the parking lot.

An hour and a half later, Morgan walked into the house. Charlie and Abby jumped up and ran to the door like greyhounds in a dog race.

"Are you okay?" Charlie asked.

"Is any of us?" Morgan asked.

"If anyone should be drinking, it should be me," Abby said. "You guys found your father. I'm still an orphan."

"You aren't an orphan," Charlie said. "Just because he didn't know Mom might've been pregnant when she left doesn't mean you aren't his. Besides, you can't be an orphan when you have us."

Abby smiled, but the smile didn't reach her eyes.

"We're all messed up right now," Charlie said. "But, Morgan, you can't run away by self-medicating again."

"I know, but I feel like I've slipped off the edge of a mountain, and I can't hold on much longer," Morgan said, shaking her head back and forth. "How are you guys okay? We have a mother who killed herself, a father who rose from the dead, and until recently, we didn't even know our actual last names or birthdays. I'm not sure who I am anymore."

"You're the same person you've always been," Charlie said, putting her arm around Morgan's shoulder. "When it gets hard, you need to lean on Abby and me."

Abby nodded in agreement.

"Thank you both for rescuing me today," Morgan said.

"You'd be there for us if the situation was reversed," Abby said.

"Yes, but as the oldest, I'm supposed to be taking care of you guys. Instead, I'm selfishly wallowing in my own stress," Morgan said.

"We all handle things differently. I work through my stress with strawberry ice cream," Abby said. "It's not as much fun as alcohol, but at least I'd remember if I slept with a stranger."

"That only happened once that I can remember… but you made your point," Morgan said. She looked at her sisters, and her hands stopped clenching, and her features softened.

Morgan pulled out her phone and called her sponsor. Then, she looked for another AA meeting to go to that afternoon. She needed to double up for a while. Besides her sisters, it would be the only thing that could save her from herself.

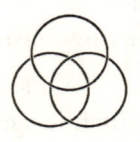

CHAPTER 30

Charlie

Charlie's stomach had been in knots since Rick asked her to marry him or, rather, *told* her they were going to get married. *The thought of marrying him is worse than a pocket-size alien coming from a far-off galaxy, shooting me with a freeze ray, and enslaving me on his planet. Morgan and Abby will kill me for letting things get this far.*

Tonight was Charlie's turn to cook dinner, so she decided to make spaghetti. Something she could make in her sleep—and thank goodness, because she felt like a walking zombie.

She poured what she thought was spaghetti sauce into a pan but then discovered it was BBQ sauce. She dumped the pan out in the sink, washed it, and started over. This time, she made sure to use spaghetti sauce and put the burner on to simmer. Next, she grabbed what she thought were mushrooms and threw them in the sauce—then realized they were carrots.

She stuck her fingers into the pan and tossed one carrot at a time, into the sink. She caught herself before she substituted matzo meal for spaghetti.

Charlie forced herself to concentrate on her cooking; she wanted to offer her sisters a good meal before they murdered her. She split open a baguette, slathered it with garlic, butter, and parmesan cheese, then put it in the oven and made a salad. When everything was ready, she called Morgan and Abby to the table.

"Everything smells good," Abby said, as they all sat down.

Morgan and Abby dug into the meal, but Charlie didn't lift her fork.

"I hope the reason you aren't eating isn't because you're trying to poison us," Morgan smirked.

"Wait, what?" Abby said with her mouth full.

"I'm not trying to poison you. Although, depending on how you react to what I'm about to say, you may have given me a good idea."

"Just say it," Morgan said.

Charlie cleared her throat. "I'm trying to figure out how to tell you something and not get blasted for it." She took a bite of garlic bread.

"Well, swallow first," Abby said.

"Rick wants to get married."

"To whom?" Morgan said.

"To me, you idiot." Charlie's leg bounced nervously under the table.

"After all these years?" Abby said, her eyes wide.

"You can't marry him," Morgan said. "Tell me you aren't considering it."

Charlie put her garlic bread down. "I'm not... I won't... but I have to think about it."

"Did you just hear yourself?" Abby asked.

"I'm trying not to listen," Charlie said.

"You have to break up with him," Morgan said meeting Charlie's eyes. "You've known that for a long time."

"We've been together for eleven years and I've been waiting for him to propose," Charlie said.

"Did he take you someplace romantic and get down on one? Did he say he can't live without you and wants to be with you forever?" Abby asked.

"Or did he propose in a text with the hug emoji," Morgan said.

"Alex proposed to me in a cabin in front of a roaring fire, with snow falling quietly from the heavens. He gave me one red rose and he had champagne on ice," Abby said.

Charlie began scratching her arm. A tic she picked up in middle school when she knew she was about to do something wrong. When it got really bad, Carla would wrap Charlie's arm with gauze so no one would think she'd gotten in a fight with a feral cat.

Morgan got up from the table and crossed over to Charlie.

"Look what you're doing," Morgan said. She gently pried Charlie's fingers off her arm so she'd have to stop scratching. As soon as Morgan returned to her seat, Charlie unconsciously began to scratch again.

"Drawing blood is not a sign that you want to get married to the love of your life," Abby said.

"Okay, so it wasn't a romantic proposal, but does that matter?"

"Yes," Abby and Morgan said simultaneously.

"Think hard. Do you *want* to marry him?" Abby asked. "If the answer is a definite yes, then we'll try to support you."

"If the answer is no, we'll throw a party," Morgan said.

"I don't know. It would be easier than starting over with someone else," Charlie said.

"That's not a yes," Abby said.

"Fine, I don't want to marry him," Charlie exclaimed. "I said that out loud, didn't I?"

"And you stopped scratching," Morgan said.

Charlie looked down at her arms. "I'll break up with him. I'd rather be alone than trapped in a marriage with no skin left." As soon as the words were out of Charlie's mouth, she felt her shoulders relaxing. She knew she was about to jump out of the way of a runaway boulder. A boulder that wouldn't have just crushed her; it would've decimated her future. "I'll call him tomorrow," she said.

"Call him tonight," Abby said.

"I'll call him *tonight*," Charlie said. Her heart skipped a beat.

After dinner, while Morgan and Abby relaxed, Charlie closed the door to her bedroom and picked up her phone.

"Hey, there," Rick said. "I told my parents we're getting married."

"You what?" Charlie said, lying down next to Albert on the soft down comforter. She wished she could disappear into it.

"I said we didn't know when, but just that we'd decided."

"Rick…I don't want to get married."

"You don't?"

"No."

"I don't either. I thought that was what you wanted."

"Years ago, it was, but not anymore."

"That's great. Then we can keep everything the same."

"Not exactly." Charlie sat up, bracing herself. "I want to break up," she said.

"Very funny."

"It's not a joke. I know it's not ideal to do this over the phone, but I need to tell you today. You said yourself, our relationship has been lacking."

"Yes, but I didn't want to end it."

"We've both been going through the motions because we're scared to let go."

"I'm not scared, I love you."

"I love you too, but this relationship isn't right for me anymore."

"Is this coming from your sisters?"

"No. Both of us have changed."

"I haven't."

"Well, I have."

"You'll be back, you need me," Rick said.

"Rick, *you* need *me*." Charlie could imagine him shaking his head in denial. "Before I get back in town, please get anything of yours from my apartment and leave the key on the coffee table."

"Wow. You're serious."

"It's best that we don't have to see each other right now."

"So, that's it? After eleven years, you never want to talk again?"

"I don't know. Maybe after we each have time away for a while, we can be friends."

"I don't need a friend," he said.

"Take care of yourself." Charlie hung up before she changed her mind or let him try to change hers.

"I did it!" she yelled loudly. "Goodbye, Rick!" Albert sensed her excitement and thought she was offering to take him for a walk. He jumped up and down and ran around the room.

"Aren't you proud of me, Albert?" Charlie danced to a rhythm she'd created in her head. "We're free, we're free, no more boyfriend!" Then, suddenly she froze. "No more boyfriend. I'm all alone now. Who am I going to go out with on a Saturday night? Who's going to be my emergency contact?"

She sat on the floor and cuddled with Albert, who licked her cheek. After a few minutes, Charlie stood up. "I can do this. I've helped clients get through break-ups. I'll be okay." She hoped that would be true.

CHAPTER 31

Abby

That evening, Abby stood in the shower, enjoying the warm water running down upon her. What she loved most was not hearing a herd of little fists banging on the door. She missed her family but couldn't help appreciating the time she had to concentrate on herself. It had been six years since she'd had a full night's sleep without someone's feet kicking her in the stomach. And when was the last time she could have a conversation on the phone without it being grabbed out of her hands to play Kids Doodle?

She had convinced herself that harmless flirting with Greg fell into self-care. While she took the time to shampoo her hair and scrub her scalp, she thought about her life.

I've been only a wife and mother for so long; I deserve to feel like a woman again. Does that make me ungrateful when I've been blessed with a loving husband and four adorable children?

She applied a hair mask and sat on the bench in the shower to wait five minutes for it to work. *Maybe my family have been happier without me. I wonder if they miss me. Alex is probably a better mother than I am. Geez, I gave up everything for kids who don't even care that I'm gone.*

Abby shook her head, trying to ward off these thoughts. Then she washed the mask off, not waiting for the full five minutes. She turned off the faucet, rubbed the water out of her eyes, and stepped out of the shower. Soaking wet, with a towel wrapped around her, she went into her bedroom not caring that she had been dripping water onto the carpet. She was about to reach for her clothes when her phone rang.

"Hey you," Alex said.

Why does he sound so relaxed? I never sound that mellow when I'm at home.

"Hi," Abby said.

"How are things going with my beautiful wife?"

"Pretty much the same since we spoke last night."

"I know you have a lot to process."

Abby hit the speaker button and grabbed her PJ shirt and panties.

"How're the kids?" she asked.

"They're good. We found our rhythm, and everything's going smoothly now."

"Really," her voice was almost monotone. "I guess that's good." Abby got her shirt on, but when she went to put her panties on, they fell behind the bed.

"You don't need to worry about us," he said.

Abby felt tears come to her eyes. *I was right, they don't need me, they're doing fine without me.* "Okay, well, I'm glad you checked in," she said, trying to reach behind the bed, but she couldn't quite grasp her panties.

Then she heard a clatter as something hit the floor. Alex was swearing, his voice suddenly sounding far away. "Is everything okay?" she asked.

"Hudson, don't do that!" Alex said. "Levi, give me back my phone!"

The sounds in the background got louder, then softer, and then loud again. "Hello? Alex?" Abby yelled.

"Give it to Daddy now!" Alex said. "Abby? Are you still there?"

"Yes, what happened?"

"Hudson rolled his toy dump truck in front of me, and I tripped and dropped my phone, and the screen cracked. Then Levi swooped in and grabbed it." Alex said, huffing and puffing as if he had fought off a bull.

"Is that Mommy?" Hudson and Levi asked.

"Yes," Alex said.

"Mama!" Abby recognized Emma's voice.

"We want to talk to her!" Hudson said.

"Okay, give me a second," Alex said.

Alex put the phone on speaker. "Mommy! We miss you so much," the kids yelled.

"Oh, my babies, I miss you too," Abby said, almost laughing out loud. Even though they weren't on FaceTime, out of habit, Abby grabbed the towel from the floor and held it up to her body. She was still naked from the waist down.

"Daddy doesn't know how to sing the 'Baby Shark' song," Levi said.

"And he doesn't make macaroni and cheese the way we like it," Hudson said.

"I want a hug," Addison said.

The smile on Abby's face was brighter than the neon lights on the Las Vegas strip.

"I love you all so much," Abby said.

"Okay, let me finish talking to Mommy, and then I'll read you all a story," Alex said.

"Bye, Mommy," Addison said.

"Come home," Hudson said.

"Hold on," Alex said, taking her off speaker.

"I'm sorry," he said.

"For what?"

"I didn't want to burden you with how much we need you here," Alex said.

"I'm glad I know. Thank you for giving me this time, though."

"I love you. Take all the time you need. Well, maybe not all of it." Alex laughed. "Now I get how much easier my job is than yours."

"I appreciate you saying that," Abby said.

"Thank *you* for all you do."

"I love you," Abby said, then noticed that a text from Greg came across the screen of her phone. She quickly swiped up to get rid of it, as if Alex could see it from where he was. "Should I come home for a quick visit?" she asked.

"That'll be harder on the kids when you leave again. We're fine, don't worry."

"You're the best," Abby said.

"I do miss cuddling with you, though."

"Me too." Abby got down on her hands and knees and retrieved her panties. "Finally!" she said.

"What?"

"Oh, nothing," she said as she slipped them on.

"I better go, honey," he said. "I need to go read to the animals in our zoo."

When they hung up, Abby clicked on the text from Greg.

Hey Kelsey, I missed talking to you today. Let's find a time to meet again in person. I can come there if that works for you.

Abby held her finger over the keypad for a moment. *Greg, you were the perfect distraction I needed from my real life—one I could easily continue.* She shook her head. *But it's not worth the risk. I'd be giving up too much.* She found Greg in her list of contacts, blocked him, and deleted his number.

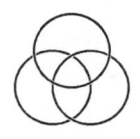

CHAPTER 32

Carla

Getting pregnant with a third child was not part of Carla's plan. Brian had promised to get a vasectomy, but that had turned out to be another one of the things he didn't follow through on. She didn't tell him about the pregnancy because she knew he'd only bet more money and say it was for their growing family.

When they left New York, Morgan and Charlie were still so young, so Carla hoped they wouldn't remember much from this time in their lives. Someday, they'd have lots of questions about their father, and when that time came, she'd tell them that he passed away. To Carla, that part of her life would be dead anyway.

After she married Brian, she should have been smarter about staying financially

independent. Before she got married, she had always worked and saved money. At a young age, she taught herself to type fast, so at fourteen, she worked for a neighbor doing medical transcribing. When she was sixteen, she got a job selling costume jewelry in a department store. And all through college, she worked on campus in the admissions office.

If Carla had learned anything from watching her mother scrimp and save when her father divorced her, Carla might have stashed more money away. By the time Carla left Brian, she had gotten together enough money for the first and last month's rent for an apartment and even had job interviews set up in Los Angeles.

Carla had been so busy getting the girls settled and passing the California real estate exam that she almost forgot she was pregnant. She'd gained less weight with this pregnancy because she was running around town with her clients, so at nine months, she didn't look more than seven months pregnant.

Carla had recently entered her first million-dollar sale into escrow and was walking through the property preparing it for the inspector when she felt a contraction. She ignored it because it was just one of many she'd felt for the last couple of days. She knew what labor felt like and was sure this wasn't it.

The inspector, Stan, a tall, lanky man who looked like he could have been a fitness instructor, arrived. When Carla shook his hand, she noticed his grip was firm, yet his palm was soft. Since she'd been pregnant, all her senses had been heightened. Stan wore jeans that flattered his physique and a plain T-shirt that was so white, she wanted to ask how much bleach he used to keep it looking that way. She didn't see a wedding ring on his finger or a tan line.

The sun's reflection through the windows brought out gold specks in his chocolate eyes. He smiled at her as he took in her pregnant belly.

"Is this your first kid?"

"No, my third, but it's my first without my husband in the picture."

"Really," he said. "You look so young." Carla thought he got closer to her, but she wasn't sure if she imagined it. "You have that glow about you," he said.

Carla wasn't one to blush, but she felt her cheeks get warm. She smiled at him, and then suddenly, she felt a wetness in her pants.

I haven't been turned on like this in a long time, but I don't remember peeing a little when I was, she thought. After another second, a whoosh of water poured through her leggings. Stan looked down at the floor and then moved quickly backward.

"Oh, my God, my water broke," Carla said, pulling her legs together, hoping that would hold something in, but she knew from having Morgan and Charlie that it wasn't going to work. And it didn't.

This would have to happen when I meet a cute guy who finds me attractive, even when I'm carrying another human being inside me.

"I'm sorry, Stan, but I think I should go," Carla said.

"You shouldn't drive like this. Do you have someone who can take you to the hospital?"

"I'll call my friend Ginny. Finish your inspection; I wouldn't want my giving birth to get in the way of the Wilson's escrow."

"Are you sure?" he asked. "I don't feel comfortable leaving you like this."

"It's fine."

He nodded and moved out to the backyard. Ginny arrived in record time with a beach towel that Carla wrapped around her waist.

"I called Julia," Ginny said. "She'll pick up Morgan from school and Charlie from daycare and watch them overnight."

"Thank you so much," Carla said.

Ginny helped Carla to the car, and they headed to the hospital.

"How did I not realize that I was going to have to give birth all alone?" Carla began hyperventilating. Ginny did her best to calm her down by agreeing to be her birthing partner.

"Are you sure you're okay with that?" Carla asked. "You've never wanted kids."

"As long as it's you, not me, that something is jackhammering inside of and ripping apart, I'm fine."

"You were born to be a birthing coach," Carla said, laughing until a big contraction hit. When they arrived at the hospital, Carla had to sit in the car, inhaling and exhaling slowly, until the last contraction stopped.

"Let's get you settled," a nurse said as she pushed Carla in a wheelchair into a room with Ginny walking alongside them. The nurse put a cup of ice chips on a tray beside the bed. "Your doctor will be in soon. Your wife can help you change," she said, putting a blue hospital gown on the bed. Carla and Ginny had a good laugh after the nurse left and closed the door.

Six hours later, Abby came screaming into the world. After cleaning her up, the doctor put her on Carla's chest. Ginny looked at the baby, her eyes glistening. "She's gorgeous," Ginny said.

"Isn't she? Morgan and Charlie wanted another sister."

"Babies are so cute," Ginny gently touched the top of Abby's head. "It's a shame they have to turn into adults."

"Yep, that's usually the way it works," Carla said, not taking her eyes off her newborn.

Two days later, when Ginny dropped Carla and Abby home from the hospital, Morgan and Charlie were in a screaming, drag-out fight. Asleep in Carla's arms, Abby awoke with a start and added to the hysterics. Carla nursed Abby while negotiating with Morgan and Charlie, whose turn it was to feed their baby doll. Carla took the doll away when she couldn't stand their arguing anymore. Morgan and Charlie began crying, and then Abby stopped breastfeeding and started crying, which made Carla cry along with them all.

Julia knocked on the door having heard the commotion through the walls. "Let me help," Julia said. She took Morgan and Charlie into the other room and Abby calmed down and was able to latch back on.

"What was I thinking about having another baby by myself?" Carla said to Julia when she came back into the room. "I'm never going to be able to do this."

"You will. It's like having three dogs—two is no harder than three, there's just more poop."

"Where did you hear that?" Carla asked. "I've only had three for a few hours, and I'm already pulling my hair out. Maybe I shouldn't have gotten divorced."

"I can't answer that," Julia said, "but you're a smart woman, so I'm sure you had a good reason to leave. And besides, even though you're divorced, he should be here helping. They're his kids, too."

Carla wasn't about to tell Julia the truth; she would have to learn to go it alone. She told herself they'd be okay with only one parent as long as she was an attentive and supportive mother. Carla didn't know if she believed that, but what choice did she have?

It's Brian's fault that I had to give up everything that made me who I was, she thought. *Having to start over, reinvent myself, and create a new history was not in my plans.*

It took years before Carla got used to all the lies. She felt like a fraud because she was.

When the girls became old enough to question why their father wasn't there, Carla told them that Brian had walked out on them. He didn't want to be a part of their lives. A few years later, when Morgan wanted to talk to her father, Carla said that she had heard he'd died. It was the only way she knew how to make things final.

Being the head of the household meant Carla had to work hard, but no matter how much effort she put in, she had still taken the most important male role model away from them. Carla knew from all her college psychology classes that this decision might affect her daughters. As the years flew by, she realized she was to blame for many of the bad choices the girls made in their lives.

When Carla discovered that at thirteen, Morgan had started drinking, she should have put her foot down or gotten her into therapy. Instead, she denied it and dismissed it as typical teenage rebellion. She convinced herself Morgan would grow out of it.

A year later, when Morgan's destructive behavior had continued, Carla confronted her, and Morgan stopped speaking to her for weeks. When Morgan became addicted to pain pills after one of her car accidents, Carla didn't say a word.

After Morgan finally got sober, Carla would hold her breath every day and pray Morgan wouldn't relapse. She knew Morgan resented the constant pressure, but she couldn't help herself.

Carla also blamed herself for Charlie staying with a man for years when it was leading nowhere. Charlie had been independent when she was younger but changed dramatically when she started dating Rick. He took advantage of her, and Charlie acted like she didn't see it, or she didn't think she deserved better. Charlie was taking after Carla who had not been the best judge of character. After all, she picked Brian and she hated seeing Charlie making the same mistakes she did.

Abby was the baby Carla didn't know she wanted until she was born. The child that was all hers and the one she had the most in common with, but not always in the ways Carla wished. Abby didn't like to take risks, and Carla worried it was because her own fears had rubbed off on her daughter. At least Abby had chosen a good man, even if Alex was the first boy she had ever talked to. Alex took good care of her and treated her well, things all mothers wanted for their daughters.

Carla wished that Abby hadn't followed in her footsteps by marrying young and having kids so quickly. She would've wanted Abby to experience more of life first and be able to follow her passion for acting. Carla knew Abby could've been a star. Unlike Beverly, who never would have made it big, Abby had talent and that special spark. If she only had half the confidence that Beverly had and more time, she would have been famous.

When Carla looked back on Morgan's drinking, Charlie's staying with Rick, and Abby's need to create an instant family, she wondered if she'd done the right thing keeping their father from them. Did her lies predetermine her daughters' lives?

The one thing Carla knew for sure, was if anyone discovered what she'd been hiding all these years, she'd have to disappear. And until that viral video of the fire, no one had found her.

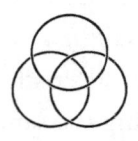

CHAPTER 33

Morgan

Morgan woke up—if you could call what she'd done sleeping—before sunrise and walked the two blocks to Starbucks. It was so early that she thought she would be the first customer there, but the place already had a handful of people waiting for their morning pick-me-up.

The espresso machines gurgled and hissed as each barista politely took ridiculously complicated orders from picky customers. The microwave dinged periodically as it warmed up croissants and egg tartlets for those same people. The baristas called out the customers' names while Morgan waited for her cappuccino with no extras, under the name Pumpernickel. She realized she wasn't alone in giving a fun fake name. Today, she heard Radcliffe, Obama, and her new all-time favorite, Uncle Mikey.

The tables around Morgan began filling up with early risers infused with liquid energy. Some were already clicking away on their laptops, two clusters of moms chatted and laughed—probably about their kids, and an earnest man in an ill-fitting suit discussed his resume with an intense red-headed woman in black slacks and a silk blouse.

After Morgan had been sitting at the same table for two hours with her hands wrapped around a cold cappuccino, she considered ordering another one, but the line had stretched out the door and into the parking lot. She knew if she got up, she'd lose her table, and she was enjoying the time alone.

In Brooklyn people patiently waited in long lines in the cold to order their coffee, Morgan thought. *It's rarely under sixty degrees In Los Angeles, and I can hear complaints every time the door opens.*

The sun had finally emerged from behind a cloud, so people inside began shedding their hoodies and light jackets and draping them off the backs of their chairs.

The chatter inside grew louder as each new table became occupied. The voices rose and fell like Muzak to Morgan but less annoying. She eavesdropped on the couple next to her having a heated discussion about who would get custody of the parakeet if they decided to separate. She tried hard to use all the background noise as a distraction from the thoughts doing somersaults in her head.

How will I ever trust anyone again when my own mother lied about the most important things? How could someone supposed to love us betray us and then kill herself so we can't ask why?

She wanted to scream, and she would have if she didn't think the baristas would call the police or kick her out. Morgan rubbed her forehead hard, trying to push the thoughts onto a more productive path, but like ornery children, they refused to listen. If nothing else, maybe all the rubbing would help smooth out her wrinkles so she could at least look like a youthful, crazy person.

Morgan had always thought Carla was rational and made good decisions, so she had to have had a valid reason for hiding Brian from them. Now, she and her sisters would only know his side of things, and after this many years, how would that explain why Carla took her own life?

Morgan pondered what it might be like if they met their father in person. *What if he didn't like them? She and Charlie aren't the cute toddlers he remembers. What if we don't like him? Has too much time passed to have this man. a total stranger, come into our lives?*

Her thoughts were interrupted by two college-age girls standing in front of her table glaring at her. She knew they wanted her to relinquish her seat. Although Morgan took pleasure in the mere implication that they thought they could influence her with their stares, she decided she'd been there long enough.

As she reached behind her and took her purse off the back of her chair, Morgan noticed a young man looking for a table coming up beside her. He was the epitome of the guys she wished liked her. He wore a polo shirt but had hair down to his shoulders and a tattoo of a roaring lion on his upper arm. She would have flirted with him if he had been ten years older and didn't look like he drove a muscle car.

"Would you like this table?" she asked him, "I'm about to leave."

He thanked her and she stood up so he could sit down. The girls sneered at Morgan. *You snooze you lose,* she thought as she gave the girls a big smile. *Learn to be more polite to older people, then next time, maybe you will have won out over the cute guy...although I doubt it.*

By the time Morgan had walked back to Carla's house, it was nine o'clock. She assumed her sisters would be awake, but the house was silent, and even Albert was asleep in his furry bed.

Morgan needed to vent to someone. She returned to the front door, opened it, and then slammed it so hard the walls rattled.

Within seconds, Charlie and Abby sprinted into the living room. Charlie rubbed her eyes, and Abby stretched her arms over her head.

"What was that banging?" Charlie asked.

"I heard it, too. It woke me up," Abby said.

Morgan shrugged her shoulders, hiding a smile. "I didn't hear anything. But, since you're both up, we have some things we should discuss."

"Okay, but we need coffee first," Charlie said, yawning. "Do you want any, Morgan?"

"I'll have a little," Morgan said, then realized she had forgotten to bring back their vanilla lattes.

Charlie made coffee and then handed Abby and Morgan mugs. Morgan rarely drank more than one cup because it made her jittery, so she pretended to sip hers, but then she let out a loud belch.

"Nice manners," Charlie said.

"Who cares about manners," Morgan said.

"No wonder you don't have a man in your life," Abby said.

Abby and Charlie laughed lightheartedly.

"Am I the only one who's freaking out about finding our father?" Morgan said. "How can you both seem calm?"

"Who says we're calm?" Abby said.

"I haven't been able to think about anything else," Charlie said.

"Except maybe good manners," Abby smirked. Then she took her napkin and, daintily wiped the corners of her mouth with her pinky in the air.

Morgan narrowed her eyes into a piercing stare. "We didn't ask enough questions when we talked to Brian," Morgan said. "We need to ask him what happened between him and Mom."

"We don't even know him. Why should we believe what he says?" Charlie asked.

"Well, we know we can't trust Mom's version. She said he left us and then died, and now we know at least one of those things is not true," Abby said.

"So, Mom lied about him being dead; I'm sure she had her reasons. Maybe we need to give her the benefit of the doubt," Morgan said as she sprinkled two Stevia packages in her coffee.

"When people get divorced, there can be a nasty custody dispute. One person might not want to share parenting responsibilities," Charlie said.

"Are you saying Mom could have wanted us all to herself?" Abby asked.

"Wouldn't that be kidnapping?" Morgan asked and Charlie shrugged.

"Oh my God, we were kidnapped," Abby said.

"You weren't. Brian didn't even know about you," Morgan said.

Abby pouted.

"Abby, whether you're his or not, you're still our sister," Charlie said, and Morgan nodded in agreement.

"Thank you," Abby said. "And I agree that even if he's not *my* father, we should call him again."

Abby looked at her recent phone calls to get Brian's number. She called him, placing the phone in the center of the kitchen table. It rang four times before they heard his deep and mellow voice.

"Hello," Brian said.

"Hi," the sisters said in unison, Abby's voice not quite as loud as her sisters.

"I'm so glad you called," Brian said. "I haven't been able to think about anything other than all of you. Even you, Abby."

Morgan patted Abby's hand and Abby smiled.

"Would it be okay if we asked you a few more questions?" Charlie asked.

"Of course."

"We need to know everything about your relationship with our mother," Morgan said.

Brian started by telling them how he and Carla met when they got married and about Morgan and Charlie's births. Then he paused for a moment. Morgan figured he must be gathering his thoughts.

"When Morgan and Charlie were toddlers," he said, "I wanted Carla to be able to stay home with them, but we needed some extra money. I began betting on sports. I didn't think it was a big deal. At first, I made small bets, but I won most of the time, so we had more than enough to pay our bills. As time went on, I got greedy. I didn't want to just pay our bills, I wanted to buy other things that we couldn't have afforded before. I started making bigger bets and winning less and less. Carla had no idea that I was maxing out all our credit cards and taking out new ones."

He went on to say that Carla had been busy with Morgan and Charlie, so she wasn't aware of how in trouble they were until the bank left a message on their home machine that their account had been overdrawn. They owed thousands on their credit cards, and their bank account was depleted.

"I had to come clean about how much I owed to a loan shark, and Carla was rightfully upset. I promised I would stop gambling, but by then, I was a full-blown addict, and I couldn't stop. Your mother freaked out even more when the men who worked for the loan shark threatened her and you girls. I assume that's when she decided to take you and run."

Morgan looked at her sisters, her face filled with sadness and compassion. She knew what it was like to be an addict.

"I had gotten home from a business trip to find no one home and your closets empty. And then there was a knock on the door. I ran to it, thinking you were back, but instead, I got served with divorce papers. I was devastated. I couldn't get out of bed for a week, and I almost lost my job."

"Why didn't you look for us?" Charlie asked.

"I tried. I hired private investigators, but no one could find where she took you. Now it makes sense since Carla had not only moved across the country but also changed your last names. After a few years and a lot of money, with no results, I had to give up."

"How could you not know about me?" Abby asked, shaking her leg under the table so hard that the table vibrated.

"Carla never told me she was pregnant. I guess she didn't want me to know, or you aren't mine. I'm hoping it's the former."

"Me, too," Abby said quietly.

"So, what happened with your gambling?" Morgan asked.

"After sinking into a deep depression; the high from gambling was the only thing that helped. When one of the bookies broke three of my fingers and threatened to cut off my hand, I left New York and got help for my addiction. I'm now a member of Gamblers Anonymous."

"I'm glad you got your life together," Morgan said.

"Same here. It took years, and by the time I was sure I was in a good place, you and Charlie were teenagers. I could finally be a good father to you, but I didn't know where you were, until I saw that video of your mom saving her neighbor. I finally had her new name, where she worked, and an email address. I wrote her immediately."

"We looked through her emails and didn't see anything from you. What email address did you write to?" Abby asked.

"Her work one."

"It never occurred to us to look through her work emails," Charlie said.

"What did you say when you contacted her?" Morgan asked.

"I told her that I'd stopped gambling years ago, and I wanted to see my two daughters."

Morgan watched as Abby got up from the table and walked toward the kitchen with her head down.

"What did my mom say?" Charlie asked.

"You and Morgan were doing well without me and meeting me would upset you both. She refused to tell me where you were. I had no idea if your last name was the same as hers, or if any of you had gotten married and changed your name."

"Thank you for telling us all this. Would it be okay if we call you back another time?" Morgan asked.

"I hope you do," Brian said.

After Morgan hung up, Abby brought a glass of water back to the table and sipped it. "It's not fair," she said, tapping her fingers as if she were playing a silent piano. "I need to know if he's also my father. And if he's not, who the heck is mine?"

"One step at a time," Charlie said. "I'm sure he'd be happy to take a DNA test."

The next morning, Morgan called Carla's real estate firm and told the assistant, Kathy, that she was one of the executors of her mother's will and needed to get into her work email. Kathy explained that she wasn't supposed to give anyone outside the firm a password for their computers. Morgan begged, and eventually, Kathy relented and said she would send her a code to get in.

Morgan sat at Carla's computer for twenty minutes until Kathy sent the code. Morgan carefully inputted it and her mom's work email popped up.

"I'm in," Morgan said to the empty room.

As she weeded through emails about open houses, commissions, and conferences, she prayed her mother hadn't deleted Brian's emails. Finally, she found seven between her mother and father. They were all dated a week before Carla died.

Carla,

I'm sure I'm the last person you expected to hear from. I searched for you and the girls for years, but eventually, I had to give up because hoping I'd find you and not succeeding took a heavy toll on me. When I saw that video of you online, I finally knew where you'd gone.

I'm not writing today to blame you for leaving. I understand why you felt you needed to, but that doesn't mean it didn't kill me to lose you, Morgan, and Charlie from my life forever. I admit that I didn't deserve to be a husband and father during that time. When you tried to tell me that you and the girls were threatened and you didn't feel safe, I thought you were blowing things out of proportion. I regret more than I can say that I didn't protect our family. I loved you and the girls; I'm so sorry for how scared you must have been.

After you left, my gambling got even worse, and Antonio Sr. and his men came after me. The last time, they hurt me, and that's when I moved from Brooklyn to Connecticut and got help. I assure you I'm not the same person I was back then. I haven't gambled in years, and I make a good living. I'm a member of Gamblers Anonymous and I attend meetings three times a week. I want to come to California to see you all. I think we have a lot to talk about.

Brian

Brian,

I'm sorry it took me a few days to get back to you. I was shocked to get your email, and I've been trying to absorb what you said. I'm happy you got help and are doing better, but it's been a very long time since we've known each other, and I don't think there's anything to talk about. I'd appreciate it if you didn't contact me again.

I wish you the best.
Carla

Carla,

If you don't want to see me, that's fine, but I want to get to know my daughters. I'm sure it wasn't easy for you to raise them on your own, and I know my showing up when they're adults isn't ideal, but I truly believe they would want me in their lives. I have always loved them and will continue to love them. If you send me Morgan and Charlie's information, I will get in touch with them and leave you out of it.

I hope you will seriously consider what I'm asking. I'd rather not go around you.

Brian

Brian,

When the girls were young, I told them that you had passed away. I thought it would be easier for them than to wait and wonder where you were. They adjusted fine, and now it would be shocking for you to contact them. I have been their mother this whole time and raised them on my own because of the actions you took. It's better if we keep things the way they are and go on separately. Please leave us alone.

Carla

Carla,

You're being unreasonable; they will get over the shock. They deserve to have me in their life as much as I deserve to have them in mine. They'll understand when we tell them why you left me and why you told them I had died. If the truth comes from you, it will go over better. Since the girls are now adults, they can decide for themselves if they want to get to know me. And now that I know where you are, I will make it happen.

Brian

Brian,

Is that a threat? Even if you come here, I won't tell you their last names or where they live, so don't waste your time.

Carla

Carla,

I'm sorry you're upset, but if you don't comply, I'll have to contact a lawyer. I don't want to go that far, but what you did was kidnapping. I hope you won't leave me with any other choice but to file felony charges against you. Either way, I'll find my daughters—of that, I can assure you.

Brian

The final email was dated two days before Carla ended her life. Morgan read each of them two more times. She felt anger rising inside her like steam from a pressure cooker.

Morgan couldn't understand why her mom reacted that way. *If no one gave me a second chance, where would I be? Mom, no matter how old we became or how much time had passed, you knew how much Charlotte, Abby, and I wished we had a father. What were you so worried about?*

Morgan rubbed her neck; her back was aching, and she hadn't even been sitting that long. She turned on the printer, which came to life with a low rumble, a geyser erupting after being dormant. She printed three copies of the emails. Were these some of her mother's final words?

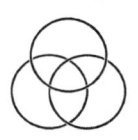

CHAPTER 34

Charlie

Charlie sat on her bed, holding the emails Morgan had given her and trying to digest their enormous meaning. She had been holding them so tightly that her fingers throbbed. She opened her hands and let the papers flutter to the floor.

The emails verified everything Brian had said. He hadn't walked out because he didn't want to be a husband and father; her mother had left him. She could understand how painful it must have been for him when he looked for them and got nowhere. Charlie had been too young to remember Carla telling her and Morgan that their father had died, but she had spent her entire life thinking he was gone.

Charlie shivered and went to get a warm woolen scarf to wrap around her. She glimpsed her reflection in the full-length mirror on the closet door. Losing her mother had done a number on her, and all the stress had made her appear gaunt. She'd only been able to stomach half her food since this nightmare began. Sometimes, she'd be nauseous; other times, she'd get full too quickly. Her insides always felt as though they were filled with rocks the size of boulders, and those boulders were rapidly turning into a monolith.

Charlie's life had changed entirely in a matter of weeks. She'd lost her mother, gained a father, and broken up with her long-term boyfriend. Any one of those crises on its own would have ramped up her anxiety, but all three together made her wonder how she'd ever get through it. The world was no longer safe, and she didn't know if it ever would be again.

To top it all off, Rick wasn't going away quietly. He'd been texting constantly, asking her where to find various items in his house. Charlie figured it was an excuse to talk to her, but she still tried to help. The eighth time he texted, she told him he'd have to find the hammer himself. She knew she had made the right decision, but she needed someone other than her sisters to vent to.

Charlie stood up, her legs weak and unsteady like a newborn giraffe's. She sat back down.

Would it be so bad if I called Rick? There were times he could be so supportive. No, that would be a bad idea. She got her phone from the side table, pulled up all her contacts, and studied them. *I could call Susan, Cayla, Jill, or Lori,* she thought as she scrolled through a long list of friends. *But they didn't know my mom well, and I've never told them anything about my father. I could post something on Facebook asking for advice, but that would probably look deranged.*

Charlie always called her mom when she was in a bad place. Charlie's fingers hovered over the buttons, and the next thing she knew, she heard a gruff, condescending voice on the other end.

"I knew you'd change your mind," Rick said with what Charlie could tell was a satisfied tone in his voice.

What have I done?

"Charlie, say something," Rick said. "It's okay, I forgive you." Charlie's vocal cords had gone on strike. "Just admit you love me and can't live without me," he said. "You know it was a bad idea to break up with me. We can continue like this was a small blip in our relationship."

Charlie finally found her voice. "Sorry, butt dial." She hung up and put her hand on her chest, then smacked herself in the head. "You idiot," she said, then laughed in embarrassment. If she told her sisters she'd called Rick, they'd take her phone away as if she were a misbehaving child.

She dragged herself into the living room. Abby was on the couch reading their mother's emails.

"Hey," Charlie said.

"Hey."

"Where's Morgan?"

"She took Albert for a walk."

"You're sure that wasn't an excuse to go to another bar?"

"Not unless Albert has taken up drinking," Abby said.

Morgan opened the front door, with Albert panting so hard he couldn't walk over the threshold. She leaned down, picked him up, and carried him into the living room, where he fell in a heap.

"He looks drunk to me," Charlie said to Abby.

Morgan reached down, unhooked Albert's leash, and filled his water bowl. Albert didn't move, so Morgan put her hands on his collar and gently tried to get him to go with her. Albert still didn't move, as his body had melted into the floor. Morgan gave in, picked up the water bowl, brought it to him, and placed it under his mouth.

"While I was out, I started thinking there's not a lot more we can do here," Morgan said. "It's time we go home to our own lives."

"I agree," Charlie said. "I need to get back to my clients before they decide they're mentally healthy."

The tags on Albert's collar, clinking against the bowl, echoed throughout the room.

"I want to see my kids and relieve Alex," Abby said. "He'll be happy to have me back for several reasons. I can list four off the top of my head."

"That husband of yours is a saint," Morgan said.

Abby nodded. "I know, right?"

Morgan and Charlie got on their laptops to make their travel plans. After Charlie's flight was booked, she contacted her clients to tell them she would be back in her office in two days. Next, she started looking for condos for sale. Her current home held too many memories of Rick, and she needed a fresh start.

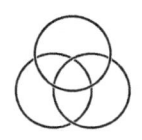

CHAPTER 35

Abby

Abby's homecoming was filled with happy tears. All four of the kids were up waiting for her. They were afraid that if they went to sleep, she would be gone when they woke up. This broke Abby's heart, and she assured them she would be there in the morning.

After Addison was the last kid to conk out on the couch, Abby carried her to bed. When she returned, she found Alex pouring them each a glass of wine. Abby sat down next to him, leaning her head on his shoulder.

"What if Brian isn't my father?" she said, sipping her drink.

"You were born six months after your mom moved to Los Angeles. It's more likely that she decided not to tell him she was pregnant."

"I hope that's true; I can't handle any more surprises."

Alex kissed her on the forehead. "I'm impressed with how strong you've been during all this."

"It's a façade. I keep wavering between being sad that my mom died and then being filled with rage at her. And then my anger makes me feel like I'm a bad daughter."

"You were a great daughter," Alex said.

"Thanks. I'm hoping someday I can forgive her."

"I bet you will."

"What's really crazy is that I'm thirty years old and didn't know my actual birthday or maiden name."

A tiny male voice screamed out. "Mommy!" Abby and Alex looked at each other.

Abby stood up. "I'll be back."

When she returned fifteen minutes later, Alex pulled her onto his lap and wrapped his arms around her.

"Hudson has been having the hardest time without you," Alex said. "Did you have to read *I'll Always Come Back?*" Alex asked.

"No, he wanted to hear *Heather Has Two Mommies.*"

"Should I be insulted?" Alex asked.

Abby laughed. "His kindergarten friend brought the book to class for the teacher to read to them. Hudson thought it was fascinating how two mommies could make a baby without a daddy. I was too tired to explain it, so I told Hudson they could have a baby the same way mommies and daddies do. God drops one off at their house…I'm a terrible parent."

"We have time to tell him that his mom is delusional," Alex said, falling back on the couch and pulling Abby on top of him. He kissed her passionately. After a few minutes, they came up for air. "I missed that," he said.

"Me, too." She kissed him again. This time, when they pulled apart, she moved off him and sat back up. "I need to talk to you about something," she said.

Abby wanted his full attention, so she got up and went to the chair across from him. If she stayed where she was, she might not be able to say everything she wanted to, especially since Alex's lips looked soft and luscious.

"Should I be concerned?" he asked.

"I don't think so."

"So you still adore me?"

"Couldn't you tell from that kiss?"

"Good point. So, what's going on?"

"I love being your wife and the mother to our kids, and I never want that to change, but these last few weeks have made me realize I need more."

"Okay..." he said.

"I understand now why my mom lived life like someone would take it away from her. She had to be careful that her secret wouldn't come out, so she couldn't fulfill her dreams. I think growing up, I sensed her fear, and I took it on. I can't be afraid to take risks anymore."

"So, what are you saying?" he asked.

Abby thought she heard his voice crack for a moment. *What does he think I'm about to tell him?* Before his thoughts took on a life of their own, she continued. "I need something outside of this house to remind me that I'm more than someone who cares for everyone else. I'm going to take acting classes again and maybe get involved in the local theater."

Alex smiled; he looked relieved. "I think that's great."

"You do?" She stared at him. "I thought you'd push back on the idea since the kids are so young. If I get a part in a show, you know I'd have to be gone in the evenings."

"Are you trying to get me to change my mind?"

"I am my own worst enemy," Abby said, going back to sit next to him.

"I'm all for anything that makes you happy. We're a team. We'll make it work," Alex said, and Abby hugged him. "I've always known how talented you are, and truthfully, I've felt guilty that we got pregnant so fast just as your career was taking shape." Alex took her face in his hands and looked into her eyes. "If you weren't so damn sexy, I could've kept my hands off you, and you'd be famous right now."

"You're amazing," Abby said. "The classes I've researched are only one night a week."

"No problem. I've become an expert at making them dinner, getting them bathed, and putting them to bed. I have the routine down pat."

"That's not what I heard," she said.

"Those snitches will have to put up with me, and so will you."

"How could I not? You're too sexy to resist," Abby said.

Alex picked her up like a baby, carried her to their bedroom, and locked the door.

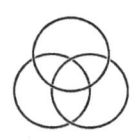

CHAPTER 36

Carla

When Carla first arrived in Los Angeles, she lived as if Brian might pop up at any time. Whenever she left her home, she stayed vigilant of her surroundings. During those first few years, she'd shudder if anyone got near her or the girls. Once, she almost punched a man when he approached them to say how cute the girls looked in their Halloween costumes. As the years went by, she began feeling safer. Brian had not found them.

When she got close to women friends and they asked her about her past, she would tell them she divorced her husband when the girls were young. She said he had met someone else and then, a few years later, passed away. She talked about her life as tragic, explaining that after her divorce, her parents died in a car accident. When she was called upon to relay these stories, she made her chin quiver so the person would feel sympathy for her and change the subject. It always worked.

Ginny was the only person Carla had told that she had grown up in Brooklyn, gone to college there, and moved to Los Angeles when she got divorced. Carla didn't mean to divulge all that information, but one night, when she and Ginny had too much wine, her mouth forgot to stop talking.

Carla's life with the girls made all the secrecy worthwhile. She loved being a parent and wished they never had to grow up. One night, she told Ginny that one of her biggest fears was that the girls would someday move away—and that's exactly what eventually happened. One by one, her daughters left Los Angeles.

It took Carla a while to accept their absence from her life, but she looked forward to their annual weekend away together. She also visited each of them as often as she could, or they came to see her. She began driving down to Abby's every other month when she became a grandmother. She loved her grandchildren as much as she loved her daughters.

Everything changed for Carla on the night of the fire. She didn't have a moment's hesitation about saving Martha but never considered that someone would film her or that her picture and identity would be broadcast across America.

All those years she had spent hiding from Brian and the loan sharks who were chasing him had gone up in smoke when she got an email from Brian on her office account. Carla read his first email many times over. She waited two days to answer him, trying to figure out what to say. When she finally wrote back, she told him that too much time had passed, and it was a bad idea for him to see the girls. She knew Brian and that he wouldn't stop asking, but maybe it would buy her some time so she could figure out what to do.

Carla didn't sleep that night and felt weary and delirious when her alarm went off. *I have to get out of here, I have to get out of here*, her brain kept repeating. She hoped Brian would leave her alone if she disappeared again.

She pulled two large suitcases out of the garage and packed as much as she could fit into each one. Then, she drove to the bank, pulled her passport out of her safety deposit box, and withdrew over three thousand dollars in one-hundred-dollar bills. When she got home, she googled foreign countries where they spoke English.

She sat down to make a plane reservation when it hit her that what she was doing was insane. Was she really going to be able to outrun the past? She hid all the money in her clothes and shoes in her closet in case someone robbed her.

Her computer dinged to announce an email. She had a sick feeling it was from Brian. She didn't want to read it but couldn't stop herself. He was determined to see the girls.

There's no way I can tell the girls that for their whole life I lied about their father. I know how much damage not having him around has done to them. Even if I explained that I was protecting them, they'd hate me for all the nights they mourned their father when I could've given them hope.

Carla felt a panic attack coming on. She hadn't had a bad one in years. She got down on the floor with her legs pulled up to her chest in the fetal position. Feeling as if she was about to pass out, she took deep breaths, blew them out slowly, and worked on steadying her heart rate. Then she grabbed a bottle of vodka and wrote back to Brian. She told him that Morgan and Charlie were fine without him and that meeting them would do more harm than good.

At least he doesn't know that Abby exists. The subsequent few emails only got worse. In Brian's final email, he threatened that he would see their daughters no matter what, even if he had to have her arrested for kidnapping them across state lines. Carla knew from police shows that there was no statute of limitations for kidnapping.

She clutched her chest. *I'm going to lose my daughters and go to jail. There's no way to fix this; it's too late, and my girls will never speak to me again. I'd rather die than have them all turn against me.*

Carla was sobbing so hard she could barely find her way to the bathroom. She pulled out the new bottle of Xanax that she kept for emergencies. Things had been going well, so she hadn't taken any in a long time. She took a blanket and curled up on the couch with a pad of paper and a pen. Since the pills were so small, she popped four at a time in her mouth and swigged the Vodka before she could think about what she was doing. Ten minutes later, there were no more pills and much less Vodka. Albert jumped up on the couch next to her.

"Forgive me, Albert," she said, gently patting his head. "I promise you'll find a nice home with someone who'll love you as much as I do." She leaned down and kissed him.

Albert snuggled up into her as if he knew something was off. As she continued talking to him, her words became slurred, and her speech slowed dramatically. Albert licked her face. When she tried to push him away, she couldn't pick up her arms anymore; they were dead weight.

Right before she fell unconscious, her eyes fluttered open. She had a moment of regret for what she was doing.

"I'm so, so tired. Good night, Albert."

Carla closed her eyes for the last time.

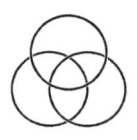

CHAPTER 37

Morgan

Morgan shifted in the plastic chair but couldn't get comfortable. She'd never seen so many people at an AA meeting before. A few latecomers didn't have seats and had to stand in the back of the room.

Morgan had been attending as many meetings as she could since she'd almost fallen off the wagon. Still, she hadn't felt comfortable sharing, which was ironic because AA meetings were where she felt the safest to be vulnerable. She thought about ducking out, but something told her to stay.

When the meeting started, the first speaker shared for fifteen minutes. Three other attendees followed. When there was a momentary break, Morgan began to stand up, then sat back down again. When the hour was almost over, and the meeting seemed to be ending, Morgan, with her pulse racing, pushed her feet firmly into the floor and stood.

"Hi, I'm Morgan, and I'm an alcoholic."

"Hi, Morgan," the others responded.

Morgan couldn't help thinking she would be judged by what she was about to reveal, although AA had taught her that she was the only person in that room who was judging her.

Morgan continued with her eyes cast down. "After recently getting my four-year chip, I'm embarrassed to say that I got very close to drinking last week. I would have gone through with it if my sisters hadn't talked me out of it."

When she looked up, Morgan noticed many people nodding along as she spoke.

"When life gets heavy, and everything seems to crash down on me, all I want to do is hide inside a whiskey bottle. In the past, I got good at convincing myself that alcohol was the solution. I'd drink enough to become numb and hopefully blackout. I'm grateful that my sisters stepped in this last time, but they won't always be there, so I need to be able to stop myself. I'm going to get back into therapy and work through my pain and survive it, which is the only way I know I'll stay sober."

Morgan bowed her head and collapsed back down in her seat. An intense heaviness lifted from her shoulders, replaced by restored energy. Even the chair felt more comfortable under her.

When the meeting concluded after the serenity prayer, several people approached Morgan to thank her for sharing. They, too, had similar stories, reminding her that every day might be a struggle, but all she had to do was get through one day at a time. Going to AA fueled her, and when she spoke and people understood and related to her, it filled her heart.

Several friends had called to get together, but Morgan needed time to reacclimate and take care of her mental health. She also had to start working through her grief. Concentrating on her anger had been a distraction from mourning the loss of her mother and the emptiness that had consumed her life.

Morgan made sure she attended an AA meeting a day and found a new therapist. Rachel worked with her to understand that Carla may not have kept their father away for malicious reasons when they were growing up. As their mother, she thought she was protecting them.

"Imagine how stressful a life your mom led, trying to keep such a huge secret," Rachel said.

Morgan had compassion for her mother, but that didn't stop the little girl inside her who wouldn't have cared if her father gambled. That child had been crying for the man she remembered as a doting and affectionate father.

It took a while, but Morgan's anger lessened. It would be even longer before she could forgive her mom and think of her the way she used to.

When Morgan wasn't at a meeting or in therapy, she caught up on sleep. In the past, she'd always been a night owl; if she got to sleep before one a.m., that was an early night. Now she'd go to bed at eight-thirty and be asleep by nine and then wouldn't wake up until her alarm went off at seven-thirty.

Rachel suggested that when Morgan wakes up in the morning, she writes down her feelings, hopes, and dreams for the future. Morgan was not one of those people who manifested her life; her life fell into her lap like a car crash.

In the past, Morgan had quietly made fun of her friends when they said they were creating a vision board. She thought they were a waste of time, but still, she decided to make one. Morgan pulled out a bunch of old magazines and cut out anything that spoke to her. The words accomplishment, success, inspiration, love, and relationships were the most meaningful. She added pictures of people getting healthier through nutrition and exercise, things she had neglected in her own life.

Then she filled the board with images of people that inspired her: Michelle Obama, Oprah Winfrey, and Princess Diana… Morgan held all these women in high regard for their generosity and giving of their time to various causes. When she filled the entire board, she glued one last thing on it: 2025. This would be the year her mental and physical health would be her main priority.

Little by little, Morgan was no longer the woman who hid from issues but the woman who dealt with them.

One rainy Sunday, when thunder crashed outside her window, and droplets the size of marbles were falling from the sky, she grabbed a cup of coffee and settled back in bed. She reached for one of her old journals and read from the beginning.

The one thing that she had written repeatedly was that she wanted to use her experiences to help others. *I can counsel people on how not to make the same mistakes I made. I'd be good at that.*

She looked at her watch; it was still early. Without thinking, she snatched her phone and dialed. While it rang, she placed the notebook back on the end table. A moment later, she heard her mother's voice on her greeting.

"Hi, this is Carla. I can't come to the phone right now…"

"Shit," she said and hung up, but stared at her phone. "I hate you for leaving me. How can I tell you the good stuff that happens to me or vent about the bad? Why didn't you love me enough to stay here?"

As Morgan sobbed, her phone began ringing. She wasn't going to pick up until she saw it was Charlie. She answered but couldn't say anything.

"Morgan, what's wrong?" Charlie asked.

"Everything," Morgan said.

"You were thinking about Mom, weren't you?"

Morgan nodded as if Charlie could see her.

"It still hits me every night when I get home from work. As soon as I put my keys down, I remember I can't call her and I start crying," Charlie said.

"Are we ever going to feel normal?" Morgan asked. "The grief sits on me and won't move. It's like this bulldozer that refuses to bull or doze---you know what I mean." Morgan took her phone into the bathroom to get a tissue to blow her nose.

"I hate to admit it, but sometimes I wish Rick was around to distract me."

"Please tell me you aren't thinking of going back to him."

"No, but right now I wish I'd waited a little longer to end it."

"Eleven years wasn't long enough. You ended it at the right time," Morgan said, throwing her tissue in the trash and taking iced tea out of the fridge.

"So, other than sobbing uncontrollably, how're you doing?" Charlie asked.

"Let's see…well, I just called Mom." Morgan took a sip of her drink.

"Did she answer?"

Morgan couldn't help but laugh. In the process, she did a spit-take, spewing iced tea all over her pj shirt. "Now look what you made me do," she said as if Charlie could see her.

Morgan tried to wipe the tea off, but the liquid had already soaked in and felt sticky against her skin. She gave up, yanked the shirt over her head, and dropped it on the floor.

"I'm tired of being angry and sad," Morgan said, grabbing another shirt from her bedroom. "I want to feel like me again."

"Wouldn't you rather feel like someone better than you?"

"You can't see this, but I'm sticking my tongue out at you," Morgan said, and she knew Charlie was smiling.

They talked for a while, trying to give each other moral support. After they hung up, Morgan sat at her desk. She placed her glass on top of a file folder that had a stack of papers sticking out of it. Then she remembered what was inside that folder and opened it. She combed through all the research she'd been collecting on how to become an addiction counselor. She had gone over the information many times over the last year but hadn't moved forward.

She signed on to her computer and contacted the admissions offices at a few different colleges around the country that had substance abuse counseling programs. She was ready to move into the future and create the life she wanted for herself.

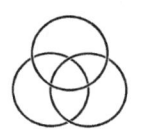

CHAPTER 38

Charlie

Charlie was busy all week with a full load of clients. By Friday night, she didn't want to go anywhere, do anything, or talk to anyone, so she kicked herself for letting her friend Amy talk her into checking out the new escape room in town. Charlie didn't feel like she could cancel, because Amy was so excited and had put in for a reservation the moment she'd heard it was opening.

"This is going to be so much fun," Amy said when they pulled into the parking lot at what looked like a commercial office building.

"I'm not sure my brain will be much use for escaping anything. We could get trapped in the room forever."

"I'm an expert at puzzles. We'll be out in less than thirty minutes, and then we can go for a drink."

"Or we could just go straight to the drinking," Charlie said.

The women lined up at the desk to sign in behind two men. Amy insisted on paying for Charlie, and Charlie didn't have the energy to fight her. The two women put their purses in the lockers against the wall and moved to a bench to wait for instructions. The two men stood a few feet away from them. Five minutes later, an energetic staff member in her early twenties stepped up.

"Hi, my name is Natasha, and I want to welcome you all. Before you go in, there are a few things I want to go over. You'll have sixty minutes to solve all the puzzles and find your way out. Stay in the designated areas and don't use force to move the objects because if you break something, you will be charged. We can hear everything you say, so call out if you get stuck, and a team member will give you a hint. And if there's an emergency, stay calm, and we'll come in immediately."

"Does I have to go to the bathroom count as an emergency?" Charlie whispered to Amy, who stifled a laugh.

"No, it doesn't," Natasha said, then continued. "The theme of tonight's escape room is the sinking of the *Titanic*. Are you ready? If not, I don't care because here we go!" Natasha opened the door. "The timer starts the moment I close this door."

As Charlie and Amy were about to walk into the room, Charlie noticed the two men were also heading in.

"We aren't together," Charlie said to Natasha.

"Oh no, did I double book again?" Natasha said, looking panicked.

"Again?" Charlie said. Then turned to Amy. "Are you sure you want to go in there? We may very well sink."

"We'd be happy to join these women," one of the men said.

"Oh, thank you," Natasha said before Charlie or Amy could reply. "If the owner—my dad—finds out I screwed up, he's going to fire me. Again."

Charlie shot Amy a look that she hoped relayed, 'Let's get out of here right now and get that drink.' Charlie just wanted to hang out with her friend, but she didn't have the interest to be social with men she didn't know.

"It's fine. We love meeting new people," Amy said.

Either Amy didn't understand the look I was giving her, or she could've been pretending not to, Charlie thought, then sighed. *I need to get this people-pleasing thing under control.*

One of the men, wearing a navy T-shirt and distressed jeans, gestured to the women to indicate they should go in first. Charlie and Amy entered, and as soon as the men crossed the threshold, the door slammed behind them. Charlie jumped.

"Tell me that wasn't intimidating," Charlie said.

The room was dimly lit and divided up into various sections of the *Titanic*. One area was decorated as a first-class passenger cabin, another as a lower-class bedroom, and the crew lounge. There was even a chandelier that hung precariously over a replica of the main dining room section.

A loud voice came over a speaker, which Charlie recognized as Natasha. "The timer is on; you have sixty minutes, so you better get moving," she said, then tried to do her best evil laugh but failed to pull it off.

Charlie felt her stomach clench. A ticking clock made her anxiety begin to ramp up. It would have gotten a firm hold on her if the other guy, who had a ponytail and was wearing shorts with flip-flops—even though it was cold—hadn't admitted that he was feeling nervous also.

"I'm Collin," the guy in the navy shirt said, "and this weirdo is Colby."

"I'm Amy, and this weirdo is Charlie," Amy said.

"She doesn't look that weird to me," Collin said.

"Thank you?" Charlie said.

"Stop talking. We need to solve these puzzles, or we're going to drown," Colby said, his voice vibrating with either excitement or doom.

"You do know there's no water here, right?" Collin said.

Amy suggested they start with the puzzle in the first-class cabin section. It was a word puzzle that they needed to solve to open Lady Duff Gordon's trunk. They had to figure out what the initials RMS meant that preceded *Titanic*. Each one of them called out a guess.

"It's Royal...I can't remember what the M stands for," Collin said.

"Mail," Charlie called out. "Try Royal Mail Ship."

Collin did, and the trunk opened. Amy cheered, and they all high-fived. Inside the trunk was a clue to the next puzzle located where the lifeboats were. The group would have to figure out how many passengers would fit into the remaining lifeboats after all the women and children were boarded first.

"I'm one of the many women who are good at math," Charlie said, stepping in front of the others.

"Good, because I'm one of the many men who stink at it," Collin said.

"He's lying. He aced all his classes," Colby said. "He even went on to AP Calculus."

Charlie picked up the passenger manifests left inside the lifeboat and went through them as Collin looked over her shoulder. She calculated the number of people on the ship and the number of lifeboats there were. It took a few minutes, but she solved the puzzle. A porthole opened and the next clue had been wedged inside.

"See, you can do everything by yourself," Amy told Charlie. "You don't need Rick."

"Who's Rick?" Collin asked.

"Charlie's ex. They just broke up." Charlie nudged Amy.

"Just like Collin," Colby said. "He and his girlfriend broke up last week."

Collin shrugged and smiled warmly at Charlie.

As Collin made his way over to the next puzzle in the third-class quarters, Charlie looked at him. Even in this low light, she could see how attractive he was. He had a perfectly oval face with symmetrical features and a dimple on his right cheek. He had stubble on his chin, but the kind that looked sexy, not scratchy. He was thin but not muscular, and she could see the glint of sweat on his forehead, but not one piece of his hair looked damp. Collin reminded her of the guys she dated before she met Rick. The ones who were not athletic, loved to read novels and bent over backward to be accommodating.

Collin turned, and Charlie quickly looked down at the ground. *I've barely been single, and I'm all but drooling over this guy.* She hoped he had not seen her staring at him like a diabetic eyeing a donut.

Charlie emerged from her reverie when a happy yell erupted from Amy, Colby, and Collin. While Charlie was fantasizing, they had solved another puzzle. When Charlie high-fived with Collin, she felt his soft palm against hers. She hoped there were many more puzzles to complete so she could keep touching him. The thought made her skin grow slightly warm.

As Collin walked toward the next puzzle, Charlie slowed down behind him, admiring how his jeans hugged his body. *I need to get ahold of myself here.*

"Ladies first," Collin said, turning around and gesturing for Charlie to go in front of him.

"I'm surprised that this is way more—" Charlie said.

"Fun than you thought it would be?" Collin said, finishing her sentence.

Charlie nodded and laughed.

"You have a great laugh," Collin said. "That guy that broke up with you must be a real moron."

"Actually, I broke up with him."

Collin nodded as if that made much more sense. Charlie continued. "We'd dated for a long time, and it should've ended over seven years ago, but I didn't want to hurt him, so it took me a while to say anything."

"I get that. When I finally ended it with my ex, we both knew it was time to move on."

"How long did you date?" Charlie asked.

"Eight years."

"I got you beat; my ex and I were together for eleven."

"At least you and I finally saw the light."

"And now we're single," Charlie said, then realizing it sounded like she was being more forward than she wanted to be, she blurted out, "I mean, we're unencumbered, not attached--you know what I mean."

"I do," Collin said.

Charlie and Collin kept talking, their conversation flowing easily as if they had all the time in the world. Charlie found herself flirting, something she hadn't done with Rick since the beginning of their relationship. She was glad she remembered how to or hoped she did because otherwise, she had been making a fool of herself. Neither she nor Collin noticed that Colby and Amy had already moved on to the engine room.

"So, what do you do when you aren't trying to escape from a sinking ocean liner?" Collin asked.

"I'm a psychologist," Charlie said.

"Seriously?" Collin laughed.

"Why is that funny?"

"Because I'm a psychiatrist."

"That's wild," Charlie said. "Do you have a card? I'm always looking to refer clients."

He pulled a business card out of his wallet and handed it to her. "I'd love to have your business card, too. I have lots of patients who need talk therapy."

"Mine are in my purse. I'll get you one as soon as we get out of here."

"Hey, you stragglers back there," Colby yelled out, tapping his fist on a table like a nun with a ruler. "Are you planning on helping us with this safe?"

Collin and Charlie shrugged, then joined Colby and Amy. The engine room area was filled with levers and valves and a life-size mannequin of Edward J. Smith, the captain of the *Titanic*.

A voice boomed over the loudspeaker. "You have eight minutes to complete the last puzzle, or you'll feel the icy fingers of the Atlantic," Natasha said, then gave a better, ridiculous, evil laugh.

"Did you hear that?" Colby said.

"Yes, we might actually get out of here," Amy said.

They stood in front of a safe trying various combinations.

"I've been trying to open this for the last five minutes, and none of the numbers I put in are working," Colby said.

"What about the date the Titanic went down?" Abby said.

"I already tried that," Colby said.

"We've come this far; we have to beat the clock," Amy said.

"I know I can do this," Charlie said, pushing her way through.

First, she put in the date the *Titanic* set sail, but the safe didn't open. She looked around the room for any clue that might help. She felt everyone breathing behind her as if their living or dying were on her shoulders. She liked the power that came with that.

Finally, she entered the captain's birthdate. She'd seen it on one of the documents in a lifeboat and remembered it because it was the same date that Morgan was born—or at least the date on her fake birth certificate.

The click of the safe opening echoed through the room, and inside, they found a key to the door. They all looked up at the clock at the same time. There was one minute left to get out. Colby grabbed the key and opened the door as everyone cheered.

"You can't leave until I get a picture of the first people to escape," Natasha said. "Granted, we opened a day and a half ago, but still."

Natasha took a picture of the group, and then they all walked outside. At first, Charlie and Amy were ahead of Collin and Colby, but the closer they got to the parking lot, the closer the guys got to them.

Amy turned. "You guys can follow us, but you should know we don't take strange men home," she said sarcastically.

Charlie held her hands at her side because she wanted to smack Amy, although she should've been used to it. Amy loved to embarrass her.

"Good to know," Collin said, smiling at Charlie. Charlie smiled back.

"We're just going to our car," Colby said. "It's right there." He pointed to a black Corolla in a parking garage filled with cars.

"How funny, our car is right next to yours," Charlie said, pointing to Amy's Nissan Sentra. *I wonder if that's what they call kismet,* she thought.

Amy got into her car, but Charlie dawdled. "Bye," Charlie said, her eyes on Collin as she slowly opened the passenger door. Before she got in, she reached into her purse. "Oh, I forgot. Here's my business card," she handed it to him.

"Great," Collin said. "And please let me know if you have any referrals for me."

You can bet I will, Charlie thought, but only nodded and waved goodbye.

Amy turned on the car and started backing out of the parking space. "Someone has a crush," Amy said.

"I don't even know him," Charlie said, not sounding convincing to her ears. Charlie couldn't tell how much of the stirring inside her was caused by excitement or how much from hunger, but she figured it was mostly the former.

"He's cute. Even the wax ship captain in the boiler room could see he was into you," Amy said as she drove down the street.

"He was *just* being friendly," Charlie said, while thinking she hoped that wasn't true.

The following day, Charlie was about to pick up her next client from the waiting room when she noticed a voicemail alert on her phone. Something inside her told her to listen to it. When she hit play and heard Collin's voice, she grinned.

"Hey, it's Collin…from yesterday… I just wanted to ask you a professional question. No, that's a lie…I wanted to say I had a nice time meeting you. No, that's a lie, too. I mean, I did have a nice time meeting you, but I meant I was lying about why I called. Oh, God, can I erase this message and start over?

I sound like an idiot." Charlie heard him take a breath, then he continued. "Okay, I called to see if you wanted to meet for coffee this week. You're probably busy or possibly met someone and got married, but if you have any time and are still single, call me. Then again, you don't even have to be single. Just kidding, please call me. Did I say it's Collin…from the escape room." Charlie heard him groan, and then he hung up.

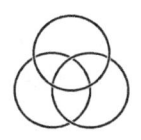

CHAPTER 39

Abby

A week later, Abby sat in her first improv class in years, located in the theater department of the local high school. Three people stood in the center of a small wooden stage, lit by a few overhead lights. In the corner was an open trunk packed with props, a horse mask lying on the top.

As she watched the actors on stage, Abby started second-guessing why she had signed up for this class in the first place. She'd always been intrigued by improv but had been nervous about attempting it. The thought of failing miserably on her very first night made her queasy. *How could I compete with these people who've been doing this for years?* She looked at her watch and wondered what story Alex had read to the kids that night. *I should be home putting the kids to bed. I still have time to sneak out.* She was sure the door was beckoning her.

Before she could decide, the other students clapped for the actors who exited the stage and were replaced by two more. Abby noticed that the instructor, Milo, was standing next to her.

"You're next up, Abby," Milo said, glancing at her name tag.

"Can't I just observe since this is my first class?" she asked.

"Those who only watch don't learn. You don't have to be good; we're just having fun here," Milo said.

Abby's hands grew clammy, and as she stood up, she wiped them on her jeans. She walked toward the stage like a turtle in a relay race. The two students, a man and a woman, were waiting for her. Abby guessed they were probably in their twenties. *How can I feel ancient when I'm only thirty?* She glanced at their name tags, Meredith and Tom. Milo told them to improvise a job interview and assigned Tom as the interviewer and Abby and Meredith as the applicants. The two women would be applying for employment as a zombie killer. Tom and Meredith seemed ready to go, but Abby looked down at the floor and said nothing.

"Miss, what qualifications do you think you have that would make you an expert zombie killer?" Tom asked.

When Meredith didn't answer, Abby realized Tom was talking to her. She blurted out the first thing that came into her brain. "I have four kids."

Laughter and clapping exploded in the room. Abby looked at Milo who was nodding his approval. She lifted her chin and gazed out at the audience, marveling at the other students who seemed to be enjoying themselves. Her posture became erect, and her voice grew louder with each line she threw out. By the end of the exercise, the student's rapturous applause made her giddy. Abby returned to her seat, smiling so widely that the muscles in her cheeks hurt.

"I'm having a hard time believing that you've never done improv before," Milo said.

"Being a mom, I've had to make things up to get my kids to do their chores. I hadn't thought of it as improv before; I thought it was just lying," she said.

Abby couldn't believe how much she enjoyed the class; she already couldn't wait to return. When Milo dismissed them, he asked that they bring in five to ten prompts for the following week. Abby already had some ideas.

As Abby walked to her car, she looked at her phone. A voicemail from Morgan had come in, so she hit the play button to listen to the message.

"Hey, I hope things at home are good. I just got a call from Mom's lawyer that we need to go back to Los Angeles and clean out her house so it can be put on the market. Charlie and I think it's a good idea because we can pay off the mortgage and split the equity after it sells. We can all use the money. If it's not a good time, Charlie and I can do it without you. Call me when you have a chance to discuss it. Bye."

Abby put the phone back in her purse and got into her car. It hadn't crossed her mind that they'd have to sell the place where they grew up in. They had lost their mom, and now they were going to lose their childhood home. She knew keeping it didn't make sense when none of them lived nearby.

As if watching a movie montage, Abby saw her sisters and mother lighting the Hanukkah candles in the living room, all their Passover Seders, and the birthday parties they had in their backyard. The memories came crashing down on her, and her chest ached.

By the time Abby got home, it was after nine o'clock, and Alex had fallen asleep on the couch with Emma on his chest. Emma opened her eyes and reached out her arms to Abby, who, as smoothly as possible, picked her up and took her to her crib. She covered Emma with a quilt and gave her what felt like a thousand kisses on her tiny cheeks and forehead. Abby breathed in her sweet baby smell and knew someday it would be gone, replaced by teenage sweat and dirty socks. She wished her daughter sweet dreams, then closed the door and went back into the living room.

Abby looked at Alex with his legs curled up to his butt, happily sleeping. She felt a silly grin cross her lips, and her heart filled with pride that this man was hers. She wanted to reach out and run her hands through his hair, but she didn't want to wake him; he looked so peaceful. She gently lay down next to him, wanting to feel the warmth of his body against hers. She took in the fragrance of his aftershave and lightly brushed Cheez-Its crumbs off his shirt. Alex didn't awaken, but he must've sensed she was there because he rolled over and laid his head on her chest, and she closed her eyes.

When she woke up, Alex was gazing at her.

"What time is it?" Abby asked.

Alex looked at his watch. "Three forty-five. How was class?"

"Amazing. I'll tell you all about it in the actual morning." Abby rolled off the couch. "Let's go to bed before our favorite people wake up," she said.

When they got into their room, Abby was so tired she didn't have the energy to change into her pajamas. She took off her pants and crawled under the covers in just her T-shirt and panties. She kissed Alex before turning over to get as much sleep as she could before the light came through the blinds and little feet clomped on the floor.

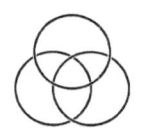

CHAPTER 40

Morgan

Morgan hated being late. She rushed up to Carla's front door, breathing heavily as if she had run from the airport. Unaware that Abby was opening the door, Morgan pushed it hard. Abby jumped back to avoid getting hit in the face.

"Jeez, Morgan," Abby said.

"I'm sorry," Morgan said, dragging her suitcase inside the house. "My flight sat on the tarmac for three hours in Oregon. Some idiot locked himself in the bathroom and kept saying he wouldn't come out until he was bumped up to first class. I don't get why he didn't tell the gate agent that it was his birthday, so if they have an extra seat, he'd appreciate getting upgraded."

Abby hugged her and said, "Well, you're here now."

"Morgan, does that tactic work?" Charlie asked as she wrapped a vase in bubble wrap.

"Yes, I've had three birthdays this year." Morgan pulled her suitcase into the corner of the living room and then took in the sea of moving boxes. "Thanks for getting started on all this."

"No problem," Abby said. "But we've still got a lot more to pack."

"And we don't much time before the painters come." Charlie said.

Abby took a framed print of *Starry Night* off the wall. "Does anyone want the pretend Van Gogh?" she asked.

"I don't, but I'll take the pretend Monet. I love *Water Lilies*," Charlie said, pulling a different painting off the wall.

Morgan surveyed all the empty wall space. "This is depressing," she said.

Charlie picked up three bronzed baby shoes off the side table. "I can't believe Mom kept these."

"I don't get why she had them made in the first place," Morgan said. "I doubt we'd get anything for them at our garage sale."

"You never know," Abby said, putting a few candles in a box "The last time I had a yard sale, some woman wanted only one of my garden gloves. Then another woman heard her and asked if she could buy the other one. I made seventy-five cents apiece."

"How do you think Mom would feel about us selling so many of the things she worked hard for?" Morgan said.

"I doubt she thought about it when she killed herself," Charlie said.

Morgan's throat constricted as if a piece of food had gotten lodged inside. "I just want to get all this behind us," she said, taking two table lamps to the garage. Abby and Charlie followed her, carrying a box filled with once-treasured knick-knacks.

"Charlie, what is Collin up to while you're here?" Abby asked as they headed back inside to pack more boxes.

"Collin? What's a Collin?" Morgan asked.

"A guy I've been seeing," Charlie said.

"You're dating someone, and I haven't heard anything about him," Morgan said.

"I told Abby before you got here," Charlie said. "If you weren't late, you would've heard the whole story."

"Early bird gets the gossip," Abby said. "Charlie thinks he's the one."

"Don't you think you're buying the food before getting the refrigerator, Charlie?" Morgan asked.

"When you know, you know," Charlie said.

"Then how do you explain the eleven years you spent with Rick?" Morgan asked, heading to the kitchen. Charlie and Abby grabbed empty boxes and followed her. Morgan pulled out the blender, a food processor, and some pots and pans and placed them on the counter.

"I'm a slow learner," Charlie said.

"I knew right away with Alex," Abby said, grabbing some crackers from the cabinet.

"Hey, hand me some of those," Charlie said. "I'm starving." Abby held the box out to Charlie, who stuffed a few in her mouth, the crumbs escaping and falling onto the floor.

"Can you two stop snacking and start helping?" Morgan asked.

Charlie and Abby each ate another cracker, then opened cabinets and piled baking pans, platters, and the waffle maker on the countertop. Morgan rushed to get everything into boxes before they ran out of room on the counter and had to heap things onto the floor.

Hours later, moving boxes filled the garage, and the kitchen was empty except for what they'd need for the next few days. Morgan wiped the counters down.

"I'll get the vacuum," Morgan said, heading to the hall closet.

Charlie and Abby went into the living room. While Charlie took the framed photos off the bookshelves, Abby arranged the books by color, and Morgan began to vacuum. The vacuum's low hum echoed off the empty walls. First, Morgan went over the hardwood floor and then pushed the vacuum onto the rug.

"Can you guys help me move the couch?" Morgan asked. "I hope Albert's hair hasn't mixed with the dust bunnies and created a new creature."

Charlie and Abby each took a side of the couch.

"One, two, three, lift," Morgan said. Charlie and Abby grunted as they pulled it onto the hardwood floors.

Abby reached down, picking up something on the carpet. "I just found a Lego," she said, holding it up. "Oh, cool. It's my mini figure of Yoda. I always wondered where that went." She blew the dust off it.

"Mom couldn't have moved this couch in years," Charlie said.

Morgan noticed a small piece of blank paper lying on the ground. She picked it up, turned it over, and immediately recognized her mother's writing, although it was messier than usual. As Morgan read to herself what was on the paper, her face went slack, and she began to cry. Abby and Charlie stared at her.

"What's the matter?" Abby asked.

Morgan couldn't say anything; she just kept crying.

"Morgan?" Charlie's hand shook as she took the paper away from Morgan. Tears streamed down Charlie's cheeks as she scanned what was written.

"What is it?" Abby asked.

"It's a suicide note," Morgan said, finally getting the words out.

"Oh my God," Abby said, taking the note from Charlie and reading it out loud.

My dear, sweet daughters, by the time you read this, you probably already know I've been lying to you about your father. I lied to him, too. He didn't have any clue that I was pregnant with Abby when I took you and ran away. I am so sorry for all the damage I caused in your lives by not letting you have your father. I know that the three of you will be so angry at me that you'll cut me out of your life, and I don't blame you, but I can't live with that. I'd rather disappear than be on this earth knowing my girls hate me. I love you all so much and I'm sorry for all the pain I caused.

Abby barely got through the final sentence before she began sobbing.

"I didn't think I had any more tears in me," Abby said.

Morgan handed her a tissue, and she blew her nose. "So, Brian is my father," Abby said.

"I'm glad," Morgan said.

Charlie's crying stopped. "Mom makes it sound like she had no choice, but she always had a choice. She could've told us the truth; the lie wasn't worth ending her life over."

"Didn't she know we would've forgiven her if she'd been honest with us?" Morgan asked.

"She thought it was too late," Abby said.

"It's never too late," Morgan said. "We would've been mad, but we would've gotten through it. There's no way we would have stopped speaking to her."

"I guess she didn't trust that," Abby said.

"How could she not know how much we loved her," Charlie said.

Morgan sat down on the couch. "Part of me feels sorry for Mom," she said.

"I don't," Charlie said. "She made life-changing choices for us."

"And that was wrong, but when Brian found her after all that time, she must've felt trapped," Morgan said. "And then he threatened her."

"If Alex hid my kids from me for thirty years, I'd go far beyond threatening him," Abby said.

"I agree with Abby," Charlie said. "Not being a good husband is different than him being a bad father. When we turned eighteen, we should've been able to decide whether we wanted contact with him."

"Exactly. Mom left him; we didn't," Abby said. "My entire life I thought he abandoned us after I was born. That royally screwed me up in so many ways," Abby kicked a box.

"Mom thought she was protecting us from him," Morgan said.

"Why are you defending her?" Charlie asked.

Morgan shrugged. "I can't be mad at her for doing what she thought was right. Besides, she's dead, so it's stupid for us to be angry."

"Are you saying we're stupid to feel pissed off and betrayed?" Charlie said.

"Just because you can pretend things didn't happen doesn't mean we can," Abby said.

"We can't change what Mom did. We need to move on," Morgan said.

"Yeah, you've always been good at running away from problems," Charlie said.

"How dare you?" Morgan said.

"That's why you got drunk," Charlie said. "So, you wouldn't have to deal with anything."

"Don't think you can analyze me just because you're a therapist," Morgan said.

"I don't have to be a therapist to recognize the toll your drinking took on our family," Charlie said. "It used to make me so mad how Mom would always clean up your messes. I told her she should let you hit rock bottom, but she was sure she could help you."

"I never asked her to help," Morgan said, her voice rising.

"Well, you got her attention," Charlie said.

"She was always taking care of you," Abby said. "She forgot to pick me up from elementary school once because she got called to come to your school when you showed up drunk. And she had to leave in the middle of two high school plays I starred in to get you from the police station."

"And she almost missed my grad school commencement when you disappeared for two days, and she couldn't find you," Charlie said.

"I didn't know that," Morgan said.

"Because you were too drunk to notice or care how you were affecting us," Charlie said.

"I need some air," Morgan said, picking up her phone and keys and walking toward the front door.

"Yep, run away," Charlie said. "Just like Mom did."

Morgan slammed the door without looking back.

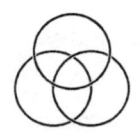

CHAPTER 41

Charlie

Morgan had been out past when Charlie fell asleep, but Charlie hadn't stayed awake worrying. If Morgan ended up in a bar again, that was on her. A part of Charlie felt guilty that she had gone after Morgan, but another part thought Morgan needed to hear it. Morgan had never acknowledged how much stress she had added to their household.

The following morning, Charlie made herself coffee and then went back into her bedroom to finish boxing up the rest of her old belongings. Carla hadn't touched the room since Charlie moved out other than to change her twin bed to a queen. The wallpaper was still the same pattern, with colorful butterflies flying around a blue sky with white clouds in the background. Charlie had been obsessed with butterflies; she identified with their transition from ungainly wiggly caterpillars into beautiful creatures that soared. Everything she bought when she was younger had butterflies, her purses, earrings, and a turquoise necklace.

Charlie had not opened all her desk drawers in years. Inside one, she found her prize ribbons from elementary school when she competed in gymnastics. She was promising but quit as soon as she grew breasts. A few years ago, she attempted to do a cartwheel, hurt her back, and was laid up for a week.

In another drawer were her high school yearbooks and notebooks covered in doodles she drew when she was bored. She opened one and realized she had saved her tenth-grade U.S. History notes.

Before she had put all her photo albums in a box, she grabbed her prom picture out of one of the sleeves. She knew Collin would crack up when he saw her hair in tight curls and she loved that he'd make fun of her date in his powder blue tux. She could already hear Collin's warm, heartfelt laugh in her mind.

Collin had infiltrated her life in the best way. After their first date, Charlie decided he was it for her, and she would marry him immediately if he asked, which was entirely out of character for her. She realized she had stayed with Rick because he wouldn't commit, which was ideal because she didn't trust men. Collin had overcome that distrust in a remarkably short time. When Charlie thought about the future with him, instead of scaring her senseless, her body ached with excitement, and she felt herself smiling so big and bright that she imagined she must look like the smiling, open-mouthed emoji with heart eyes.

She and Collin had gone out six times in the past two weeks. On their first date, they went for sushi. Charlie loved sushi, but Rick hated it, so he'd never go with her. On the date with Collin, she held up a piece of tuna sashimi as if it were a live puppet.

"Hi, Collin," she said while the piece of fish flopped all over the place. "Is something fishy here?"

Collin picked up his piece of salmon. "I can't tell if anything is fishy because I have no eyes," he said.

Charlie laughed so hard she knocked her water glass over. A bunch of ice scattered across the table, one piece landing in Collin's lap. He flicked it at her, and she cracked up even more. She knew they were being immature, but she'd forgotten how much she enjoyed being silly with a man. If she had ever acted that way with Rick, he would have looked away and made it clear that she had embarrassed him.

When Charlie finished packing up her room, she looked at the barren space and felt a familiar melancholy she had unfortunately gotten used to. Before she could sink into it, she heard a knock at the door.

"Come in," Charlie called out.

"Hey," Morgan said, opening the door but remaining in the doorway.

"Hey," Charlie said.

"Are you still mad at me?"

"No. I shouldn't have said anything."

"I wish you'd said it a long time ago," Morgan said. "Can we talk?"

Charlie cocked her head in a gesture for Morgan to come in. Charlie stood up and joined Morgan, who had sat on the bed.

"I hadn't thought about what I put you and Abby through," Morgan said.

"I know you didn't. And I don't hold it against you...most of the time," Charlie said.

"I made amends with Mom a long time ago, and I know she forgave me, but I didn't with you and Abby. That was wrong, and I'm deeply sorry."

Charlie could see how sincere Morgan was. Charlie looked up, and noticed Abby had been standing in the doorway. Abby walked into the room, sat beside Morgan on the bed, and put her arm around her.

"We've all gone through things," Abby said to Morgan. "You drank, Charlie stayed with Rick, and I married the first boy who was nice to me. Even though Alex is—"

Morgan cut her off. "The greatest man who ever lived. Yes, yes, we know."

"It's going to take time for us to come to terms with the damage both our parents did to us," Charlie said.

"I've had enough emotional upheaval in my life," Morgan said. "It's better for my mental health to put all the anger behind me."

"We're all entitled to our feelings," Abby said, then turned to Charlie. "Just because you and I are upset doesn't mean Morgan has to be—even if she's wrong," Abby smirked.

The sisters sat for a moment, each bathed in their own thoughts until the silence was broken by the chime on the clock in the living room. It played Greensleeves every time it hit the hour.

"That clock is the worst," Morgan said, then turned to Charlie. "I told Mom to leave it to you in her will."

"Ha ha," Charlie said. "Mom used to tell me if I ever came home after curfew, she'd make me sleep in the living room as a punishment."

"I always wanted to stomp on it, but I didn't know how I'd explain how my foot had climbed that far up the wall *accidentally*," Morgan said.

"I miss Mom and the crazy ways she disciplined us," Abby said.

"Me, too. And now we're sad orphans," Morgan said.

"We still have a father out there," Charlie said.

"We should call him again," Abby said.

"The realtor is coming by with a photographer soon, so let's call him after they leave," Morgan said.

"I still have a few more things in my room to pack up," Abby said.

"I'll finish going through the books in Mom's office," Morgan said.

"I finished my room, so I'm going to nap. If I don't get a few minutes of sleep, I'm going to kill myself," Charlie said, then cringed. "Sorry, poor choice of words."

Morgan and Abby chuckled and then their laughter got louder and slightly hysterical. Charlie joined in, and they laughed so hard that Abby fell off the bed.

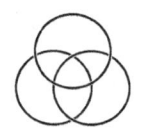

CHAPTER 42

Abby

After the agent and the photographer had left, Abby surveyed the house trying to see it from a buyer's perspective. There was nothing personal left. No family pictures on the mantel and none of the funny magnets on the refrigerator from the road trip they all took to Yosemite. Even the Hanukkah dish towel Carla kept out year-round because the girls had saved up to buy it for her was in a box in the garage. Their childhood had disappeared, and now the house seemed sterile and plain. Charlie came into the living room.

"It looks like no one has ever lived here," Abby pouted.

"You get more money for a house that looks like Mr. Clean owned it," Charlie said. "It will be perfect for some new family to start their own traditions in."

"I'm going to miss all the holidays we celebrated here."

"Me, too,"

Morgan came in from the garage. "I took the last box out. Hopefully, no one goes into the garage, or they'll disappear amongst the boxes, and never be seen again."

"Hey, Abby, why don't you go out there?" Charlie said.

"You just ruined our special moment," Abby said.

"It's still a special moment. It's just a special moment for me now," Charlie said and Abby laughs.

"Hey, if you two are finished, we could call Brian now," Morgan said.

The sisters sat side by side on the couch. Abby put her phone in the middle of the coffee table, dialed Brian's number, and hit the speaker.

"Hi," Brian said. "Can you give me a second?"

"If this is a bad time, we could call you back," Charlie said.

"No," he sounded panicked. They heard shuffling, and then his voice was back. "It's fine; I'm here," he said. "I'm so glad you called."

"We have a few more things we wanted to ask you," Abby said.

"Of course, but before you do, there's something that has been weighing on me." He paused for a moment, then continued. "Once I found your mother, I was desperate to meet my daughters. I shouldn't have threatened her, but I never thought she'd do something so drastic," he said, his voice breaking. "I'm so sorry."

"None of this is your fault," Morgan said.

"I still feel like I'm somehow responsible. I'm devastated that I made her think she had no choice."

"You didn't *make* our mother do anything. She had to have known we'd be devastated losing her, yet she still left us," Charlie said pursing her lips together.

"We found her suicide note," Morgan said.

"You did?"

"She admitted you didn't know she was pregnant with me when she left," Abby said. "I'm your daughter."

"That makes me so happy, Abby," Brian said. "I can't believe I was looking for two daughters and found three."

"Mom hid a lot from all of us," Morgan said.

"I'm a parent," Abby said, "I know it would destroy me if I couldn't see my kids."

"I have grandchildren?" Brian asked.

"You have four," Abby said.

"Oh wow," Brian said, "I've always wanted grandchildren."

"Be careful what you wish for," Charlie said, and Abby lightly elbowed her.

"I've been thinking about something since we last talked, and I want to run it by you all," he said. "Please feel free to say no if it's too much. How would you guys feel if I flew out there to see you?"

Abby looked at Morgan and Charlie, but before any of them could say anything, Brian blurted out. "No problem. If you're not comfortable, it's okay. I don't want to intrude."

"We would be thrilled to have you come here," Abby said.

"Really?" he said, and Abby could hear the smile in his voice. "That's great. I'll get a plane reservation and let you know when I'll be there." Brian exhaled as if he'd been underwater and had come up for air.

They all said goodbye, and Abby hit the button to hang up.

"I guess we're no longer orphans," Charlie said. "Unless he comes and realizes he doesn't like us."

"That's impossible, we're all likable," Morgan said. "Except maybe Abby—he's never met her."

Abby couldn't help but laugh. "We have a dad!" Abby said.

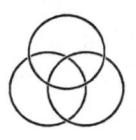

CHAPTER 43

Morgan

Four days later, Morgan awoke before the sun came up. She tried to go back to sleep but knowing that her father would be there that afternoon made her whole body vibrate with anticipation, nerves, and anxiety. She hoped she wouldn't throw up. She put on her best sundress and cleaned the house, even though they had someone come in and do a deep cleaning a few days before. Dusting kept her mind busy.

When the doorbell rang, Abby and Morgan jumped up as if they had just won the lottery. Charlie followed slowly behind.

When they got to the front door, Charlie held up her hand. "We have no idea who this man really is. You two need to calm down."

"Screw that," Abby said, flinging the door open.

Brian stood on the doorstep in nice black slacks and a white button-up shirt.

"Hi," he said, "If I got the address right, I'm your father." He ran his fingers through what little hair he had left. He had wisps of light brown on the sides of his head but was completely bald on top, and he had lines on his face from a hard life. Morgan remembered a more youthful father, with all his hair and no wrinkles etched around his eyes. *The last time he saw me, I was so young; I looked different, too,* she thought.

"I'm Morgan."

"And I'm Charlie or Charlotte."

Abby stepped forward. "I'm Abby, the one you placed in a womb but never knew."

"It's so nice to meet all of you," Brian said, then turned to Abby. "My grandmother's name was Abby. Carla loved her, and she adored Carla."

"Really? I was named after someone?" Abby said.

"Would it be okay if I hugged you all at some point?" Brian asked.

"Sure," Abby said, and Morgan nodded.

They stepped towards Brian, but Morgan noticed Charlie was silent and didn't move toward him. Clearly, Charlie had reservations, but for Morgan, hugging her father didn't feel awkward; it felt natural.

"Why don't we let Brian come inside," Abby said, almost pushing her sisters out of the way so he could enter.

"Thank you." Brian walked in and looked around. "Nice house. Is this where you grew up?"

"Yes," Abby said. "And we wish we didn't have to sell it."

"If I could afford to buy it myself, I would," Morgan said.

"But you live in Oregon," Abby said.

"I've been toying with the idea of moving back here," Morgan said. "Cal State Northridge has a great addiction counselor program, but it's expensive to rent in Los Angeles. I might have to stay in Oregon and go to Portland State University."

"Have you had any offers on the house yet?" Brian asked.

"No," Morgan said. "The agent said it should go fast, though."

"Can I get you something to drink?" Abby asked as they led Brian into the living room.

"Water would be great," he said. He sat in a chair across from where Morgan and Charlie were sitting. Abby brought in four bottles of water and sat next to her sisters on the couch.

Sitting in a row across from Brian, the sisters looked like they were employers appraising his qualifications for a job. Brian seemed uncomfortable in his dress clothes, and Morgan wondered if he had gotten dressed up for their first meeting. After all, she and her sisters had looked their best. Morgan even put on more makeup than she normally wore during the day, and Abby and Charlie had spent last night picking out their outfits. Abby curled her hair, and Charlie had on her favorite necklace and earrings.

"How was your flight?" Charlie asked just for something to break the silence.

"It was fine," Brian said, staring at them. After a pause, he continued, "I can't believe I'm in the same room with my daughters. I'm so grateful you let me come here. I didn't think this would ever happen."

"Since we were told you were dead, we never thought it would happen either," Morgan said.

"What did you do when you realized we were all gone?" Abby asked.

"The first thing I did was call Carla's mother. I hoped that's where Carla had gone, but Beverly had no idea where Carla was, and she was incensed that Carla hadn't called her in a few days. That same afternoon when I got served with divorce papers, I still thought your mom must be bluffing, but quickly, I realized she meant it."

"You must've been devastated," Abby said.

Brian nodded. "I'd lost everyone I cared about at once. And then six months after you were gone, my dad passed away from a heart attack, and five months after that, my mother died in a car accident,"

"That's so sad," Charlie said.

"It took a while, but eventually I realized I was responsible for ruining my life, and I had to change. I moved to Connecticut, and got help. It's been a struggle, but I haven't gambled since."

"I'm glad you got support," Morgan said. "I'm in AA."

"I hope you didn't get the addiction gene from me," Brian said.

"I might have, but more so, I think it was not having my father around," Morgan said.

"If I could go back and change it all, I would," Brian said. He picked up his bottle of water and chugged down half of it.

"Our mom made choices for you," Abby said.

"But if he hadn't lost all their money and put us in danger, she wouldn't have left," Charlie said.

"Charlie!" Abby said, loudly.

"It's true. Mom had to take care of us all on her own," Morgan said.

"It's okay, Abby," Brian said. "Charlie and Morgan are right."

"We can't change the past, and at this point, I just want my father in my life," Abby said.

"Me too," Morgan said.

Brian looked expectantly at Charlie.

After a moment, Charlie said, "I'm willing to try, but it might take me a little longer."

"Take all the time you need," Brian said. "I'm not going anywhere; I plan to make up for the last thirty years."

Morgan launched into every question she'd thought of since she found out he was alive. She wanted to know his favorite color, what music he enjoyed, and what he did for a living. She needed to find a connection she could build on. Brian answered each question with specificity and details.

They talked for hours until the outside porch light clicked on.

"Do you want to stay for dinner?" Abby asked. "I could make something, although we only have eggs and bacon right now."

"That's sweet of you, but I'll head back to the hotel. I don't want to overstay my welcome on the first day."

"Will you come for brunch tomorrow?" Abby asked.

"I'd love to," Brian said, standing up. The sisters walked him to the door. "Would it be okay if I hugged you all again?"

"Sure," Morgan said, stepping forward. Abby followed, with Charlie stepping up last. Brian's expression looked as if he'd won the lottery.

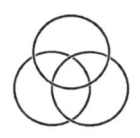

CHAPTER 44

Charlie

When Charlie dressed the next morning, she wore her favorite pink flowered dress. She was happy that she had a good reason to wear it. While Morgan made a vegetable frittata, Charlie arranged bagels, lox, and cream cheese on a platter. Charlie knew her sisters were as overwhelmed as she was since the only sounds in the room were the steady whir of the coffee grinder's blades crushing the beans into dust and the refrigerator constantly opening and closing.

The women had brought in some of Carla's things from the garage so they could make brunch special. Although having empty counters worked for home buyers, Charlie felt the room was barren and cold, like she needed a blanket and slippers whenever she wanted a snack.

Abby put the ground coffee in the coffeemaker and hit start. Within thirty seconds, Charlie could smell the coffee brewing, and her mouth watered.

At ten o'clock sharp, when they opened the door to Brian, he smiled warmly. He held a bouquet of white hydrangeas in one hand and a manila envelope in the other. This time, he was dressed in jeans and tennis shoes. Charlie noticed his Nirvana T-shirt. *I like this casual father more than the one who was here yesterday. And he has great taste in music.*

"It's me again," Brian beamed. "You said not to bring anything, but I didn't want to show up empty-handed." He gave Charlie the flowers and she thanked him.

"Come on in, breakfast is just about ready," Morgan said. Since the vases were all in boxes in the garage, Charlie went to grab a tall glass from the cabinet.

On the table was a linen tablecloth the color of lush foliage in an emerald forest, Carla's best china, and cream linen napkins at the side of each place setting. Silver candlesticks with candles to match the tablecloth sat in the center.

"Is all this for me?" Brian asked.

"No, we're expecting the President of France," Charlie said, and Morgan and Abby laughed.

"Cool, I'm honored to get to dine with him."

Abby brought the platter of bagels in from the kitchen in one hand and the frittata in another.

"Can I help?" Brian said, jumping up.

"Thanks, but this is nothing. I feed four starving kids and a husband three meals a day. I could carry this, do laundry, and walk the dog at the same time."

Brian sat back down and put his napkin on his lap. "I feel like a king," he said.

"Then you'll get along with the French President," Charlie said.

"I hope he likes me," he said.

"If he doesn't, then you have to go." Charlie chuckled, then froze and pressed her lips together in a slight grimace.

I hope he knows I'm joking, she thought, then her shoulders relaxed when she saw he was snickering.

Morgan poured coffee for everyone and sat. Charlie reached into the middle of the table for the creamer at the same time as Brian did, and their hands touched. Brian's strong hand made Charlie think about what it must've been like to have him hold her as a child. Brian gestured for her to use the half-and-half first.

After brunch, everyone pitched in to clean up the table. Brian insisted on washing the dishes, so Morgan dried them, and Abby put them away. Charlie shook out the tablecloth and threw it in the washing machine.

"What's in the envelope?" Abby asked.

"Pictures of Morgan and Charlie when they were little."

"Oh," Abby said, trying to hide her frown.

"I wish I had some of you too, Abby."

"It's okay, how could you," Abby said.

Charlie could tell Abby was trying to rally back from the disappointment. Brian opened the envelope and scattered about twenty pictures onto the table. "This is everything I have. Carla took the rest with her when she left," Brian said.

There were a few shots from Brian and Carla's wedding, some of Brian holding Morgan the day she was born, some of him holding Charlie, one of Brian and Morgan in the park in Brooklyn, and one of Brian holding Charlie up to help her blow out the candles at her first birthday party. When they got to the family photos of only the four of them, Charlie noticed Abby was barely glancing at them.

"Are you okay?" Charlie asked Abby.

"It hurts that you're both in these pictures, and there aren't any of me."

"I hate that, too," Brian said. "I would've been so proud to bring you home from the hospital when you were born."

Morgan put her arm around Abby. "Mom has a lot of pictures of you," Morgan said to her. "Why don't you grab one of the photo albums in the garage so Brian can see what you looked like back then."

"That would be great!" Brian said.

"Okay," Abby said and went out to the garage.

"She was a cute baby," Charlie said.

"She was. She looked just like me," Morgan said.

"That's so not true," Charlie said, holding up a picture of Morgan as an infant. "Abby didn't have your giant pumpkin head—that's unique to you."

"At least I didn't have a big toe that was longer than all the rest," Morgan said.

"You girls are a riot. I bet your mom had a blast watching you grow up." He looked away, his eyes misting up.

Abby came back in carrying a couple of photo albums. She regaled Brian with pictures and stories of her from birth to college.

"Can I take a couple of these? I promise to give them back. I want to make copies."

"Sure, which ones?" Abby asked.

Brian picked out all the pictures that were milestones in Abby's life. "It's heartbreaking knowing I wasn't there for any of you. I couldn't dry your tears when you were sad or laugh at your favorite jokes. And I wish I could've helped out financially. I would've happily paid for your education."

"I still have loans from grad school," Charlie said.

"How much?" he asked.

"I'm kidding; I paid them off a long time ago. You don't need to give us anything," Charlie said.

"But I have a lot to make up to you guys."

"We're fine," Morgan said. "Our mom may have screwed up with you, but she was amazing to us. We had everything we needed."

"Except a father," Charlie said.

"Except for a father," Abby conceded.

As the morning turned to afternoon and the clock struck three o'clock, Brian gathered all the pictures back in the envelope and stood up.

"I should get going and let you all relax." As they walked him to the door, he asked if he could take them to lunch the next day, and they readily agreed.

"He seems like a good person," Morgan said as the front door closed. "I wonder how different we would be if he'd been a part of our entire life."

"If I could've gone to him for advice, maybe I would've had the self-respect to break up with Rick a long time ago," Charlie said.

"And I would've had a dad to walk me down the aisle and dance with me at my wedding," Abby said.

"I feel for him," Morgan said. "It must've been heart-wrenching for him to know we were out there somewhere, but he couldn't find us."

"I judged him too quickly," Charlie said. "Even though he made mistakes, I need to give him a second chance."

"I can't wait for him to meet his grandchildren," Abby said.

"We just got him back. Maybe you should ease him in slowly," Morgan said.

"You're mean," Abby said.

"Your kids are adorable," Morgan said. Then, without Abby seeing, she shook her head at Charlie, who covered her mouth, trying but not succeeding in stifling a laugh.

"What?" Abby said.

"Nothing," Charlie said. "I was agreeing with Morgan about how cute they all are," Charlie said.

"So cute that I'm getting my tubes tied soon," Morgan mugged and stuck out her tongue at Abby.

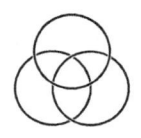

CHAPTER 45

Abby

Abby grabbed a sweater from her suitcase and called to Morgan and Charlie. "We need to go, or we're going to be late for lunch with Brian."

As they walked to the front door, Abby's cell phone rang. "Hello," she said. "Oh, hi, Jennifer, hold on a sec." Abby mouthed the words 'real estate agent' to her sisters. They hurried over and huddled around her as she put her phone on speaker.

"Okay, we're all here," Abby said.

"Good," Jennifer said. "A great offer just came in on the house. It's all cash, full asking price, a twenty-day escrow with no contingencies, and the buyer wants to keep all the furniture."

"Really?" Morgan said.

"I doubt you'll get a better offer than this one," Jennifer said. "So, do you want to accept it?"

Abby looked at her sisters to get their reactions, but neither Morgan nor Charlie said anything. "Can we call you back?" Abby asked.

"Sure, but don't wait too long," Jennifer said, and Abby hung up.

"What do we think?" Abby asked.

"I thought we'd have a little more time to get used to selling it," Morgan said.

"Me, too," Charlie said. "If we take the offer, a new family will live here in less than a month. We won't be able to come here again."

"If I had the money, I'd buy it," Morgan said.

"Me, too, even if it was only an investment to rent it out," Abby said. "I'd love to keep it in our family."

"We don't have a choice; I think we have to sell," Charlie said.

"No matter what we do, Mom is never coming back here," Abby said.

"We'll still have all our memories," Morgan said.

"And the toaster that burned our bread every morning," Charlie said.

"And the waffle iron that didn't cook the inside of the waffles," Abby said.

"We also have Albert, who constantly falls off the couch," Morgan said, then turned to Abby. "Accept the offer before we all change our minds."

Abby called Jennifer back, who said she would send the paperwork later that day.

"We better go. Brian's waiting for us," Morgan said, and they headed outside.

"Do you think we should call him Brian or Dad?" Abby asked, unlocking the car.

"Whatever you're comfortable with," Morgan said, and Abby's eyebrows scrunched together in contemplation.

Abby drove to El Torito, a Mexican restaurant in Sherman Oaks that they frequented with their mother. It seemed crowded for lunch; all the bar stools were taken by people drinking margaritas and munching on chips and salsa.

Brian was already there, seated at a booth in the corner. "Is everything okay?" Brian asked. He must have noticed the three of them had the same expression, and their shoulders were sagging as they walked up to him. "If you guys have changed your mind about getting to know me, I'd understand."

Abby saw Brian's leg jiggling under the table. "No, it's not that," Abby said. "We just accepted an offer for Mom's house, and we're having a tough time letting it go."

"Oh, that's great," Brian said.

"No, it's not," Morgan said as they scooted into the booth.

"I meant you accepted my offer," Brian said.

"Your offer?" Charlie said.

"Yes, I bought the house. I asked my company to transfer me to Los Angeles. I hope that's okay. I don't want to spend another minute without being on the same side of the country as the three of you."

"You're going to move into our mom's house?" Abby asked.

"I'm not going to live there," Brian said. "I bought it thinking one of you might want to move in."

"You know none of us live in Los Angeles, right?" Morgan said.

"I can't move my practice from Arizona, and besides, I just met Collin, and I want to be where he is," Charlie said.

"I can't move here either," Abby said. "Alex just got a great promotion, and two of my kids are in school. I can't uproot my family."

"Morgan, you mentioned you were considering moving back," Brian said. "If you lived in the house, that would eliminate the expense of renting something."

Morgan looked at him, then tilted her head from side to side as if weighing his offer. "You'd let me live there for free?"

"Of course, but no pressure," Brian said. "If you decide you don't want to move, I'll rent it out as an investment. I knew none of you wanted to part with it."

"The program at Cal State Northridge is perfect for me. Can I think about it?"

"Definitely," Brian said.

"If I decided to move in, I wouldn't feel comfortable not paying you," Morgan said.

"We can work something out. And if you do live there, your sisters will have a place to stay when they visit. Which I hope will be often."

"That is not a selling point," Morgan said, smiling.

"Are you for real?" Abby said to Brian.

"I think so," Brian said, pinching himself. "Or this is the best dream I've ever had."

Morgan, Charlie, and Abby beamed at each other.

"Dad, I don't know what to say," Morgan said.

"You called me Dad," Brian said.

"Is that okay?" Morgan said.

"It's more than okay," Brian's smile matched theirs.

Abby looked around the table at her sisters and father and knew nothing would ever be the same. And that was the greatest thing any of them could have hoped for.

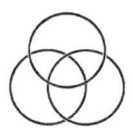

Hi,

Thank you for taking the time to read *When People Leave*. You might also like my other two novels, *After Happily Ever After* and *The Stories We Cannot Tell*.

I would be grateful if you left a review for *When People Leave* on Amazon. Reviews help other readers find my books. Sign up for my newsletter using the following link to stay updated on my new releases. I promise I'll never sell or share your information.

https://www.lesliearasmussen.com/contact

I'm always available to answer questions, so email me at Leslie@Lesliearasmussen.com. You can also follow me on Facebook at Lesliearasmussenauthor, on Instagram at Leslierauthor, or on Amazon and BookBub under Leslie A. Rasmussen.

I love to visit book clubs and discuss my books. If you'd like me to come to yours in person or virtually, contact me on my website, and I'll arrange it.

www.lesliearasmussen.com

Thank you for all your support. Readers like you are the reason I write books. I'm looking forward to getting to know you all.
Best wishes and happy reading!
Leslie

ACKNOWLEDGEMENTS

There are several people that I need to thank, as this book wouldn't exist without them.

To Annie Tucker, my talented developmental editor and someone I enjoy brainstorming with. I'm grateful also to consider her a friend. I want to also thank my copy editor, Stephanie Elliot, and Danna Steele of Dearly Creative for a gorgeous cover that makes me happy every time I look at it.

I want to shout out to all the talented authors I've met through this journey. We've shared lots of tricks to succeed in this crazy publishing business. And to the bookstagrammers and influencers who have promoted my novels, I couldn't be more grateful.

I want to acknowledge my good friend, Suzanne Simonetti, who inspires me. I have learned so much from her, and she's been there for me through all my ups and downs. She has a way of making me laugh even when I didn't think I could, and her brilliant seventeen-second rule has saved me.

Thank you to Meg Nocero, a truly generous spirit who has not only been a friend but has also connected me to some other wonderful people.

To Valerie Taylor and Liani Kotcher for sharing their wisdom and friendship with me. They have made this journey so much easier.

A special thank you to Lori Wilson, my longtime friend who is more like my third sister. I wouldn't want to do life without her. She knows my deepest secrets (don't ask her, she'll never tell) and always takes my side. I can't wait for our next girls' trip.

I want to acknowledge Jill Campbell, who has never wavered in her support for me, even when I was went down a rabbit hole. Her advice has kept me sane, no matter the issue, and I love her with all my heart.

To Debi Pomerantz for her inciteful notes on my writing and for a friendship that bloomed from a random meeting at a writers' conference.

Thank you to my close friends, who make my days happier. Cayla Schneider, Susan Nathanson, and Erin Semper. I'm grateful for all of them.

I would be remiss if I didn't thank my workout buddies at Iron Method and Carolyn McGuire, our fearless instructor. Spending the morning with these women has been a pleasure and has kept me sane for the rest of the day.

To my parents, Katherine and Howard Rieder who I literally wouldn't be here without. I grew up in a happy household with them at the helm. My father has been gone for eight years, and I miss him dearly. And to my sisters, Dee O'Reilly and Linda Gardner. I'm happy we're so close and that they both find time to come to my events and cheer me on.

To Hunter and Jake, my two wonderful sons, who have grown up to be impressive young men, and I know both of them will add a lot to this world. I'm proud to be their mom, and every day, they inspire me to keep writing.

My husband Bruce is my rock and the most supportive husband I could ever ask for. He's always there for me. I hope I'm as talented a writer when I grow up as he is.

Lastly, I want to thank my supportive readers, without who my career would mean nothing. The comments and emails I receive keep me going, and I hope to meet each of them someday. I write books to entertain and hopefully teach something, and readers' letters have made me feel like I've succeeded.

ABOUT THE AUTHOR

Leslie A. Rasmussen was born and raised in Los Angeles and graduated from UCLA. She went on to write television comedies for Gerald McRaney, Burt Reynolds, Roseanne Barr, Norm McDonald, Drew Carey, The Wild Thornberrys, and Sweet Valley High. After leaving the business to raise her boys, Leslie attained a master's degree in nutrition and ran her own business for ten years. Leslie has been published in the Huffington Post over twenty times and speaks on panels discussing female empowerment. She's a member of The Writers Guild of America, Women in Film and The UCLA Alumni Association. *After Happily Ever After* is Leslie's debut novel and has won over fifteen awards, and her second novel, *The Stories We Cannot Tell,* has won eleven awards, and she's been interviewed about it on NPR and XM radio. When Leslie isn't writing, she loves reading, exercising, and spending time with friends. Leslie lives in Southern California with her husband and two sons.